# The White Buck
of Ash Hollow

Philip Mazza

# Also by Philip Mazza

From Under a Tree Book One; The Harrow Saga

Shadow in the Flame Book Two; The Harrow Saga

Children at the Gate Book Three; The Harrow Saga

The Child of Fire Book Four; The Harrow Saga
(Coming 2026)

The Neon Hive

The Quantum Gardener

At the End of it All

Beneath the Ashen Sky

I Know God is a Cat

The Road to Stillwater

The Never-Ending Road

The Cosmic Vending Machine

The Wicked Man Cometh

Gideon Rex

Mother

The Quantum Messiah

# The White Buck

## of Ash Hollow

## Philip Mazza

⬢MNI PUBLISHERS

www.philipmazza.com

Omni Publishers of New York
ISBN 979-8-9924526-6-2
Printed in the United States of America

First Printing: September 2025

To my brother, Paul.

On Christmas morning in 1972, you gave me a wonderful gift: a hardcover, first printing of *Watership Down*. That book has lived on my bookshelves ever since; a constant reminder of the magic it first opened my eyes to—a magic we have shared all our lives. This novel, and the world within its pages, is born from the inspiration of that enduring gift. It is dedicated to you, with all my love, and in honor of all the adventures endured.

# Prologue

There was a time, long ago, when the earth wore a deeper green than any you have seen, brighter and thicker than even the slyest dream a rabbit could dream in his burrow at noon. It is not the tired green you find at the edge of spring now—the sort that gives up under sun and claw, that's gone to dust by High Day—but a vast, merry greenness, ripe as a doe's best bedding, sweet as dew on the very first dawn, unrolled across downs and hollow places alike, so thick and tall and full of singing life that the wind itself lost count of the hills. Grass then was dress for the land, a fur that needed no mending. Clover heads stood high as a kit's ear; their scent drifted for hills upon hills and made a meal in the asking. I remember it as if the memory weren't mine but borrowed— sometimes it feels older than my bones, older than the stones that lean above our chamber.

In those days, the rivers ran so bright and clear, you could see the stones sleeping on their beds, pale and glinting, with fish streaking through like arrows of sunlight. The water leapt and chattered, quick with joy. Rain came gentle and went gentle as a visitor who knows his welcome. Even the clouds in winter were honest—bringing cold, yes, bringing hunger enough for discipline, but never cruelty. Never the sort of winter to wither the roots or send a warren to silence.

Burrows were snug and plentiful, and you could dig all day and never run into poison or black stones. Even the wind in the ash trees was a friend—a voice that sang you to sleep, not the cruel warning-song it's become. In those days, the ash and the fir whispered secrets through the ground, sap and root working together as kin. The birds nested by the thousand, and each dawn was a festival of sound. You'd wake to the lark and sleep to the nightjar, never doubting your place in the endless round.

And the Twolegs . . . ah, young ones think the Twolegs have always been as they are now: greedy, blind giants, taking what they please and leaving only scars behind. But it was not so once. They walked the land as if it were their own breath—neither master nor thief, but makers of small kindnesses. They took stalk and root with a mind for the year ahead, and with the other, patient hand, they planted again: nuts and berries for badger and bird, hedges woven thick for shelter, grain left uncut at the edge that the little ones among us might eat in times of want. They'd hum their strange, soft songs under the moon, and more than one kit was named for the song of the Twoleg-spade tapping stones.

Even the foxes hunted well in those days—no need for desperate blood, just the old bargain kept: a swift chase, a quick end, and a feast for the cubs. There was a law then, deeper than tooth or claw. Not written, but lived: every creature, every root had its place and season—nothing hoarded, nothing wasted, nothing forced out of its own time.

The Twolegs remembered the standing places too. Stones older than their words or ours, set in circles under the sky, their tops polished by sun and season. They would leave carrots and seed at their feet, pour pure water at dusk, and whisper heartfelt thanks to the earth beneath. In the green time, we watched from our brambles—never chased, never trapped. I'd see the moonlight shine on their faces and hope they were dreaming the same dream we did: of the world as a kind circle, complete.

The warrens then ran deep—deeper and richer than Glenmere. Tunnels echoing below the roots, council chambers great enough for a hundred does, sunshafts letting golden ladders fall across the packed earth. I was only a kit, but I saw the Old Mothers trace their paws over sacred ground, murmuring the old names before each meal, before each birth. There were places even we wouldn't go—caverns where the Hollowkin, the Dreaming Kin, touched the waking world for a heartbeat, their voices humming in the root-deep dark. Those days, you could cross all the meadow's length and never know want sharper than February's wind. Hunger was a lesson, not a law.

But nothing in field or hollow holds forever. The longest summer finds its dusk. It began quiet: a hedge trimmed here, a stream muddied there, a ring of Standing Stones pushed aside for a road. The Twolegs grew hurried, took more than their share—first because there were more of them, then because they forgot the bargain that held the world together. The fields of clover thinned. The water went dark, and hungry foxes drifted closer, their eyes old with loss.

They forgot to leave the gifts at the stones—then they broke them, carted them away, or split them for walls and fire. The land mourned; it mourns still. The old bargain frayed. The dreams that guided the grass to grow thick and the frost to be gentle—

those dreams waned, as if the Hollowkin were falling into a far sleep no one could wake.

The little ones of today have never tasted that clover, never heard the river laugh at their paws. But believe me: it was real, and may be again. The earth remembers: sorrow, yes, but also the joy. The Hollowkin sleep, but they dream of green days, and sometimes, sometimes the White Buck appears in the dusk or a circle of dew-bright stones reminds us that kindness is only ever asleep, never wholly dead.

That is why I speak now—though my own dreams run thin and my ears lose their edge. Stories carry what paws cannot. This world will not always belong to the Twolegs. Stones do not bow forever. Let your hearts be ready for the day the Hollowkin's song rises again under the ash. And should your best hour find you in green days, remember to leave a gift, to shape the earth gentler for those who follow.

So listen well, for these words are not mine alone, but all the remembering earth. The Long Green Days are not gone. They wait, like spring, just out of sight—waiting for those steady and hopeful enough to greet them when they come.

*- Cloverleaf, The Elder*

# Chapter 1
## The Strange Season

In the days long since abandoned, when the world still wandered through the deep enchantments of its youth, when hills yet murmured with the dreams of stone and rivers remembered the first songs of rain, there lay a warren far in the western reaches of the Green Country. It was cradled beneath the gnarled roots of ancient ash trees—those towering sentinels that watched the passing of centuries with slow, unwavering grace—and it nestled close to the foot of a hill crowned by a broken circle of weather-worn stone, the remnants of some forgotten time. The place was called Glenmere, though none now living knew why or how the name had come to be. Yet it lingered, like a root sunk too deep to be pulled.

The rabbits of Glenmere had known peace for many seasons, and their memory of strife had long since faded into story and whisper. They moved through their days in quiet rhythm—waking with the dew, foraging among the sweet clover and knotgrass, curling in hollows deep beneath the soil as the sun rode high and the wind curled through the trees above.

But that spring, a wind came down from the north.

It was a dry wind, bitter and strange, and it carried no promise of warmth or rain. Where once the air had been rich with the hum of bees and the sweet, dark scent of upturned earth, it now stung with the tang of bark and ash. The clover, which should have risen thick and green across the meadows, poked up sparse and yellowing. The grass was wiry beneath paw and tooth. And the birds—those bright-throated heralds of morning—sang haltingly, their notes sharp and jangled, as if trying to recall a tune lost to time.

At the mouth of the elder tunnel, where the roots of the ash grew knotted and thick as the arms of old giants, sat a young buck named Bracken.

He was small for his kind, lean and sinewy, with a coat mottled in shades of earth and dusk that made him near invisible among the rocks. His ears, long and restless, betrayed every flicker of thought. His eyes were a deep amber, thoughtful and troubled. For many days now, he had come to sit alone at dusk, watching the light drain slow through the trees, seeking to set his mind in order—for the dreams had come upon him again.

They were not the idle, fretful imaginings of rabbits—the fleet-footed visions of running through fields or lying safe beside a warm doe. These dreams were older, deeper, and they clung to the bones like damp moss. In the dreams, Bracken saw the White Buck—pale as frost, mute as moonlight—walking a corridor of darkness, where thorns twisted along the walls and the stones themselves seemed to pulse with an ancient, humming voice. It was not a voice that spoke in words, yet it pressed meaning upon him like weight upon a branch.

Bracken stirred. The memory of his dreams slowly slipped away like fog before wind. He gave a sudden tremble, a flick of ear and whisker. The wind was rising, keen-edged and full of scent. Dusk had fallen, and with it came that prickling hush when even the trees seem to listen.

Behind him, the warren stirred in muted unease. Kits whimpered in their sleep, and mothers pressed closer to them. A young gray-bellied doe passed by, her eyes hollow, her steps dragging. She gave Bracken a glance, but no word followed. Words, these days, were scarce.

He turned when he heard the faint patter of paws upon the stone.

Sorrel.

She came silent as shadow, her rust-red coat touched with darker streaks like the last embers of a dying fire. Her eyes were keen, her step assured. She did not speak until she had settled beside him, shoulder to shoulder beneath the watching trees.

"They're saying it's the roots," she murmured, her voice barely louder than the wind.

Bracken's ears tilted toward her, but he did not turn.

"They say something's wrong underground. That the water's gone thin, the clover's grown brittle. Even the trees seem still, too still."

Bracken's gaze wandered across the dim meadow, where shadows were gathering like old regrets. "The birds," he said, "their songs are wrong."

Sorrel's ears flicked with quiet exasperation. "You and your birds."

"They don't speak to us anymore," Bracken replied. "They now sing in a different language, one not meant for rabbit ears. As though they call to something else."

She studied him for a time, her breath visible in the cooling air. "Another dream?"

He said nothing.

The wind scraped dry across the stones, and for a while, there was only the crackle of grass and the whisper of ash leaves high above.

Then, from the deep throat of the warren, a cry broke the hush.

It was not the plaintive mewl of a dreaming kit nor the bark of warning from a sentry. It was a raw, tearing sound—full of pain and ending—and it pulled them both to their feet.

Bracken knew the voice. Briarback—Cloverleaf's eldest. A strong young buck, barely past his first winter, who had been mourning the death of his father for days.

The cry fractured into silence, and in that silence, there came no return.

Sorrel's ears folded flat. "His sorrow runs like a river under the frost. You cannot see it, but it works its way through the earth, and nothing can stop its course. Death leaves a hollow in the ground where no grass will grow for a long while."

"The healers had tried lichen poultices, bark sap, the bitter milk of the elderflower," Bracken said.

"All in vain," Sorrel whispered. "When the life has gone out, no leaf nor root can draw it back. We may dress the place where it lay, but the wind will still pass over it, and in time, even the scent will fade. That is the way of all living things, Bracken. To love is to know that one day you will listen for a voice that will never answer."

Bracken closed his eyes. A chill passed through him, though the wind had quieted.

Later, as the last embers of twilight burned to soot, the sentries raised the alarm.

A shadow lurched into the hollow from the trees—a badger, thin as death, its fur patchy and hung in folds, its eyes wild with some unseen madness. It stumbled toward the old streambed, where the black rock lay half-buried in nettles, and collapsed with a grunt.

Bracken and Sorrel crept forward from the thicket, their noses low, their ears straining.

The badger writhed and scraped at the earth with dull claws. "Ash . . ." it gasped, "ash in the green . . . ash beneath the clover . . ."

Its voice was raw as if dragged over stones.

Sorrel stared, her breath caught. "I've never seen one that thin," she whispered.

The badger's eyes rolled back, and it clawed at the ground as though digging its own grave. Then it stilled.

The wind sighed once through the ash trees, and the birds fell silent.

And in the silence that followed, Bracken felt his dreams stir again, cold and sure, like something that had never left.

Back in the gathering chamber, where the root-veined walls arched above like the ribs of some ancient beast, the rabbits of Glenmere had assembled. The hollow was dim, lit only by the pale gleam of phosphor-moss and the waning memory of the day above. The earth beneath their paws was cool, firmed by many seasons of tread, and the air carried the faint, sour tang of elder-root and mildew.

Sorrel stood upon the speaking stone, her frame slight but her bearing resolute, and the quiet strength of her voice drew the murmur of the warren into stillness.

"The land is unwell," she said, her dark eyes sweeping over the gathered host. "Its bones have begun to ache. The water is low. The shoots brittle. The wind comes thin and without scent. I'm afraid we must go."

A rustle stirred the chamber—disbelief, uncertainty, and fear.

"Not all of us," Sorrel continued, unwavering. "A few. The swift. The young. The watchful. We must seek the green . . . where it yet lingers. There must be others like us, other warrens, deeper roots, untouched ground. Places where the sun still warms the earth, where the air is not tainted with the dust. We cannot wait for the world to remember us . . . we must go and find the world that hasn't forgotten. The old stories speak of hills beyond the burnt fields, of streams that run clear beneath the hawthorn. If even half of it is true, then we must try. If we don't, the silence will take us all."

At this, some scoffed. A few stamped in irritation, muttering beneath their breath.

Bracken sat near the chamber's edge, beneath a low knot of elderwood. His paws twitched upon the earth, a nervous rhythm he could not still.

"It is only a season," said old Bramblehide, her right ear notched and her fur faded to thistle-gray. "The hills wax and wane. Spoiled over the years by the Twolegs. We have seen lean times before. Wait it out. The ground does not forget how to feed us, not truly. The roots sleep, that is all, and the rains will come when they remember the sky. No use fretting your whiskers to stubs . . . hunger passes, but fear, if you let it, makes a home in the belly."

Sorrel did not flinch. "We've waited," she replied, evenly. "The clover dies faster than it grows. Kits sicken before they speak. You know it. You've smelled it in the roots."

She paused, her ears half-lowered, nose twitching as though scenting for something just beyond the breeze. "The ground remembers, yes . . . but not all memories are kind. There's rot beneath the bark, Bramblehide. The water tastes of stone, the sky yawns wider each morning, and I saw a crow last dusk . . . alone, silent, circling low. Even the carrion birds are waiting for something. You speak of seasons as if they always turn. But what if this one has stuck? What if it means to stay?"

Hombeer, a younger buck with the copper-bright sheen of youth upon him and the stiff pride of one who has not yet been truly tried, pushed himself forward into the open space. "You'd have us chase after Bracken's dreams, would you?" he said, his voice sharp as thorn. "Dreams of white shapes flitting in the dark, of deep places lost and dead things that move when they should not. Do the roots beneath us speak now, too? Shall we sit and listen for the fall of leaves, and call it wisdom?" His eyes darted from one face to another, restless, glinting. "We've hidden before . . . from fox, from the long-legged Twolegs, and from worse . . . and still the green fields have come again. Are we to quake now because some young buck kicks in his sleep? Dreams are only wind, stirring behind the eyes. They pass." He stamped the ground once, hard enough to send a tremor through the earth. "I will not bow to fog and shadows."

The laughter that followed was uneasy.

But Bracken rose, though his voice trembled at the edges.

"There were warrens before ours, lives beneath lives," he said. "Burrows so deep the light forgot them. And in those depths walked more than fur and bone. What I saw was not born in this season, nor the last. It walks still. Not toward us . . . but waiting. Waiting for those who have forgotten too much. I do not speak of dreams. No. I speak of memory. The White Buck walks beneath the hill. He bears no name, no shadow. The way is not found . . . it is remembered."

The words, once loosed, hung in the air like frost.

The chamber fell to stillness.

Sorrel stood high upon the speaking stone, her ears still and her eyes catching the dim light that filtered through the roots above. The silence held a long while after Bracken's words faded, thick with thought and memory. Then she spoke, her voice low but clear, shaped by the wind and soil of her many seasons. "You've felt it," she said, her gaze sweeping the gathered rabbits. "The sweet grass wilts before its time. The bark tastes of ash. Even the brook runs slower, as though the hill itself tires of feeding us." A murmur stirred the chamber, but no one spoke. They knew it was true.

"I've thought on it," Sorrel continued. "The old stories say nothing stays rooted forever . . . not trees, not rivers, not rabbits. There comes a time when even the strongest warren must look beyond its walls. I will go. Not alone, but with those willing. We'll find what lies beyond the thorns, past the old creek, where scent and sky shift into strange shapes. We'll search for a place where the grass still sings and the earth remembers kindness."

Her voice did not tremble. "When we find it . . . we will return . . . to lead you to it. I promise you that. This is still our home. I would not leave it behind like a shed husk. But the hill grows thin. The roots twist in uneasy sleep. If we stay, we fade. If we go, we carry the warren with us, in our hearts and our scent and the stories we tell to the stars."

A hush settled again, deep as leafmold. Bracken looked up at her, and others too—old, young, hale, limping—all watching the rabbit who dared speak change aloud. Sorrel stood firm against their silence, ears tall, the light behind her turning the edge of her fur to silver. "Not all must come," she said gently. "But some must. The world beyond does not wait forever."

That night, Bracken dreamed again.

Yet he was not himself.

He walked on white paws, pale as mist, through a tunnel not made by claw or tooth, but shaped by something older. The earth was smooth beneath him, not cold, but warm—alive. Roots laced the earthen walls like the veins of a leaf held to sunlight, and from within the soil came a pulse, deep and slow, a rhythm not heard but felt, as though the stone itself harbored a sleeping heart.

There was no sound in the dream, and yet a voice spoke.

Not with words, nor in breath—but in shape and symbol, in image and pulse, as the fire tells stories in its flicker, and the water in its turning.

He saw trees—twisted, contorted in wicked ways, and taller than the hills, hollowed by age and time. Its bark was split down the center like a wound left open to the wind, and from the cleft poured light, not golden or silver, but dim and gray as twilight. Within the hollow, rabbits moved—not playfully, but in solemn circles, their limbs tracing patterns older than memory, a rite not of joy but of remembrance and dread.

Ash fell from above, softly at first—then in thick, choking showers. Where it landed, the clover blackened, burning holes in the bright green leaves as though fire had taken root in the earth.

Then he saw a figure.

A buck stood there, more strongly built than any rabbit Bracken had ever set eyes on—stranger even than the old tales told in half-whispers under root and bramble. His fur shone silver, not the dull gray of frost-bitten fields, but the bright, glimmering hue of moonlight spilling over winter snow. His eyes were empty hollows, rimmed in a dull, smoldering red, as though something behind them still burned, slow and watchful. Upon his brow rested a crown—not of leaf or flower, but of bone, brittle and yellowed, knotted with age and time. It curled like roots twisted in the dark, too long buried. He stood beside the cleft tree—the old one that leaned like a crippled paw against the sky—his shape unmoving, a creature carved from winter stone.

The wind did not stir his fur. No scent came from him. He did not blink. And though he said nothing, Bracken felt his thoughts pressed against him like earth on a new-laid tunnel—wordless, heavy, and real. The buck belonged to no warren, bore no scent of clan or season. He was not living in the way rabbits understand living, and yet he was no shadow either. He was there, and that was enough. Bracken's paws itched to run, but his legs would not answer. The buck turned his head—slowly, as if the motion were dragged from the earth itself—and those hollow eyes met his.

Bracken did not know his name.

But dread filled him.

He woke with a cry, sharp and startled, his sides heaving like a rabbit chased to the edge of its strength. His fur was slick with damp, tangled with bits of dry leaf and grit from the burrow floor. His breath came quick, each draw a rasp in his throat. For a moment, he did not know where he was—caught between the last threads of the dream and the waking world, between roots and memory. His limbs twitched, and his ears flicked, half-expecting the tall, crowned figure to be standing over him still.

Shadows crept through the bramble-shadows above the warren entrance, long and silver-gray. The world had not yet turned to day, but night was soon to depart. Around him, the warren lay still—breathers slow and steady in the sleeping hollows, a scent of earth and fur thick in the air. Outside, a blackbird called once and fell silent again.

Sorrel stood nearby, her paws tucked beneath her, her ears tilted not in alarm but in knowing. She had been watching. For how long, Bracken didn't know.

"You dreamed," she said simply, with neither mockery nor surprise.

Bracken nodded, but the gesture came slow, uncertain. His mouth felt dry, his throat tight as though the dream had left smoke in his chest. He could not speak—not yet. The images still clung to him like burrs: the cleft tree, the bone crown, those hollow eyes.

Sorrel did not press. She turned slightly, glancing toward the tunnel-mouth where the light grew stronger, soft and bluish now.

"We leave at first light," she said. "You're coming."

He looked up at her. Her eyes were steady, dark, and clear as water under stone. He searched them for question, for hesitation, for a shred of doubt—but found none. She was not asking.

He met her gaze and held it. In the quiet space between them, something passed—like the rustle of a dry leaf on hard ground, faint but certain.

"You ask yourself why? Why me?" she asked then, though her voice was low, almost a murmur. As if she, too, already carried the answer somewhere inside her and only asked to hear it aloud.

Bracken's voice came, low and steady, drawn from the place inside him where fear and memory braided tightly together.

"Because you need my dreams."

And though neither of them moved, the hush that followed felt like the moment a rabbit shifts its paw before the first bound— the stillness before everything changes.

They departed in silence, long before the pale mist of dawn had uncurled from the roots of the elder ash trees. The wind stirred softly through the boughs above, shaking loose dry leaves the color of old parchment and age-darkened copper. They fell without sound, turning slowly in the hush like forgotten coins cast upon a tomb. Five rabbits stole away from the sleeping warren of Glenmere, no farewells spoken nor good wishes exchanged, for unease lay heavy on all hearts.

At their head moved Sorrel, lithe and sure-footed, her rust-hued fur dark against the wan morning. Close behind padded Bracken, lean and watchful, ears high and quivering at every sigh of wind. Then came Wisp, a small doe barely past her first winter, known for her twitching limbs and wide, luminous eyes that always seemed to see what others did not. The rear was held by Thatch and Reed, two young bucks as yet untempered by true hardship, whose strength outpaced their wisdom. They moved together like a shadow, silent and wary.

Their trail led them beyond the green confines of Glenmere, past the old alder stump where owls once perched in long-forgotten seasons, and down through the thinning grass where the soil turned pale and friable beneath their paws. Here, the earth was strangely brittle, and it whispered underfoot, as though disturbed in its rest. At one place, Bracken paused beside a stone fissured down its center and pressed his nose against it.

"It's hollow beneath," he murmured, ears swiveling.

Sorrel, without turning, said, "Then don't stand on it."

They moved on.

No one spoke. The hush between them was not of fear, not quite—but of knowing, of something half-remembered yet fully felt, as though the very earth beneath their paws remembered too. The world beyond Glenmere had changed, as if some old sorrow had drifted in like fog and forgotten how to leave. Trees stood at strange angles, leaning not with the stoop of time but as though shouldering some unseen grief. Their trunks groaned in the breeze, and their limbs, bare and crooked, reached upward like hands begging something from the sky that would not answer.

The air was sharp and dry. What streams remained trickled weakly over beds of brittle stone, their sound less like song and more like whispering—words just out of reach. The brambles grew thicker here, less wild than purposeful, clutching at root and stone as if trying to hold the world in place. And everywhere, silence. Not the calm stillness of resting meadows or sleepy hills, but the silence that settles after flight—the hush of something gone, something taken. No birds called. No wings stirred the air. Even the beetles seemed to crawl more slowly, and the wind, when it came, moved warily, threading itself through thorn and branch like a story told with too much truth and not enough hope.

It was Wisp who stopped first.

The young doe had ranged a little ahead, ears forward, nose twitching. She paused beside a curtain of old ivy, its edges brown with rot. Beyond it lay a clearing. The others caught up one by one and stared.

The glade was ringed with bramble so thick it looked grown with intent, the thorns curved back like talons, ancient and gray. Inside, a ring of stones stood in eerie silence—too deliberate to be natural, too precise to be chance. They were not like the tumble of old cairns or the half-buried markers of forgotten burrows. These had been placed by something that understood shape and purpose. Each stone leaned just so, forming a circle without flaw.

And within the ring, the grass was green.

Not the hopeful green of spring's first blush, nor the high summer green that hums with warmth. It was deeper, sharper, like moss in moonlight or the fierce green of something that had never learned to wither. The color seemed to breathe, to pulse ever so slightly, as though the earth within the stones held its own memory and had no intention of letting it go. Around it, the clearing was dead—shrubs brittle, roots shriveled, the soil gray as ash.

Wisp stepped forward, slow and careful, as though drawn by something older than thought. Her eyes were fixed—not with the bright flicker of curiosity, but with the quiet, reverent stillness of awe. Her paws moved without sound, pressing into the earth as if she feared to break some unseen thread beneath her. The grass within the ring bowed slightly, not from wind, but from presence— as if something had passed this way long ago and left its mark behind.

There was something there—etched into the earth, though not by claw or paw. A sigil, yes, but stranger than any mark Bracken or Sorrel had known. Twisting lines that curled like roots and branched like antlers, patterns too deliberate for chance yet too wild for any rabbit's design. None of them could name it, yet all felt its shape brushing at the edges of their thoughts—like the memory of a story half-heard in a burrow long ago, or the faint tug of a dream that wakes before its end. Wisp did not speak, but the hush around her deepened, and even the wind seemed to pause and watch.

"Don't," Sorrel said, her voice low and sharp, like a twig snapping beneath watchful trees. She moved to block her, her ears flat, the fur along her spine rising.

But Wisp had already crossed the threshold.

Her paw touched the sigil, and a hush fell heavier still. Even the wind withdrew as if it dared not pass the stones.

At first, nothing happened. The circle accepted her as if she belonged. Then her body shuddered. Her eyes, bright already, grew wide with a light that was not of the sky.

"I hear them," she breathed, her voice thin and distant. "They're speaking."

Bracken leapt toward her. "Wisp . . . "

She turned her head slowly. "The Hollowkin," she said, and the name landed like a stone in still water.

And then it was there—the murmur.

It came not from above, nor from the surrounding woods, but from beneath the very earth. A low chorus of voices, indistinct and ancient, as if the stone and root themselves were whispering the names of things that had no place in the waking world.

Wisp trembled violently.

Bracken crossed the ring and pulled her back. For a moment, the green grass resisted, tugging at her paws, as though reluctant to relinquish what it had claimed. Then it released her, and she tumbled into Bracken's chest, panting as though she had run for leagues.

"They're not dead," she whispered, barely audible.

Bracken's heart thudded beneath his ribs.

"They're dreaming."

Behind them, the wind passed through the clearing again, and the thorns rustled like bones shaken in a dark sack.

They camped that night beneath the gnarled husk of a fallen elder tree, long dead and hollowed by time, its bark worn silver by wind and rain. Moss clung to its flanks in fraying garlands, and brambles crept through the splintered hollow like the fingers of a forgotten hand. The ground beneath was damp and quiet, thick with loam and the faint scent of crushed fern. A thin mist gathered low among the roots, coiling like breath held too long.

Sorrel and Bracken slipped away from the others, finding a patch of shadow beneath a leaning birch where the air was thick with the scent of damp earth and old leaves. For a moment, neither spoke, each listening for the distant murmur of Wisp's voice or the restless shifting of Thatch and Reed. Finally, Sorrel broke the silence, her gaze fixed on the place where Wisp had stood in the strange glade. "Do you think she truly felt them . . . the Hollowkin?" she whispered, her voice barely more than a breath. "Not just the fear, but something deeper, something old?"

Bracken's ears flicked, and he stared at the ground, tracing the pattern of roots with a trembling paw. "I do," he replied softly. "The Hollowkin aren't like us, not really. The old tales say they spoke lost languages and lived in harmony with the land, long before our kind forgot such things. They're not alive, but not gone either. It's as if they're bound to the earth by memory itself . . . caught between worlds, dreaming beneath the soil. Sometimes, in places marked by strange signs or where the grass grows wrong, you can almost hear them . . . like a song half-remembered, or voices murmuring from below."

Sorrel shivered, glancing back toward the glade. "If Wisp truly heard them, then we're walking in the shadow of something ancient . . . something that remembers when magic was as common as rain. The Hollowkin are the land's sorrow and its hope, both guardian and warning. Maybe the White Buck in your dreams is one of them, or sent by them, pressing us to remember what's been lost. I only hope," she added, her voice trembling, "that their dreams mean to guide us, not lead us astray."

As Sorrel and Bracken slipped back through the tangle of the elder tree, the hush of their absence seemed to lift from the clearing. Reed, ever alert and bristling with the nervous energy of youth, raised his head and fixed them with a questioning stare. "Where did you go?" he asked, his voice edged with worry, though he tried to hide it beneath a veneer of indifference. The mist curled low around their paws, and Wisp watched them with wide, searching eyes, as if hoping for some reassurance.

Sorrel gave a gentle shake of her ears, her tone calm and steady. "We didn't go far," she replied, glancing back toward the shadowed trees. "We just wanted to see what lay ahead and sniff the air for danger. There's nothing close . . . just the old wood and the wind." She offered Reed a small, reassuring nod, though her eyes lingered on Bracken for a heartbeat longer, the weight of their secret conversation pressing softly between them like the memory of a distant storm.

As light faded into the quiet embrace of night, the rabbits settled beneath the sheltering boughs of the elder tree.

No one spoke.

Wisp curled into herself, a small, shivering bundle of russet fur. Her eyes, usually quick and sharp, now remained closed. Even in sleep—or whatever uneasy rest she had found—her ears twitched faintly, as though fending off dreams. Thatch stood just beyond a log, rigid in the half-light, his body tense with a watchfulness he did not fully understand. He kept his shoulders square and his stance proud, but the tremble in his haunches betrayed him. The young buck was trying hard to look brave—for them, for himself.

Reed had settled close to the mossy underside of the log, his back pressed firm against the bark as if seeking strength from it. His voice was low, barely a murmur, as he repeated the old half-prayers taught in his warren: quiet fragments of a song once sung to the wind and the sun and the roots. His words fell like dew upon the earth—soft, uncertain, yet somehow steady.

Bracken could not sleep.

His eyes remained wide and unblinking, fixed upward where the thick canopy gave way to a narrow sliver of sky. The stars—pale, distant—blinked slowly, like the weary eyes of ancient watchers, their gaze slipping through ragged cracks in the night's fabric. The constellations he had once known as a kit—those comforting patterns stitched by story and season—now seemed scattered, scattered as if some unseen hand had scattered their threads across the heavens. Even the Moon, usually a steady guardian in the dark, had not yet risen, as though it, too, feared to witness what lay beneath on this restless night.

Beside him, Wisp's breathing rasped low and uneven, ragged but steady. Bracken counted each breath as if it were a precious rhythm, a fragile tether to the waking world.

Then, at the edge of the tree line, at the bank of a river of black, he saw it.

At first, he thought it might be a trick of mist and shadow—an echo of a dream or the play of moonless darkness. But no. It stood there, as solid as the earth beneath his paws, as clear as the cold air that brushed his fur. Just beyond the veil of tangled branches and whispering leaves stood the White Buck.

It did not move. It did not blink. The pale glow that surrounded it was soft and eerie, as if the creature were carved from frost and moonlight, a spirit of winter made flesh. Its eyes were deep and dark, like still pools in the shadow of a wood, holding no glimmer save what the beholder carried there. The hindquarters showed the strength of hard running over open ground, the neck thick and set low, and the legs drawn up beneath as if ready to spring at the first stir of danger or need. It stood unmoving, poised as if caught between moments.

It raised its head slowly, deliberately. And stared at Bracken.

No wind stirred the leaves, but they seemed to whisper anyway, rustling in some unseen current of old magic.

Bracken's breath caught tight in his throat, a sudden stillness choking the air. A soundless word passed through him— not heard, but felt deep inside, like a thunderclap held beneath the hills or a river swelling behind a dam. The pulse reached into his bones, marking the old, secret places that stories warned of but seldom touched.

And in that moment, he knew.

There was no turning back.

Not to Glenmere, with its soft earth and familiar burrows. Not to the ways that had kept them safe and hidden. Not to the comfort of running swift and silent beneath the safe sky.

The world had shifted. Like the long, dark walks of elder tales, like rivers running dry in the summer drought, like birds who forgot their songs in the silence—something had changed. The White Buck had come. And where it passed, the old paths would fade, vanish like mist before the dawn.

When morning came, with its pale light spilling over the meadow and setting dew to sparkle like scattered glass, Bracken would speak. He would tell the others what he had seen. Sorrel and Wisp would listen with careful eyes, hearts quickening at the edge of old fears. Thatch and Reed would turn their gaze away, folding their doubt silently between their ribs, tired of the restless dreams that always seemed to haunt him like a shadow at dusk. But still, he would tell them, because the truth carried its own quiet weight, and because somewhere beneath it all, he knew the world was changing—and the old stories might soon come alive again.

# Chapter 2
## Sorrel's Path

The world outside Glenmere was not the world Bracken remembered from his kithood. The fields, once lush and humming with the secret life of grasshoppers and bees, now lay in ragged, uneven patches of brown and ochre, as if some careless paw had smeared mud over the green. Where once the clover had grown thick and sweet, the earth was bare and pitted, the few remaining tufts of grass brittle and yellowed, curling in upon themselves like old parchment. The hedgerows, which had been dense and alive with the chittering of wrens and the darting shadows of voles, were now sparse, their branches jutting out at odd angles, stripped of leaves and bark, resembling the ribs of some long-dead animal. Here and there, a faded berry clung to a thorn, shriveled and black, a memory of sweeter seasons. The air itself felt thin, carrying the faint, acrid tang of decay, and every breath seemed to draw more of the world's sorrow into their bodies.

As they pressed on, the woods loomed ahead—once a place of dappled sunlight and the soft, forgiving hush of moss underfoot. Now, the trees stood like sentinels scarred by battle, their trunks scorched and split, bark peeled away in ragged strips to reveal pale, wounded wood beneath. Branches hung broken, some dangling by mere threads, others scattered on the ground like discarded antlers. The undergrowth was sparse, the ferns and brambles withered, their stems twisted into brittle knots. No birds called from the canopy. The only sounds were the restless sigh of the wind, threading through the empty spaces, and, far off, the hollow croak of a solitary crow—a sound that seemed to echo from another world entirely.

They moved in silence, the five of them strung out in a wary line. Sorrel led, her head high and her stride sure, though her ears flicked constantly, tracking every whisper of movement. At the rear, Thatch and Reed moved with a surprising stealth, their ears swiveling as they scanned the shadows behind them. The others, their bodies tense, ears flattened hard against their heads, eyes rolling white at every snap of twig or flutter of leaf. Their fear was palpable, a living thing that clung to their flanks and made their steps falter. Wisp, the smallest of them all, huddled against Bracken's flank. Her nose worked in quick, nervous flickers, pulling in the damp stink of rot and the dry taste of dust. A faint shiver ran through her from ears to tail-tip, as if she might come apart with one wrong sound. Each strange smell set her ears twitching; each moving patch of shadow might be teeth and claws. Yet it wasn't these things that truly held her attention.

"Why is it so quiet?" she whispered, her voice barely more than a breath, as if she feared waking something that slumbered in the ruined woods.

Bracken shook his head, his own unease sharpening at her words. "I don't know. It feels wrong." He remembered the world as it had been—alive, unpredictable, but never silent. This silence was the silence of absence, of something vital gone missing.

Thatch snorted, the sound harsh in the hush. "The land is sick. Even the stoats have moved on. Only fools and ghosts remain." His words hung in the air, heavy with finality, and Bracken felt a chill crawl up his spine.

They came to a streambed, once a lively ribbon of water that had sung over stones and lapped at the roots of willow and alder. Now it was nothing but a scar in the earth, the stones exposed and sharp, their edges worn smooth by water long vanished. The bed was cracked, and the mud split into a mosaic of jagged lines. Bracken paused, staring at the ground. In his dream, he had seen this place—only in the dream, the water had run black and cold, and the White Buck had stood on the far bank, watching him with eyes that glowed like embers. The memory made him shiver, the sense of prophecy pressing close.

Sorrel did not pause. Her pace was relentless, her voice a low command: "Keep moving. We're exposed here." She glanced up at the sky, where the sun struggled to break through a veil of thin, gray cloud, and pressed on.

They passed through a copse of birch, the trees standing pale and skeletal, their bark peeling in long, curling strips. The leaves, what few remained, were shriveled and gray, clinging stubbornly to the ends of branches. A sudden gust of wind rattled the branches, sending a flurry of dead leaves skittering across the ground like a swarm of insects. The sound startled Wisp, who bolted forward in a panic, only to be hauled back by Sorrel's quick teeth in the scruff of his neck.

"Stay close!" Sorrel snapped, her voice sharper than usual, cutting through the tension like a blade. "And keep your wits sharp . . . every one of them."

Wisp's eyes shone large and bright in the dim light, the pale rims glimmering all around the dark centers. "Something's watching us," she whispered, her voice thin as wind through dry grass. A shiver passed through her from nose to tail. "I can feel it, in my bones."

Thatch grunted, his gaze sweeping the shadows. "Everything's hungry. Move." His words were not meant to comfort, but they had the effect of spurring the group onward.

The sun dragged itself up, pale and unsure, spilling a thin light that neither warmed the ground nor eased the tightness in their bellies. At last, they came upon a hollow beneath a fallen log, its roots jutting out in a snarl, like the groping claws of some long-dead thing. Sorrel stopped and flicked her ears. Without a word, they crept inside, pressing close in the cramped space, each listening to the empty stretch of the woods beyond.

"We'll stay here for the night," she said at last.

Overhead, the sky rolled on without care, vast and unmoved, while the wind slithered through the wreckage of trees, bringing with it the bitter tang of ash and something older— something that had gone wrong long before they came this way.

That night, Bracken's dreams returned, sharper now—no longer the soft wanderings of a restless mind, but vivid and urgent, like the beat of a distant drum calling through the roots. He found himself running—not through sunlit woods or soft meadow grass, but through a tangled tunnel of twisted roots and cruel thorns. The walls pressed in close, scraping at his fur with rough bark and thorny grasp, a narrow passage carved beneath the earth's skin. Ahead, like a pale flame flickering in the dark, moved the White Buck—silent, serene, impossible in its stillness.

The air in that underground way was thick and stale, heavy with the smell of rot and old leafmold, the scent of a thousand seasons buried and forgotten. Bracken's paws slipped upon slick, black earth that clung like wet cloth to his feet. Above, the roots knotted tightly together, blocking all but slender ribbons of cold moonlight that spilled in faint, ghostly stripes across the tunnel floor. The White Buck's fur shimmered softly, a glow like frost in dawn's first breath, casting wavering shadows that danced and flickered with every step Bracken took, like the flicker of candlelight in a great, hollow cavern.

He called out then, his voice trembling with urgency, "Wait! Please . . . wait!" but the buck did not pause nor glance behind. Its ears stretched high, brushing the tunnel's low ceiling and stirring the thorns, which trembled and whispered in a language old and strange, a tongue of silence and sorrow that Bracken could not understand. The path forked and twisted, narrowing until his sides rubbed raw against the cold earth, sharp thorns snagging and tearing at his flanks. He felt the sting of blood mingle with the heavy breath of the soil, a copper tang that grounded him in the dream's harsh reality.

Deeper still he ran, and the tunnel seemed to pulse beneath him, alive as some great beast lying buried beneath the land. Shadows flickered at the edges of his vision—bones tangled in roots like forgotten trophies, empty eye sockets watching from the dark with silent intent. The White Buck moved on, unhurried, unbroken, leaving no trace in the soft earth beneath its paws, a ghost walking a path no living creature could follow.

Bracken's heart thundered in his chest, a frantic, desperate drum echoing through the dream's silent halls. He tried to call again, but his voice faltered, broken and thin, swallowed by the vast hush around him. A tightening urgency gripped him, the sharp edge of something vital slipping beyond reach if he did not close the distance soon. The tunnel began to slope downward, the air growing colder and more bitter, the thorns thickening into a wall of menace. The White Buck paused at the mouth of a vast hollow chamber, turning halfway, eyes glowing with a light that belonged neither to sun nor star.

Bracken reached out blindly, desperate to touch, to understand—to ask the questions burning deep inside his mind. But as he neared, the buck stepped back, fading like mist drawn into shadow, swallowed by the cavern's darkness. Silence fell, suffocating and complete. Bracken was left alone, surrounded by the silent witnesses of the dead—bones entwined with thorn, and the memory of those glowing eyes.

He woke with a start, the taste of earth thick in his mouth, his paws caked with cold dirt. Within the hollow, the others slept, wrapped in dreams untroubled by shadows. Above, the moon hung low and distant, casting long, cold shadows across the clearing. Bracken's breath came fast and shallow, his heart still pounding with the dream's raw urgency.

He looked down at the ground. His pawprints led away from the warren, deeper into the dark woods, tracing a path that mirrored the winding tunnel from his dream. The earth was churned and damp, soft as though freshly disturbed—as if he had been digging, searching for something buried and forgotten beneath the surface.

A faint stirring in the grass made him glance back. Sorrel had lifted her head, the last threads of sleep still clinging to her eyes. The moon caught the red patches in her fur, turning them to pale fire. "Bracken? Where are you going?" she breathed, the sound quivering like a leaf in the night air.

He shook his head, words caught tight in his throat. "I . . . I don't know. I was dreaming." His voice sounded hollow, even to himself.

Her words were not cruel, but they carried the weight of all the burrows lost, of foxes that came in silence and snares that glinted too late to avoid. She did not need to raise her voice. The air did that for her—clear and still, so that every word landed sharp as flint.

Bracken's ears lowered. Shame flared in his chest like nettle-fire—quick and hot. "I didn't mean to startle you," he murmured. "I just . . . I saw something." He stared at his paws, caked with cold soil and dry grass, refusing to meet Sorrel's eyes. They were steady eyes, and his heart felt too unsteady to bear their gaze.

Thatch shifted slightly, not rising but watching with a narrowed look, as if weighing more than what had just been said.

His face, dark with age and knowing, gave little away, but something in the slope of his shoulders said he already suspected the shape of Bracken's answer.

"Did you see the White Buck?" Thatch asked, his voice quiet, but there was no mistaking the importance laid in the question.

Reed, sharp in his own right, turned toward Bracken. His tone held no wonder—only certainty. "Tell us. Did you see it?"

Bracken swallowed. The memory rose vivid and untouched—those eyes like night-pools, the white fur and twisting like smoke from a dead fire. He nodded slowly. "I did."

A silence fell then, but it was not empty. It was filled with breath held and thoughts turning. Thatch grunted, a sound low in his throat, as though something long buried had stirred in the earth beneath them.

"Dreams," he said, "are old things. Older than warrens. Older than hills. Sometimes they walk beside us. Sometimes ahead. And whether we want them or not, they find our path."

Sorrel's expression shifted—only slightly—yet something in her stance slackened, and her ears leaned toward Bracken. A glimmer passed over her face, quick and pale as sunlight slipping between briars.

"We stay together," she said, her tone gentler now, though it still carried the surety of hard ground underfoot. "We can't have any of us gone astray. Not now."

Bracken nodded, though the tightness in his chest did not ease. The others turned back toward the hollow of earth for a wink or more of sleep and roots, but Bracken lingered, staring at the world that awaited as if it might speak again. Inside him, the pull of the dream had grown stronger, not weaker. It coiled within his ribs like a thread drawn taut, humming with something ancient and unseen. It was not fear. Not exactly. It was a summons—low and quiet, rising from beneath the earth like sap in spring—urging him toward the dark, toward the places no rabbit named aloud, into whatever lay beyond the edge of known paths.

The next day dawned no brighter. The sky hung low and colorless, a lid pressed over the world, and the air itself felt thin, as if the land were holding its breath. Dew clung to the grass in sullen beads, cold and tasteless, and every sound—paw on earth, the snap of a twig—seemed to echo in the emptiness. They traveled in a line, Sorrel at the front, her stride purposeful but tense, Bracken behind her, then Wisp, and at the rear Thatch and Reed, who now lagged and whispered together in voices too low for the others to hear.

Reed's ears flicked constantly, his eyes darting from shadow to shadow as if expecting foxes or worse. Thatch's nose twitched, but he seemed to shrink in on himself, his pale fur dulled by dust. Bracken tried to catch their eyes, offering a quiet word or a gentle nudge, but his reassurance felt brittle, like a shell that would crack with the next sharp word.

"Only a little farther," Sorrell murmured, glancing past a clump of nettles that leaned over the narrow track. "There's a hollow just ahead . . . quiet ground, and maybe a trickle running."

But Thatch turned his head aside, and Reed, with his stillness, told all there was to tell.

The land about them took on a restless strangeness as the sun climbed higher. No hollow lay ahead—only great matted swells of bramble, sprawling in confused heaps, their leaves curled and rimmed with dull gray. A faint, sour taint drifted on the air, thin but clinging. Even the birds had gone, it seemed; only a single magpie gave a sharp, solitary call before the silence folded over them again.

By the turn of the sun, Sorrel flicked his ears and brought them to a stop among the brambles, their thorns dulled with the dust of the track. They crouched in the threadbare shade, sides heaving, easing their pads against the baked ground. The air was close; even the flies moved slow, drifting in the heat-haze. Thatch padded a short circuit, nose low, muscles tensing and easing under his coat as if some private unease kept pace with him. At last, he stood still, sides quivering.

"We ought to turn back," he said, the sound rough in his throat. "It's wrong to go on. Glenmere may be ailing, but its paths are known to us. This—" he glanced beyond the bramble edge to the wavering horizon "—this is a place for strangers, not for our kind."

Reed nodded, his ears flat and his gaze fixed on the ground. "We're sorry, Sorrel. We can't go on. Not with . . . all this." His voice faded. "Not with Bracken's strange sleep. Not with dreams that bled into waking."

Sorrel's jaw tightened, but she did not try to stop them. Her eyes, dark and steady, flicked from Thatch to Reed and back. "If you go, go quickly. And be careful. There's nothing left for you at Glenmere, but the world is no kinder here."

Thatch looked at Bracken, and fear was plain in his eyes—fear not just of the world, but of Bracken himself. "You see visions. Things that aren't there. It's not . . . normal. It's not . . . safe." His words were sharp, but his voice was small, as if he expected Bracken to vanish before his eyes.

Bracken could not answer.

His tongue felt thick, his mouth dry as sun-baked earth. The words that stirred in his chest—of dreams strange and shivering, of the White Buck who walked like a ghost through sleep, of the land itself pulling at his paws like a stream against a stone—clung to his throat and would not come. He stood there, silent.

Wisp edged closer to Bracken, pressing her side to his. Her fur was soft and warm, a balm against the cold growing in his chest. She said nothing at first, only leaned into him, her breath light against his shoulder. Then she spoke, so softly it might have been the wind threading through the grass.

"Don't listen to them," she whispered. Her voice, though quiet, held the firmness of deep roots. "I believe you, Bracken. I see things, too. Not always clear. Not always in dreams. But the world . . . it's shifting beneath our paws. The trees smell different, and the ground murmurs when I run. I feel it in the way the stars sit wrong in the sky. The old ways are cracking, like ice on the river. We have to change with it, or we'll be left behind."

Her eyes were wide, dark pools reflecting more than just starlight. She looked at him not with the gaze of one seeking comfort, but with the steady trust of one who had already chosen her path—and meant to walk it, even into shadow.

Bracken swallowed hard. His throat felt dry, as though he had swallowed dust and bark, and no words would rise to meet the moment. Yet something within him—tied tight as a hawthorn knot—began to loosen. Not because his fear had left him; it lingered still, sharp as thorn and cold as morning frost. But her belief in him—quiet, steady, unspoken—pressed against his doubt like a paw against nettle, enough to keep it at bay, if only for a little while.

Reed, who had watched too many hopes dry and blow away, gave a small grunt—not in scorn, but more like the groan of a gate long left to the wind. "The weak drop behind," he said, half to himself. "That's how it runs. Always has. The ground decides who keeps on and who lies down, and the ground's never been kindly."

There was no cruelty in his voice—just a tired sort of knowing, shaped by wind and hard soil. He did not look at Bracken, nor at Sorrel, but stared ahead as if already watching the grass swallow them whole.

Thatch and Reed turned without another word. Their bodies were drawn tight as bowstrings, eyes narrowed, ears flat against their heads. They moved together, bramble-sharp and sure-footed, slipping into the underbrush. A flick of Thatch's hind legs, a final rustle of dry grass, and then they were gone, their shapes swallowed by the field's hush and the brittle gold of late-season stems. The silence they left behind was not empty, but full of tension, like the air before a thunderstorm.

Sorrel turned to Bracken once more. Her gaze held no answer, no comfort—only the quiet steadiness of one who had seen too much to pretend otherwise. The bramble-shadow played across her face, drawing lines that might have been weariness, or worry, or something older still.

"We go on," she said. "The rest of us."

Her voice was steady, yes, but there was something softer underneath—like the muffled beat of a bird's wing in tall grass, or the hush of water moving through roots far beneath the earth. She did not name the ones they'd left behind. She didn't need to.

And so they moved on.

Fewer now.

The hush between them was deeper than before, not empty but full of what could no longer be said. Their paws pressed into the damp soil, one after the next, the rhythm slower, the path less sure. A crow called in the distance—once, twice, then fell silent. The wind moved gently through the high grass behind them, closing the way they'd come as if the land itself was erasing their passing.

Above, the sky shifted into gray. Beneath, the earth waited.

And the world, it seemed, was holding its breath.

By the next morning, the sun was pushing itself up, pale and unhurried, sending thin, slanting bars of light across the frost-touched field. Bracken moved from the shelter of the tall grass, nostrils quivering, ears forward, every sound and scent pressing close. Somewhere behind his eyes, like the last ripples after a stone is thrown, lingered the quiet, unblinking stare of the White Buck. The grass behind them shivered in the breeze, closing over their path as if they'd never passed at all.

Sorrel moved close, her body pressed low to the ground, eyes narrowed against the pale sky. She paused, nose lifted, whiskers trembling. "It's too quiet," she murmured, glancing sidelong at Bracken. "Even the larks are holding their tongues."

Bracken's paws pressed the hard, bare earth, each step sending a hush rippling through the emptiness. "They know something we don't," he said softly, more to himself than to the others.

Wisp lingered at the rear, pausing at every shifting shadow. She cocked her head, listening, as if the earth itself was whispering secrets. "The ground feels strange," she said. "Like it's waiting for something."

They moved on, hunger gnawing at their bellies. Sorrel stopped to nibble a wilted stem, chewed down to the root. She spat it out. "Bitter as old nettle," she muttered. "There's little enough left for any of us."

Bracken stopped and lifted his head, drawing the air along his whiskers. There was a change there—faint, but sure enough to quicken his pulse. He glanced back at the others, ears tipping forward and back.

"There'll be better ground soon," he said, though the tone was less certain than the words. "We must keep on. I think there's a hollow ahead."

They pressed on, their steps measured and soft, as though the earth itself might be listening. Overhead, the sky had dulled to the color of old pewter, and the hush of the fading afternoon lay across the land like a heavy cloth. A stillness lay over the fields, the kind that comes before a change in the weather—as though earth and trees were holding their breath together. Then from somewhere ahead drifted a sound, low at first, then rising: the hollow roar of wind caught in some hidden cave.

And there it was—far off in the distance—the dark line no one could mistake for anything else. The trees hunched together as though they'd turned against their own kind long ago, boughs twisting and clutching in silent knots, every branch seeming to wrestle some unseen enemy.

Bracken stopped, staring. "That's it," he said quietly. "The Crooked Wood."

Sorrel came up beside him, nose twitching. "It doesn't look right. The way they lean . . . it's as though the wind's never touched them."

"Perhaps it hasn't," murmured Wisp. She kept her eyes on the shadow ahead. "The Old Ones said not even the sun stays long in there."

From here, the stillness was like something held tight in a closed fist. No bird broke from the canopy, no leaf shifted. The air—even this far—seemed to hold the memory of damp earth that had never been dry. Bracken felt the stories pressing in on him: the tales the Elders told of paths that led travelers back to where they began, and of a place where a day might pass without moving at all.

Wisp shifted her paws and flicked an ear back. "I don't like the look of it," she said at last. "Something in there's waiting, and it's not waiting for good."

Sorrel glanced at her, then toward the shadowed fringe again. "We won't be going in," she said, trying to sound sure. "Our path keeps us to the open ground. We'll skirt it."

Bracken gave a short nod. "Aye. Best not to fret over shapes and stories. The old tales grow darker with telling."

But even as they moved on, angling their course toward the low heath, the Crooked Wood stayed in sight—a black seam against the pale reach of sky, warped and waiting.

"Shhh," said Sorrel, halting mid-step. "Listen."

Bracken and Wisp stopped beside her, ears lifting.

"Yes," said Bracken, a spark of gladness in his voice. "There . . . the sound of water."

Muted and far off, a thin murmur reached them—the sound of a stream winding unseen through roots and stones hidden from the sun.

Bracken led on, the others close behind. They slowed as the ground sank to a shallow dip, and there he stopped. His ears twitched, turning to catch what the breeze carried. Lifting his head, he drew in the air—a scent older than any rainstorm, rich and dark. "This is it," he murmured, hardly louder than the stirring grass. "What I sensed earlier. Old earth. Something deeper. Hidden, maybe."

He stepped forward warily, his paws finding purchase in the soft loam. The others followed, crowding in close, their eyes sharp and bright.

There, nestled beneath a spill of bramble and nettle, lay a dark mouth in the bank. A badger's sett. Quiet and unassuming, but old and well-kept. The creek whispered nearby, but not too near.

"Easier to dig away from the water," Bracken said, half to himself, as though repeating something long remembered from a tale told beneath the elder bushes.

Sorrel crept forward, sniffed the air, and flicked her ears. "Abandoned," she said, voice low. "Scent's still there, but much faded. Badger's been gone a long while."

Wisp peered into the gloom, her eyes wide. "Will it be safe?" she asked, voice barely above a whisper.

Sorrel nodded. "Safer than the open, with the wind turning cold."

One by one, the rabbits slipped into the cool darkness, the earth closing around them with a hush that was almost kind. Inside, they pressed close, flank to flank, breath mingling in the stillness. Sorrel settled herself near the entrance, ears half-cocked. Bracken stretched out, feeling the old earth beneath him, the scent of musk and memory filling his nose.

Wisp nestled beside him, her voice soft. "Do you think your dreams will follow you here?"

Bracken hesitated, then shook his head. "Maybe. But for now, let's just rest. The land will keep its secrets until morning."

Inside the old badger sett, the air was cool and close, and the darkness seemed to settle on their fur like a second skin. Sorrel kept her post at the entrance, ears pricked, eyes narrowed to slits as she watched the shifting shadows outside. Wisp pressed herself deeper into the earth, her flanks rising and falling with each quick breath.

Bracken lay quietly, letting the hush of the place seep into his bones. He remembered the tales his mother had told him as a kit, stories of the old badgers who had dug these tunnels—creatures slow and wise, who knew the secrets of earth and root. He wondered what had become of them, if any still lingered in the deep places, dreaming their slow, heavy dreams. The scent of badger was only a memory now, faded and thin, but it seemed to lend the sett a kind of dignity, as though the earth itself remembered its old inhabitants.

Bracken looked at Wisp. She was small, nervous, but there was something else in her now—a quiet strength, like the first green shoot pushing up through frost-hardened ground. He wondered what secrets she carried, what lessons the land had whispered in her ear.

For a time, they rested, sharing the warmth of the close earth and the comfort of one another's presence. The fear that had haunted them since Glenmere seemed to case, if only a little, replaced by a fragile sense of belonging.

Bracken found himself thinking of his dreams—the White Buck, the hollow tree, the voice that spoke without words. He wondered if the path they followed was truly their own, or if they were being led by something older and deeper than any of them could understand. The thought was both comforting and frightening, and he felt the weight of it settle in his chest.

As the light began to fade, a thin gleam seeped along the tunnel, touching the walls with a dim, greenish sheen like lichen under water. Sorrel shifted on her paws and spoke, her voice low but steady. "Best we stay here for the night," she said. "It's as safe a place as any, and we could do with the rest. Come morning, we'll be on again and see what lies beyond."

No one argued. The day's fear and tension had left them weary, and the thought of venturing out near the Crooked Wood after dark was more than any of them could bear.

As they settled in for the night, Bracken lay awake, listening to the slow, steady breathing of his companions. The earth was cool against his belly, and the scent of old leaves and distant rain filled the tunnel. He felt the old stories stirring in the darkness, the memory of badgers and rabbits and all the creatures who had come before. For the first time since leaving Glenmere, he felt a flicker of hope—a sense that, whatever path lay ahead, they would face it together.

That night, Bracken's dream was sharper than ever, as if the border between sleep and waking had thinned to a mere membrane. He found himself drifting through a tunnel lined with bones—long, delicate ribs and broken skulls pressed into the earth, their hollow sockets watching him with silent accusation. The air was thick with the scent of ash and something older, a bitter tang that clung to his fur and seemed to seep into his very bones. Each step he took sent a faint shiver through the ground, as if the earth itself remembered pain.

Ahead, the tunnel forked, darkness yawning in both directions. At the crossroads stood the White Buck, impossibly tall and radiant, its fur glowing with a cold, inner light that made the shadows shrink away. The buck's eyes were pools of pale fire, ancient and unreadable, and Bracken felt both drawn and afraid.

"Where are you leading me?" Bracken whispered, his voice swallowed by the hush of the tunnel.

The White Buck did not answer. Instead, it turned with measured grace, paws silent on the ashen floor, and began to walk down the left-hand path. Bracken hesitated, feeling the pressure of unseen eyes behind him, then followed. With every step, the air grew heavier, the walls pressing in, roots dangling from the ceiling like the fingers of some buried giant. They brushed his back and shoulders, cold and slick, leaving smears of black earth on his fur.

The tunnel widened abruptly, opening into a vast chamber beneath the earth. Roots hung from above, thick and twisted, their pale lengths resembling the ribs of an ancient beast long dead. The chamber's walls were veined with glimmering minerals, and the air shimmered with a faint, unnatural light. In the center of the chamber rose a mound of earth, its surface cracked and pulsing with a strange, pale glow, as if something alive struggled beneath the soil.

Bracken's heart thudded hard in his chest. The mound seemed alive, swelling and sinking with the slow pulse of something buried far below. Scattered all about were the bones of rabbits, half-lost in the soil, their shapes contorted as though they had once struggled upward and found no release. At the far side stood the White Buck, watching him—eyes sad yet full of an authority that needed no words.

"Is this near to where we'll find our new home?" asked Bracken, and his voice had a tremor in it.

The White Buck lowered its head, the motion slow and deliberate. Bracken felt—not in his ears, but deep within himself—a murmur that was neither sound nor thought alone. It was the echo of old tongues, half-forgotten, laced with caution, and carried through the far-spreading roots that clutch the earth.

"You seek Ash Hollow," the White Buck told him. "Beyond the bones."

The mound pulsed brighter, casting long, flickering shadows across the chamber.

Suddenly, Bracken was falling, the earth opening beneath his paws, roots snatching at his legs. He tumbled through darkness and cold, the scent of ash choking him, until—

He woke with a gasp, his breath ragged, his paws buried deep in the cold, damp soil. He was standing at the edge of a clearing, the same clearing he had seen in his dream. The others—Sorrel, Wisp—were behind him, still curled in uneasy sleep, unaware of his absence. The world was silent, save for the faint rustle of wind in the grass.

He stared at the ground where his paws had dug, heart pounding. The dream was not just a dream. It was a map, a memory, a warning. He could still feel the chill of the roots, the weight of the White Buck's gaze.

Turning back, the first hint of dawn touching the sky with pale gold, Bracken made his way to the others, his mind racing with questions and a new, terrible certainty.

Sorrel stirred as he approached, her eyes sharp even in the half-light. "Are you alright?"

Bracken nodded, though he was not sure it was true. "I think I know where we're going."

Wisp's eyes gleamed in the dimness, ancient and knowing. "Then lead on, dreamer. The land is waiting."

# Chapter 3
# The Crooked Wood

Bracken stirred first, though the light had barely sifted through the ragged canopy above. A thin grayness hung in the air, smelling of damp soil and old bark. He raised his head from his paws, ears pricked, listening to the faint scuttle of a beetle under the roots and the far-off call of a jay. Beside him, Sorrel twitched and murmured in his sleep, his hind legs giving a small kick. Wisp lay curled tight, nose tucked against his chest, his breath shallow and quick.

Soon Sorrel blinked awake, blinking as if the day itself had come too soon. She stretched her forelegs, scratched idly at the soil, and turned toward Bracken.

"You were muttering," Sorrel said softly. "Was it a dream?"

Bracken hesitated. Dreams were not spoken of lightly in the warren, least of all those that carried a shadow of meaning. Yet Sorrel's gaze was steady, and Wisp was rousing as well, his ears half-cocked, waiting.

"Yes," Bracken said at last, his voice low, as if the trees themselves might overhear. "I saw him . . . the White Buck."

Wisp lifted her head sharply. "The White Buck? You're certain?"

Bracken nodded. "He came to me in my dream, through the trees without sound. His fur shone, as though light were caught in it. He led me to a dark place of earthen tunnels. He stood before me and spoke. He said the place we seek is called Ash Hollow. He told me it lies just beyond the bones."

Neither Sorrel nor Wisp answered straightaway. The Crooked Wood creaked faintly as a breeze rattled through the twisted branches. At last, Wisp asked, "Bones? What bones? Does he mean the bones of fox or hare? Or some place where the ground is filled with death?"

Bracken shook his head, his whiskers trembling. "I don't know. He spoke, and then he was gone. I felt no fear of him, only a pull . . . as though he wished me to remember. Beyond the bones, he said, and nothing more."

Sorrel pushed herself upright, her fur clotted with scraps of leafmold. She sniffed at the air, testing the scents of morning. "Dreams or not, the day is here. If Ash Hollow lies beyond the bones, then the way is set for us to find it. No use crouching in roots, gnawing at words. Let's see what the new day brings."

She flicked his ears toward the east, away from the dark forest, where the light was spreading in long, pale streaks between the trees. The shadows bent and straightened, as if the Crooked Wood itself were stirring awake.

Wisp gave a doubtful glance at Bracken, but she rose to her feet all the same. "The White Buck does not come to every rabbit," he murmured. "If he has chosen you, Bracken, then we follow."

Bracken swallowed, the dream still alive in his chest. He could almost see the gleam of the White Buck's eyes, hear the whisper of his words. Ash Hollow, beyond the bones. The meaning was hidden, yet it pressed against his mind like a thorn under the pelt.

With Sorrel leading, they left the long-abandoned badger sett where they had slept and set off among the trees, the damp earth soft beneath their paws, the day waiting to show them what it would bring.

The air met them sharp and thin, brushed with the scent of old roots and the faint, sour tang of ash that clung to memory. Behind them yawned the sett's black entrance, still and empty as an unused burrow—nothing there now but chill and recollection. Ahead, the ground dipped into a shallow hollow where stones littered the turf like old bones, and dead grass stood up in brittle tufts.

Bracken paused. His nose twitched. The world seemed strangely thin about him, as if one misstep might splinter it. He looked to Sorrel, her ears pricked, muscles coiled like wire, and then to Wisp, who stood close against him, her eyes round and shining in the pale half-light.

"There," Sorrel whispered, her voice thin as the wind through dry weeds. "Darkness lies there. We'll keep away from it."

The Crooked Wood rose before them, in the distance, a jagged blackness lay across the horizon. It did not stand like a normal wood, but seemed to crouch and hunch, as if some great harm had been done to it long ago. Even from here, it looked ill-omened—branches twisted as though they had suffered long seasons of strain, their shapes clawing at the paling sky. The ground beneath those trees was bare, marked not by grass but by patches of leafmold and rot, though the very earth flinched from what lay within.

Bracken felt an old chill stirring as they drew near the dark wood. It crept into his belly, a fear rabbits know too well—born of pawprints vanished at the edge of silence and of tales told in low voices after nightfall. He remembered huddling close to his mother's side, ears pressed flat, as she spoke of silent woods where birds held their songs and the wind carried the trailing echoes of stranger voices, never quite animal nor entirely ghost. It was that sort of silence here: not an absence, but a presence—a hush so thick he fancied he could almost make out the words, murmuring just beyond his hearing.

"Was this all the work of Twolegs?" he asked, his voice no more than a tremor among the moss and stones.

Sorrel shook her head, eyes narrowed on the strange, ruined clearing. "Twolegs make plenty of misery, that's true," she answered quietly, "but I don't think even they could bring such a blight. Not this deep. There's something older at work here, I think . . . something that remembers before ever Twolegs set foot in these woods."

Wisp shivered. "It's cold there," she whispered. "Colder than it should be."

Sorrel's eyes were steady. "As I said, we'll go around. No sense crossing shadows that don't want crossing."

So they turned their path, keeping to the open ground where the dawn crept slow and gray, a thin, cold light spilling across the frost-bitten grass. The earth gave no warmth, but it gave enough to see by, and their paws made small, certain prints upon the hard soil. A crow called somewhere to the east, its voice carrying far in the still air, and Bracken felt his fear loosen its hold, if only by a whisker's breadth. Perhaps, he thought, the old tales were no more than stories—blown about on the wind like dry leaves.

"Ouch!" Wisp's cry broke the quiet, sharp and startled. She had fallen back, her head low, one paw raised.

Sorrel stopped at once, wheeling round, and in two bounds was beside her. "What's wrong?"

"It's . . . ah! Something's in my foot," Wisp said, her voice thin with pain. She tried to set the paw down, only to lift it again at once.

Bracken came up as Sorrel nosed at Wisp's forepaw. "Hold still, you little fidget," the older doe murmured. The fur had spread apart, and there, lodged deep between the soft pads, was a long blackthorn.

"Just as I thought," Sorrel said. "You've gone treading where you shouldn't."

"It hurt before I knew it," Wisp whimpered.

"Well, it won't hurt much longer." Sorrel gripped the thorn between her teeth and gave a swift, firm tug. Wisp let out a startled squeak, more from surprise than pain, and the thorn came free. Sorrel spat it into the grass, where it lay like some tiny, wicked spear.

"There," she said, her tone gentling. "Now let's see the rest of it."

She bent and began to lick the paw, slow and thorough, smoothing the fur and washing away the faint bead of blood. Wisp's ears lowered, and she leaned into Sorrel's warmth. Bracken stood close by, keeping watch on the open ground around them, though his eyes softened at the sight.

When Sorrel was satisfied, she gave the paw one last lick. "Try it now."

Wisp set it down cautiously, then hopped once, twice, and managed a small smile. "It's better. Thank you."

"Good," Sorrel said, brushing past her to take the lead again. "We've still ground to cover before the sun's high."

And so they went on, the three of them, paws falling in quiet rhythm, the morning light stretching long behind them. The thorn lay forgotten in the grass, its brief harm already fading to memory. Then a scent came, sharp and musky on the wind. Bracken froze, his ears going flat.

Sorrel's voice was no louder than a blade of grass. "Down. Now."

They dropped where they stood, bodies pressed low, breath held. The grass here was sparse, and there was no real cover. They could do nothing but lie still and listen. Bracken sniffed again: earth, ash—and there, unmistakably—stoat. Fresh.

A shadow flickered—long, low, sinuous, slipping through the grass with a terrible ease. The stoat's eyes glinted, its body all hunger and muscle, moving with purpose.

Wisp whimpered, barely audible. Bracken felt her shaking beside him. The stoat moved nearer, its head weaving, tasting the air. It was hunting. It had caught them.

Sorrel met Bracken's eyes. No words passed between them, yet the meaning lay clear, sharp as frost along the edge of a leaf.

Bracken nudged Wisp gently with his nose. "Run," he whispered. "Not straight. Wide arcs. Twist back. Leave scent everywhere."

Wisp's fear sharpened into quicksilver resolve, and she sprang forward. A streak of fur and trembling limbs, weaving through the hollow, slipping under brambles, vaulting over roots. The stoat hissed and lunged, blind with hunger, snapping at shadows that were not her.

Sorrel and Bracken darted in the opposite direction, scattering scent in crooked patterns, doubling upon their own tracks, teasing the trail. Clods of earth and tufts of grass flew from their paws, marking false lines, turning the pursuit into confusion. Behind them came the hiss, the snap, the relentless surge—and then, gradually, silence.

The three rabbits pressed themselves beneath the low arch of a fallen branch, fur damp, chests rising and falling as if they were breathing the night itself.

"We did it," Wisp gasped, eyes bright, glinting like dew under moonlight.

The stoat's cry had faded, its presence gone from the air, yet another scent now threaded through the wood, more insistent, more unnerving.

In the effort to mislead the predator, they had lost all sense of where they were. Darkness pressed in on every side, and the hollow seemed swallowed by unfamiliar shadows.

Bracken lifted his head. The warmth of the night drained from him as dark, sinister trees loomed above, curling and knotted, their limbs hung with lichen and the quiet weight of age. They had slipped, without realizing, into the Crooked Wood, a place older than memory and thrumming with unspoken danger.

"What have we done?" he whispered, voice tight.

Sorrel's reply was flat, almost cold. "We traded one danger for another."

Bracken swallowed. The air was thick here, like something rotting in its sleep. The old stories had not lied. The Crooked Wood was real, and it had found them.

And something within it had opened an eye.

They crouched in the hush that followed, wrapped tight in the silence of that place. The trees seemed to lean in, their boughs blotting out the last of the morning. The light that filtered through was sickly green, tinged with damp. Bracken breathed it in and tasted mold and stone and something older still.

Wisp's whiskers flicked. "It's too quiet," she whispered, the words falling like leaves. "No birds. No wind."

"Keep close together, tight," Sorrel murmured, sweeping the gloom with her eyes. "Don't wander. Not for anything."

Bracken steadied himself. He thought of the White Buck from his dreams, the thorns, the hollow trees. Was this that place? The roots beneath his feet throbbed faintly. Somewhere nearby, a whisper curled in the air.

They moved with careful steps, ears alert, paws sinking lightly into the dark soil. The trees were old beyond measure, their bark cracked and darkened with sap that glistened like amber in the dim light. Limbs arched and twisted, draped with curling moss and lichen. Bones dangled in some places, small ones, delicate as swallows.

Once, Wisp stumbled. The ground gave, revealing roots twisted like grasping fingers.

Bracken led now, though he felt no boldness in him. Only the need to go forward. The branches thickened behind them, closing the way like gates. The cold deepened.

Then a sharp crack. A branch, somewhere deeper in the dark. All three stopped.

Silence again. And something unseen, waiting.

They pressed close together, small and still, the world vast and unkind around them. Bracken felt Wisp's trembling and Sorrel's steadying breath. He remembered the words passed down by old rabbits long dead: When the world turns strange, the wise keep together.

So they did. They waited. And the Crooked Wood watched. And something else too.

The Crooked Wood pressed in around them, a world of tangled branches and sour earth, where the light itself seemed to shy away. Bracken led the way, his paws silent on the bare, root-laced ground, every muscle taut with the tension that had settled into his bones since they'd entered this place. Sorrel moved close behind, her eyes sharp and wary, while Wisp, smallest and most sensitive, kept to the rear, her nose twitching at every strange scent.

"No matter which way I turn," Bracken said softly, "the horizon offers no promise of light. I cannot tell which way to go."

He pressed onward, sniffing the air for a trace of clarity, with Sorrel and Wisp following closely.

"Perhaps this way," he murmured, "will lead us from this dreadful place."

The trees here were older than memory, their trunks twisted and split, bark peeling away in long, curling strips. Some leaned together, forming archways of shadow, while others stood apart, their roots clawing at the earth as if trying to drag themselves free. No grass grew beneath these trees, only a thin, gray moss, and the scattered bones of small creatures who had not been so lucky as to find a way out.

The silence was absolute. Not a bird sang, not a beetle scuttled, not even the wind dared to stir the branches overhead. The only sound was the soft, rapid thud of three rabbit hearts, and the careful, measured steps as they picked their way through the gloom.

After a time, Bracken slowed, his ears flicking back and forth. "We shouldn't go further," he whispered, voice barely more than a breath. "The wood gets thicker ahead. We could lose ourselves."

Sorrel nodded, her nose working the air. "We need to think. If we can keep to the edge, we might find a way out, or at least a place to rest until it's safe to move on."

Bracken shifted uneasily, his paws testing the leaf-mold as though it might give way beneath him. "I'm not sure where the edge is," he murmured. His ears stood forward, straining for sound, but there was nothing, only the hush of the trees pressing in. He glanced beyond the thickets and saw no gleam or softening of the dark. "There's no light at all out there . . . beyond the trees it's as though the world ends."

Wisp crept closer, keeping low. "Then we're already inside it," she whispered. Her eyes shone faintly in the dim hollow, wide with unease. "I don't like it here. It feels wrong. Like something's watching."

Sorrel shook herself, as if to rid her fur of the chill that clung to it. "If we've blundered in, then we can find our way back out. Listen . . . it's only trees, however bent they look. We'll keep to them as close as we may, and when the ground tells us we've gone far enough, we'll stop."

But as they moved again, the Crooked Wood seemed to tighten about them. Bracken's heart thudded with the steady tread of paws, and still no gap opened, no glimmer of sky. The air smelt of soil that had never known the sun, dead leaves compacted deep as stone. He thought of the tales told by Elders, in which rabbits wandered these trees until their whiskers grayed and fell, never finding the way they sought.

Yet, he tried to muster a reassuring smile, even though his own fear was too near the surface. "We'll be all right," he said, though the words felt thin in the heavy air.

They paused beneath the gnarled limbs of a massive ash, its roots rising from the ground like the ribs of some ancient beast. The three huddled together, their bodies pressed close for comfort and warmth. For a moment, they simply listened, as if the wood itself might reveal its secrets if only they were quiet enough.

Then, on the edge of the silence, came a scent—sharp, musky, undercut with something cold and metallic. Bracken's nose twitched, and his heart lurched in his chest.

Sorrel's ears snapped forward. "Do you smell that?"

Wisp's voice was a trembling thread. "What is it?"

Bracken didn't need to answer. The scent was unmistakable, even to a rabbit who had never seen its source. Feline. Cat.

Fear gripped them, cold and absolute. The stories from the warren came flooding back—stories of the great cats that moved like shadows, their eyes burning in the night, their claws silent but deadly. Stories of rabbits who vanished without a trace, save for a tuft of fur and the echo of a scream.

"Run," Sorrel hissed, and in a heartbeat, all three bolted deeper into the wood.

They darted between the roots and branches, their bodies low and swift, panic lending speed to their limbs. The world became a blur of shadow and movement, the trees rushing past in a tangle of limbs and darkness. But the scent of cat grew stronger, filling their nostrils, driving them onward.

Bracken's lungs burned, but he did not slow. He could feel Wisp at his side, her breath coming in short, terrified gasps. Sorrel led the way, her path weaving through the densest thickets, always searching for cover, for safety.

At last, they stumbled into a small hollow, hidden beneath the roots of a vast, ancient yew. The roots arched over them, forming a low, tangled ceiling, while the earth beneath was soft and dry, scattered with old leaves and the faintest trace of dying moss.

It was barely large enough for the three of them, but it was shelter, and for a moment, it felt like sanctuary.

They huddled close, their small bodies taut with weariness and the cold trace of fear that still clung to their fur. The scent of cat—sharp, sour, and death-tainted—was fainter now, dulled by the thick roots and the dampness of the soil, but it hadn't vanished. It hung at the edges of their senses like a storm just beyond the hilltop, not yet gone, only waiting.

A few mice skittered through the undergrowth, quick and quiet, their movements nervous. One paused to sniff the air, then vanished into a tangle of ivy without a sound.

Bracken lowered his head. "They've scented it too," he murmured. "It's not far."

Wisp shivered beside him. "I hate that smell," she said. "It smells like death."

Sorrel's ears flicked. "Keep low. And don't trust the quiet."

Her eyes fixed on the narrow opening that led back into the wood. She was about to speak, her mouth opening to give the order to run, when a sudden, heavy sound came.

Thud!

All three rabbits flinch.

Something had landed just outside their hollow.

Bracken peered out, his eyes wide with terror. A shape lay sprawled on the ground—a stoat, its body twisted and broken, blood matting its fur. The wounds were unmistakable: deep, ragged gashes, the marks of sharp teeth and cruel claws. The stoat's eyes stared sightlessly, its mouth frozen in a final snarl.

The scent of cat was now a suffocating fog, thick and acrid, curling up from the black soil and winding through the roots like a living thing. It clung to fur and throat, a silent, invisible threat. In the cramped hollow beneath the ancient tree, the three rabbits pressed together, hearts fluttering wildly, all warmth and hope driven out by that cold, predatory promise.

Wisp whimpered, shrinking so close to Bracken he could feel her trembling. "It's here. It's right here. What do we do?" Her voice was a mere thread, barely audible over the pounding of his own heart.

Sorrel's answer came steady, but Bracken, who had known her since kit-hood, heard the tremor beneath her words. "We have to run. Now. Before—"

She never finished. The air split with a sound that did not belong in the world of rabbits: a low, guttural laugh, rolling through the darkness like distant thunder. It was a sound that spoke of hunger and cruelty, and the terrible, simple joy of the hunt. The laugh came again, closer, echoing through the roots and branches, making the very ground seem to shudder beneath their paws.

Bracken pressed himself flat, ears pinned, every muscle screaming to dig, to vanish, to become nothing more than a shadow among shadows. But the hollow was a trap, and the cat— whatever it was—knew it.

A shape slid into the edge of their vision, a ripple of darkness, sleek and terrible. Two eyes gleamed in the gloom, catching the faintest glimmer and turning it to fire. The voice that followed was soft, almost playful, but beneath it lay the unyielding promise of death.

"Well, well," it purred, the words winding through the roots like smoke. "Little coneys, hiding in the dark. Did you think you could escape me?"

The cat's form was only half-seen, a shifting shadow among shadows, but its presence filled the hollow, pressing in on all sides. The dead stoat—its body twisted, fur matted with blood—lay sprawled at the entrance, a message written in violence and fear.

Sorrel bared her teeth, her body taut and trembling—though whether from fear or fury, even she might not have known.

"We're not afraid of you," she said, but her voice quavered, a lie spoken for courage's sake.

The cat gave a low, rumbling laugh, a sound like dry bracken crackling under a hunter's paw. It sent a chill through Bracken, down to the roots of his fur. There was something ancient in it—cruel, knowing, and amused.

Without warning, a mouse darted from the undergrowth, a blur of desperate courage. Too quick. Too hopeful. The cat moved with dreadful ease, one heavy paw coming down like a thunderclap. Claws unsheathed, curved and sharp, split into the little creature with no more effort than snapping a twig. The mouse's squeak was brief—a life ended in a heartbeat.

The cat's eyes gleamed, and the air itself seemed to hold its breath. "Pesky little things," he said, almost idly, as if the act had cost him nothing at all.

He stepped into the pale, sickly light that filtered through the roots, and at last, the rabbits saw him fully. He was of pure, predatory darkness, his fur the color of dried blood, muscles coiled beneath the hide, moving with silent menace through the shadowed undergrowth. His eyes were chips of obsidian, reflecting nothing but the faint, malevolent gleam of the moonless night. His ears, perpetually flattened, were notched from countless silent skirmishes, and his whiskers, stiff as wire, twitched with a supernatural sensitivity to the tremors of fear.

He moved like a ripple in the fabric of the forest's gloom, a phantom among the gnarled roots and whispering thorns. His paws, deceptively soft, landed with a silence that preceded doom, each step carrying the coiled power of a spring.

He looked down at the rabbits, his mouth curling in a slow, terrible smile as he snapped his teeth. "Gnash," he said, as if the name itself was a warning. "That's what they call me. The mice, the stoats, even the Dark Ones."

Bracken swallowed, his throat dry as old bark. "Dark Ones?"

Gnash's eyes narrowed, and he flicked his tail, the tip twitching with amusement. "They are coneys like you are, yet not as you are. They are different, terribly so. Their fur is black, their eyes sharp, and they dwell deep in the Crooked Wood. They do not nibble on tender grass—none flourishes here. They take what comes to them. Mice. Stoats. Sometimes, things far worse. The Crooked Wood changes everything that lingers too long beneath its boughs."

Wisp recoiled, her nose wrinkling in horror. "Rabbits that eat meat?" she whispered, scarcely able to shape the sounds. "Such ways are not of the world we were born to."

Gnash's whiskers twitched, and he gave a low, satisfied purr. "You should be grateful, little ones. I do not hunt coneys.

Mice and stoats are tastier. But the Dark Ones . . . ah, they are clever, and fierce. I leave them be . . . to their own hungers."

Sorrel's voice was brittle as frost. "Why do you stay here, then? Why not hunt in the open fields?"

Gnash's smile widened, showing the gleam of his teeth— sharp, yellowed, and meant for killing. "Out there, the world is full of noise and light. Here, the shadows are thick, and the prey is plentiful. The Crooked Wood is mine, and all who walk within it learn to fear my name. Except the Dark Ones. They fear nothing."

"How do you escape them?" Bracken asked, his voice barely more than a whisper.

Gnash chuckled, a sound like pebbles tumbling in a dry streambed. "I can do something they cannot. I can climb the trees." He glanced up, as if to remind them that the world above the roots belonged to him alone.

A hush settled over the wood, as deep as the soil over a forgotten grave. Bracken sensed the forest closing around them, aware of what might be hidden among the roots and thorns.

He shifted closer, his ears forward. "We seek a place called Ash Hollow," he said. "Do you know of it?"

Gnash's eyes narrowed, the fur along his shoulders stirring as if with some private thought. For a long while, he was silent, only the rasp of his breath moving in the still air. At last, he shook his head, slow and final. "Whatever tales others whispered to you, little coney, this name carries no meaning for me. Ash Hollow lies beyond the edge of what I know."

Bracken felt a hollow disappointment at the cat's reply.

"Will you help us, then?" he asked.

Wisp spoke quickly, her voice trembling. "Yes, please. We only wish to leave this place. We do not belong here."

Gnash studied her for a long moment, his eyes unreadable, the tip of his tail moving in small, sharp strokes. Then he turned his head northward with a careless flick. "That way will serve you best. The trees thin there, and the ground begins to climb. If you are swift and clever, you may yet see the sun again."

Sorrel's ears flicked, uncertain. "Will you guide us?"

The cat's laugh came low and smooth, with the edge of something ancient in it—like cold water slipping through a stone crack. It was not loud, but it carried, and every rabbit in the clearing felt it down in their bones.

"Ah, little coneys," he said, his voice soft and cruel, almost fond. "I like you. You're different than the others . . . you're cleverer, and there's a sweetness to you. You belong more to sun than to shadow. But liking is not enough."

He stretched, long and languid, his tail twitching against the bark. "I have my own game, and it's not a slow one. It doesn't pause for kind eyes or brave hearts. I will not dull my claws for the sake of sympathy."

His eyes flicked from one to the next, bright as frost under moonlight. "In the Crooked Wood," he said, "only the quick endure. Only the clever live long. The rest are stories waiting to be told by someone else."

He turned then, his shape folding into the shadows as if he'd never been more than mist and wind, a flicker of crimson and black vanishing among the roots and stone. His voice lingered, sly and smooth, like a fox's tail brushing past the burrow mouth.

"Remember this," he said, as the gloom swallowed him. "The Dark Ones are always hungry. And they are not as friendly as I."

A hush followed, like the moment before a hawk's cry. Not one of them moved. The air seemed colder, as though the very ground had heard and taken warning.

And then he was gone, and only the faint scent of ash and something older remained.

For a long moment, none of the rabbits moved. The hollow seemed smaller now, the roots pressing in, the darkness deeper and colder. Bracken felt Wisp's trembling beside him, and Sorrel's steady, defiant presence.

"We go north," Sorrel said at last, her voice quiet but sure. "Like the cat said."

And so, with the scent of cat fading behind them and the warning of the Dark Ones echoing in their minds, the three rabbits slipped from the hollow and pressed on, deeper into the heart of the Crooked Wood, where even the bravest learned to fear the dark.

Beneath the gnarled roots of the Crooked Wood, where sunlight was a memory and the earth itself seemed to brood, sprawled a warren that no gentle rabbit of field or hedgerow could have imagined. Here, the tunnels were not soft with moss or sweet with the scent of clover, but carved from black, peaty soil, slick with damp and lined with the bones of birds, mice, and the brittle shells of beetles. The air was thick with rot, old blood, and the sharp tang of fear. Silence ruled, broken only by the distant drip of water or the restless shuffling of many paws.

The rabbits that dwelt in this place were not the gentle folk of fields and hedgerows, nor the bright-eyed wanderers of upland heath. These were the Dark Ones, the ones Gnash spoke of—creatures of silence and shadow. Their pelts held no color but black, the black of moonless nights and ash-choked burrows, slick with a strange sheen that caught no light. Their eyes shone like flint in a streambed, hard and quick, ever watching. Ears longer than most, thin as grass-blades, twitched with every sound, every tremble in the earth. They moved with a lean, coiled grace, their limbs made not for show but for swift, silent killing. And their teeth—sharp as a stoat's—had known more than clover and bark. Yet most troubling of all was that they had tasted meat and savored it.

The warren was called Blackroot, and the name suited it well. It wound deep beneath the hill, a place where roots grew sideways and the air never moved. The tunnels twisted like the mind of a fox, narrow in places where even a kit might struggle to pass, then opening suddenly into chambers wide enough for a gathering of many. No two paths were alike, and only the Dark Ones knew the turns by heart. Strangers did not find their way easily. And if they did, they seldom returned.

The walls of Blackroot were damp and cold, always cold, as though the earth here had forgotten the touch of sun. The roots that curled down from the ceilings were pale and gnarled, and in some places, bones jutted from the floor or walls—bleached white or stained dark with age. Some said they were from old prey, others from enemies who had wandered too far. Either way, they stood as warnings. Nothing lived here by chance.

And yet, there was an order to it all. A silence that spoke of law, not chaos. For the Dark Ones were not mindless beasts. They were rabbits still, bound by their own tales, their own rites and reckonings. But theirs was an old law—harsher, colder. A law carved in root and blood. They trusted only their own, and even then, only as far as hunger allowed. They had learned to hunt in silence, to strike without warning, to vanish into shadow before any could mark their passage. All creatures who dwelt in the Crooked Wood knew to fear their name.

In a half-dark chamber, two young rabbits grappled over the scrap of mouse. Their black coats fluffed out, they scrabbled and bit with furious energy, eyes gleaming in the gloom. It was more than play—there was a sharpness, a need, to every strike of their paws.

Their mother, a doe named Nightfall, sat close by, muscles still beneath her scarred flanks where a stoat's teeth had once tried to close. Her gaze never wavered, fixed on the tussle with something colder than pity.

As she watched, one of the kits lunged to seize the meat, dragging more than his share to his side, licking triumph from his paws. Nightfall's head shot forward, teeth flashing so near the other youngster that he squealed.

Her voice came like dry bracken crackling underfoot. "Do you think kindness would fill your belly? Greed is power, and you had best learn it. The world will not give, only take. If you can't fight for your share, the frost and the crow will take you sooner than hunger."

The kit crouched low, his ears flat, eyes wide with the lesson. Nightfall drew back, her gaze moving to the shadows of the den where others lay, and added, "Remember . . . it is not the gentle that see spring."

At the warren's black heart, where the earth pressed low and the roots hung down like the ribs of some buried giant, the chamber opened—hollow and still as the inside of a skull. There, upon a mound of hardened earth and old bone, crouched the leader, the Chief. Cinder, they called him. And the name was earned, not given.

He was a monstrous thing by rabbit measure—larger than any buck in the warren, his shoulders broad, his flanks knotted with old strength. One of his back legs dragged when he moved, stiff and twisted from a wound no one dared speak of, but it had not slowed his rise. If anything, it seemed to have sharpened his cruelty, like a thorn that festers rather than heals. His fur, once the black of wet stone, was streaked now with ash-gray, and patches hung ragged where old scars had taken root. One ear was gone, torn away in a fight long past, leaving a jagged edge that twitched at shadows.

Yet his eyes were the most terrible—yellow, sharp, and cold as the winter moon, and they did not blink. They had seen much, too much, and yet they watched still, missing nothing, forgiving less. When Cinder looked at you, it was as if the ground beneath your paws shrank and the dark drew nearer.

The air in that place was close, thick with the scent of old blood and burrow-musk, clinging to fur and claw. This was no gathering for stories or song, no place for the harmless chatter of does and kittens. This was the chamber of judgment, heavy with silence and shadow. And Cinder—crippled, cunning, terrible—was its voice, the dark stone at the heart of the warren.

Around the large Chief, the council crouched low, half-circle and silent, their bodies tense as wire. The soil beneath them was scored with old claw marks, traces of arguments ended, and decisions carved deep. Two bucks crouched in the back—Sable and Dusker—sharpening their teeth on a length of bone, their movements quick, practiced, and steady, as though shaped by long seasons of restless waiting and the endless need to be ready.

Sable nosed at a bare patch of earth, but his eyes kept straying to the others of the council.

"What d'you think they'll bring back?" he asked, his voice low.

Dusker twitched an ear. "If they go as far as the ash copse, there's a good chance of vole. Might be slow, this late, but I've seen them fat enough in autumn."

Sable's whiskers quivered. "Vole's good, but I wouldn't mind a scrap of blackbird. The marrow's richer."

Dusker shifted on his paws, the fur along his shoulders bristling. "Bird's luck, Sable. You take what's given. My sire always said . . . if it squeals before it dies, it keeps you sharp."

For a moment, neither spoke, listening to the wind outside snag in the crooked branches. Somewhere far off, a harsh cry cut the air, and Sable's ears stood high.

"Sounds promising," he murmured.

Dusker's teeth showed in a brief, eager grin. "Then we'll eat well tonight."

As Sable and Dusker worked their teeth against the bone, the others of the council remained still, some whispering softly to a companion, others sunk in silence. The chamber glowed with the faint, sickly light of fungus clinging to the walls, its patches swelling like damp sores, casting everything in a ghostly green pallor. The air hung heavy with the scent of meat—fresh and old, mingled together, streaking the breath with a rank sweetness that turned the stomach and lingered in the throat.

A sudden commotion at the entrance drew every eye. A young buck, slick with dew and flanks heaving, darted into the chamber and threw himself down before the Chief. This was Pitch, the swiftest scout in the warren, his nose keener than any fox's.

Cinder's voice was low and rough, like gravel dragged across stone. "Speak, Pitch. What brings you running like a stoat with its tail afire?"

Pitch raised his head, eyes shining with excitement and a flicker of fear. "Chief Cinder, I bring news from the edge of the wood. The cat . . . Gnash . . . hunts near the northern boundary. And he is not alone. Three rabbits, pale-furred and soft-eyed, have entered the Crooked Wood. They travel together, but they do not know our ways."

A murmur ran through the council, a ripple of interest and hunger. Shade, a doe whose muzzle was stained with the blood of her last meal, leaned forward. "Fire-pelts? Here? They will not last a night."

Cinder's eyes narrowed. "Gnash is a danger, but he keeps to himself and walks the trees when required. These others . . . the fire-pelts . . . what do you know of them?"

Pitch's whiskers quivered. "I watched them from the bramble thicket. They move like rabbits from the open fields . . . nervous, uncertain. They are afraid. The cat toyed with them, but let them go. I heard him send them north, toward the thinning trees."

Ashen, another elder, ears notched from many fights, snorted. "Fools. If they reach the edge, they'll bring others. The Crooked Wood is not for their kind."

Cinder sat unmoving, the breath in his chest slow and deep, as if drawn from the dark soil itself. For a long while, he said nothing. His eyes, dull yellow and unblinking, stared into some distance none of the others could see. Once, long ago, there had been other days—days of soft grass and skylark song, when the morning light had meant warmth, not danger. But that world had died. Burned away like bracken in a dry wind. In its place remained only hunger, and the lessons the Crooked Wood taught with tooth and silence.

He shifted, the twisted leg scraping against the mound with a faint rasp that carried through the still air. Then his gaze settled on Pitch, who crouched low, ears tilted forward and nose quivering with attention.

"You'll follow them," Cinder said, his voice low, rough as bark rubbed by the wind. "Take two others with you, no more." He lifted his head, eyes fixed on Sable and Dusker. "Go with Pitch. Obey his lead in every step."

Sable and Dusker froze, their hearts thumping beneath their fur. "Yes, sir," they mumbled, voices tight with unease.

Cinder turned back to Pitch, outlining the task. "Keep low. Stay downwind. Watch every move they make. Let them think the wood belongs to them, at least for a time. Let them tire, let them grow careless."

Around them, the other rabbits of the council remained motionless, ears twitching at every sound: a fallen leaf, the distant snapping of a twig, the sigh of wind through twisted branches.

"When night falls," Cinder continued, "and sleep drapes them in slowness, you strike. Swift, silent. No killing unless you must. Bring the fire-pelts back. Alive. The Crooked Wood is not a road for strangers to wander. It is ours. And those who enter without leave will learn what that means."

His eyes narrowed, sharp and cold. The roots above trembled faintly, as if the warren itself had shivered in recognition, holding its breath for the orders just given.

"I want them alive," he reminded them, lips drawn back in a hard sneer. "Alive! They will make for a great feast."

Pitch's eyes gleamed. "Yes, Chief." He rose, gave a quick, sharp salute—forepaws pressed together, head bowed—and vanished into the tunnel, his black fur swallowed by the darkness.

Cinder turned to the council. "Let none disturb the cat. He is a shadow among shadows, and he keeps the stoats and foxes from our door. But these strangers . . .they will fill out bellies and then feed the roots of the wood."

A ripple of approval ran through the council. Shade licked her lips, eyes shining with a cold, predatory light. "Perhaps we should send out more to hunt tonight, Chief. The meat grows lean, and the young are hungry."

Cinder nodded. "Let the young ones have the tunnels near the old oak. The mice run thick there. Leave the hunting to Pitch. He will bring us what we need."

The council dispersed, slipping away into the maze of tunnels, bodies silent as smoke. Cinder remained, his thoughts troubled. He had seen many things in his long life, but the world beyond the Crooked Wood was changing. The old stories spoke of a time when rabbits ate only grass and feared only the shadow of the hawk. But here, in the heart of the wood, the old ways had died. Hunger had taught them new lessons, and only the strong survived.

He closed his eyes, listening to the distant sounds of the warren—the soft gnawing of teeth on bone, the rustle of paws in the dark, the faint, high cries of the kits as they played at hunting in the side tunnels. This was his kingdom, carved from the heart of the wood, and he would defend it with tooth and claw.

Pitch, along with Sable and Dusker, moved through the tunnels with the ease of long practice, bodies low and silent, ears flicking at every sound. They passed through a narrow gap, squeezed beneath a root, and emerged into the cool night air. The Crooked Wood stretched before them, a tangle of shadows and twisted branches, the ground bare and cold.

Pitch paused, nose twitching, catching the faint scent of the strangers—rabbits, but not like any he had ever known. Their fear was sharp and fresh, a beacon in the night. He smiled, showing teeth sharpened on bone, and slipped into the undergrowth.

His orders were clear: follow, watch, and at night bring them to Blackroot. As he and the others vanished into the darkness, Blackroot behind them settled into its nightly rhythm—hunters stalking the tunnels, kits learning the ways of tooth and claw, Cinder brooding on his mound of bone and earth. Above, the wind rattled the twisted branches, and somewhere, far off, the cat's laughter echoed through the night.

In the Crooked Wood, the old ways were dead, and only the strong endured. Tonight, the hunt had begun.

# Chapter 4
## Shadows in the Crooked Wood

Pitch moved like a shadow through the undergrowth, his black pelt blending seamlessly with the gloom of the Crooked Wood. The air was thick with cold and the scent of rot, every breath tinged with the memory of old blood and damp earth. Above, the twisted branches of ancient trees clawed at the sky, letting in only slivers of gray light that faded quickly as dusk deepened. He paused, nose twitching, and caught the faint, unfamiliar scent of the three strangers. Behind him, Sable and Dusker waited, silent and watchful, their eyes glinting like wet stones in the half-light. Together, they pressed on, keeping low and silent, as the last warmth of day bled away and the true cold of the Crooked Wood crept in.

Ahead, Sorrel, Bracken, and Wisp moved slowly, wary at every step. The ground was bare and cold beneath their paws, the soil slick with old leafmold and the roots of trees that seemed to writhe in the gloom. All around, the Crooked Wood was alive with eyes—creatures of the black, and the deeper, hungrier gaze of the Dark Ones themselves.

Sorrel led, her ears high and alert, pausing often to listen to the silence that pressed in on all sides. Bracken moved close behind, his nose low, every muscle taut with unease. Wisp, smallest and most sensitive, lingered at the rear, her eyes wide, flinching at every shifting shadow.

"It's colder here," she whispered, her breath a faint mist. "Colder than it should be."

Bracken nodded, his own voice tight. "It's the wood. Even the sunlight is afraid to show itself."

Sorrel glanced back, her tone steady but her eyes troubled. "Keep close. We're not alone."

They pressed on, the hush between them full of things unspoken, each step a silent plea for dawn.

As what daylight there was faded, the Crooked Wood seemed to close in tighter. Branches arched overhead, blocking what little sky remained, and the ground dipped into hollows where the cold pooled thick as water. The silence was total, broken only by the occasional snap of a twig or the distant, hollow call of a crow. The rabbits felt eyes upon them—dozens, hundreds, watching from every shadow. Once, a pair of yellow glints flashed in the gloom, and Sorrel froze, nose twitching, before urging the others on.

"Don't look back," she murmured. "Just keep moving. North, like the cat said."

The path grew harder to find, the roots twisting and clutching at their paws, the air heavy with the scent of old secrets and hidden dangers. Bracken shivered, recalling the stories of this dark place—how it swallowed the unwary, how even the wind lost its way.

Night fell like a curtain, and the darkness grew thick enough to touch. The three rabbits stumbled into a shallow hollow beneath the tangled roots of a withered maple tree, its trunk twisted and bare, branches reaching up like pleading arms. Here, at last, Sorrel called a halt.

"We'll rest here," she said, voice low. "Not a lot of cover. But we can't continue running blind."

Bracken pressed close to the roots, his breath coming fast, while Wisp curled into herself, trembling.

"Do you think they're following us?" she whispered.

Sorrel glanced at Bracken, then shook her head. "If they are, we'll hear them before we see them. For now, we keep quiet."

The three huddled together, the cold seeping into their bones, the silence pressing down like a weight.

Unseen, Pitch and his companions crouched in the undergrowth, eyes fixed on the hollow where the strangers had settled. The darkness was their ally, and they waited, patient and still, as the night deepened. Around them, the Crooked Wood was alive with movement—shadows flickering, leaves rustling, the low, hungry whisper of something old and restless. Pitch signaled to Sable and Dusker, his ears flicking in silent command.

"Wait," he breathed, so low only the roots could hear. "I sense them. There. A small hollow beneath the maple. Let them tire. Let the dark do our work."

The three Dark Ones melted into the gloom, watching and waiting, their bodies tense with anticipation.

Within the hollow, the three travelers spoke in hushed voices, trying to keep fear at bay.

"How much farther is it?" Wisp asked, her voice barely audible.

Bracken shook his head. "I don't know. The wood twists itself around us. I keep thinking we're moving north, but every path feels the same."

Sorrel lifted her nose searching for a trace of clean air, but found only the scent of rot and old sorrow.

"We'll move at first light," she said. "For now, we rest. We need our strength." The words sounded braver than she felt, but she would not let the others see her doubt.

All around them, the eyes of the Crooked Wood watched and waited. The night grew colder, the darkness deeper, and the silence more complete. Somewhere, far off, a fox barked once, sharp and lonely, and was answered by the distant cry of an owl. But closer still, the Dark Ones waited, their bodies pressed low to the earth, their hearts beating in time with the old, hungry rhythm of the wood. Pitch's eyes never left the hollow, and as the last light faded, he smiled—a thin, cold smile, sharp as bone. Soon, the Crooked Wood would teach them its law, and the night would belong to the hunters.

In the tangled roots of the withered maple, Sorrel, Bracken, and Wisp pressed close, tired, drawing what comfort they could from each other's warmth. The cold seeped in, numbing their limbs, but they did not sleep. Instead, they listened to the silence, to the faint rustle of leaves, to the slow, steady heartbeat of the wood itself. They did not know what watched them from the shadows, but they felt its presence all the same. The Crooked Wood was not a place for gentle dreams, and as the darkness deepened, each rabbit wondered if they would see the dawn.

Above, the branches creaked in the wind, and the stars were hidden behind a shroud of cloud. The night stretched on, long and cold, and in the heart of the Crooked Wood, the hunt waited for its hour.

The moon hung uncertain, a pale, broken coin above the tangled canopy of the Crooked Wood. Its light, when it managed to slip through, was shredded by the clawing branches overhead, falling in ragged strips that moved with every restless wind. The wood beneath was a world of shifting shadow and muffled sound, where every root seemed to twist with purpose and every hollow held the memory of old, unkind things. Here, Pitch led his silent companions—Sable and Dusker—through the underbrush, their black coats absorbing what little light there was, their movements as fluid and silent as the mist that crept along the ground. The scent of the strangers was strong now: clover-fed, field-soft, touched with hope and the sharp edge of exhaustion. Just ahead, they slept, unaware of the eyes that watched them from the dark.

They found the three rabbits curled together beneath a bramble hollow, their bodies pressed close for warmth. Bracken lay closest to the outside, his hind leg twitching as if caught in some troubled dream. Wisp was tucked between them, her ears flicking now and again, her nose buried in Bracken's side. Sorrel, even in sleep, was taut with vigilance—her nose pressed to her paws, her body coiled as if ready to spring. It was a bad place for a nest, too exposed, but exhaustion had forced their choice. The hush of the wood pressed in, thick and watchful.

Pitch raised a paw, signaling stillness. For a heartbeat, the only sound was the faint rustle of leaves and the distant, hollow croak of a crow. Then, with a blur of movement, the Dark Ones descended. Pitch sprang first, landing on Bracken with a thud that stole the brown-furred buck's breath before he could call out. Dusker darted around the far side and seized Wisp by the scruff, dragging her from sleep into chaos. She squealed and kicked, but Dusker's grip held fast, unyielding.

Sorrel shot to her paws, eyes wide, teeth bared. She struck Sable across the shoulder, but he was already on her, pressing her to the ground. She thrashed and twisted, furious and wild, like a rabbit trapped by a stoat, but the Dark Ones had the advantage of surprise. In seconds, the clearing fell silent again, save for the ragged panting of the travelers. Wisp let out a small whimper, but Dusker struck her with a sharp blow of his paw, and she sagged to the earth, unresponsive.

"No!' bracken cried.

But Pitch clawed a tuft of fur from Bracken, who flinched at the sharp tug. "Keep still, stranger," Pitch hissed. "Or I'll tear out your tongue and have it for a night snack!"

Bracken groaned before slumping, his limbs tangled beneath him. Sorrel's breathing came in ragged gasps, then slowed as Sable pressed her down, watching as her eyes fluttered closed, his own gaze unreadable.

"Bind them," Pitch said, his voice low and certain. "We run before first light."

Sable and Dusker worked quickly, their paws deft and practiced, binding the three with cords of bark and twisted root, slick with the bitter gum of the trees above.

When the three awoke, it was not to light or warmth, but to the close press of earth and the scent of old, forgotten things. The air was thick—cloying with rot, the damp musk of deep roots, and the sharp tang of sap. They lay tangled in bonds, their limbs aching from the weight of sleep and the bruises of capture. The chamber was not shaped by kind paws or softened with moss; its walls were hard, stone-laced and cold, the floor uneven beneath them. The roof hung low, roots poking through like the fingers of the trees above reaching for something lost. Around the edges, bones lay scattered—mouse skulls, bird claws, ribs like bent twigs. Nothing here was placed by accident. This was not a burrow; it was a cage.

And they were not alone.

Beyond the thick bars of rootwood that sealed them in, at the far end of the chamber where the shadows gathered thickest, crouched a figure. Large, unmoving, more a shape than a rabbit at first glance. But then the eyes opened—a dull, predatory yellow, and they did not blink. He sat beneath a curtain of hanging roots, his bulk half-sunk into the gloom like a stone grown from the earth itself. It was Cinder. Even without the light to show his scars, even without the twitch of his ruined ear, there was no mistaking him. The way the chamber seemed to lean around him. The silence, heavy as wet leaves. He watched them as if they were not rabbits at all, but something else—something smaller, something caught.

"Ah, look what's stumbled into our ground," Cinder mocked. "Fire-pelts, nosing about where they've no place."

Sorrel pulled herself upright with a wince, her flanks rising and falling hard.

"You've no right," she said, her voice rough but steady. "We came with no ill intent."

Cinder did not move, only watched her with those unblinking eyes.

"You crossed into the Wood," he said, his voice low and full of gravel. "You walked paths not yours. You brought light into a place that does not welcome it."

Bracken groaned, lifting his head, his eyes clouded with pain and uncertainty. Wisp pressed close beside him, rousing slowly, blinking against the dimness, her body trembling with a dark chill.

Sorrel raised her chin, defiant even now. "We seek a home. That is all. We are from a place where the grass withers. The hill dies. We thought—"

"—the hills always die," Cinder interrupted, his voice low and flat, yet carrying an edge that made the air between them shiver. He shifted his bulk slightly, the muscles of his flanks tightening with the movement, and his eyes narrowed, cold as frost along a riverbank. "You did not think," he said slowly, each word measured as if tasting the ground before stepping. "You hoped. Hope is a poor guide in these woods. It can leave you stranded, gnawing at shadows where nothing waits but hunger and stones."

He stepped closer, claws brushing the fallen twigs. A faint rustle of fur along his shoulders accompanied the movement. "If you would endure here, you must watch, not wish. Listen, smell, measure each step. The world is not gentle, and the quiet is never empty."

Bracken struggled to sit up, his limbs heavy, but Cinder's gaze pinned him in place. "Tell me," the Chief said, "why should I let you leave? Why should the Crooked Wood suffer strangers who walk without invitation?"

The question hung in the air, heavy as the roots above. Sorrel met his gaze, her own eyes bright with a mixture of fear and resolve. Behind her, Wisp whimpered, shrinking into herself. Bracken said nothing, his mind spinning with fragments of dream and memory.

"Because we are not enemies," Sorrel said at last, her voice steady despite the tremor in her limbs. "We are only lost."

Cinder was silent for a long time, the only sound the slow drip of water from the roots above. Then, slowly, he smiled . . . not kindly, but with a cold satisfaction. "Then perhaps it is time you learned what it means to be found."

The roots above them swayed gently, as if stirred by some unseen breath. The chamber seemed to close in, the walls pressing tighter, the darkness deepening. Outside, the Crooked Wood was waking to its own hunger—the eyes of fox and owl, weasel and stoat, and the deeper, hungrier gaze of the Dark Ones themselves. Somewhere far off, the moon slipped behind a cloud, and the last shred of light was swallowed by the wood. In the cold, root-bound chamber, Sorrel, Bracken, and Wisp waited, caught between hope and dread, as the old law of the Crooked Wood prepared to teach them its lesson.

In the hush that followed, Cinder's council was beginning to gather in the shadows, a silent assembly of dark forms. There was Shade, lean and coiled, his fur glossy as midnight water, eyes glinting with a sharp cunning that never rested. Ashen, broader and slower of step, carried the scars of many fights across his flanks, his clack fur bristling faintly in the dim glow, and his gaze was watchful, almost mournful, as if he measured each movement before it could unfold. Nightfall lingered near them, still and quiet, her dark ears folding close to her head, watching the flicker of the fungus along the walls.

Sable and Dusker held the entrance, bodies taut and alert, muscles knotted under their fur as they waited for any hint of defiance. Pitch lingered near the rootwood bars, his gaze flicking between the prisoners and his Chief, pride and doubt warring in his heart. For a moment, the only sound was the slow, steady breathing of the captives, the soft rustle of roots, and the distant, mournful cry of something hunting in the night.

Then Cinder spoke again, his voice low and final. "You will stay here until the council decides your fate. The Crooked Wood is not a place for hope. It is a place for those who endure."

He turned away, his bulk melting back into the shadows, leaving the three rabbits alone in the cold, unforgiving dark.

The silence pressed in, thick and heavy, as Sorrel, Bracken, and Wisp huddled together, their hearts pounding in the gloom. Somewhere above, the moon struggled to break free of the clouds, but its light could not reach the roots of the Crooked Wood.

The silence of the root-bound chamber was thick as mud, broken only by the slow, anxious breathing of the three prisoners and the distant drip of water from somewhere unseen. Sorrel pressed close to Bracken and Wisp, her ears flicking at every sound, her nose twitching for any hint of change. The council of the Dark Ones gathered in the shadows beyond the bars, their black pelts melting into the gloom, their eyes reflecting the sickly glow of fungus-like cold embers. Cinder sat unmoving beneath his curtain of roots, a brooding presence that seemed to draw the darkness tighter around him.

Wisp, shivering, tried to tuck herself further beneath Sorrel's flank, but a faint, scrabbling noise behind her made her freeze. She turned, heart pounding, and squinted into the gloom. There, between two stones at the base of the wall, a tiny nose twitched, followed by a pair of bright, bead-like eyes. A mouse, fur the color of old straw and eyes sharp with curiosity, peered out from a crack no rabbit could ever hope to squeeze through.

The mouse crept forward, whiskers quivering. "Well, well," he whispered, a squeak, his voice high but bold, "what's this? Colorful coneys in a cage? That's a rare sight in Blackroot." His tail flicked, and he glanced over his shoulder as if expecting pursuit.

Sorrel, startled but relieved for any voice not thick with menace, gave a wary nod. "We're awaiting our fate," she said softly, her voice steady though her body trembled. "Cinder and his council are deciding what to do with us. What is your name?"

The mouse's whiskers twitched, and a small smile curved his face. "I am called Smig. My family and I have lived here for before time started. Or, so it seems to me." He wrinkled his nose in mild amusement. "Now, you say . . . deciding what to do with you? Oh, they will chatter and fuss, and make a show of it, but the outcome is already settled. Mark my words. Cinder always gets what he wants, and the council follows like kits after a mother." His gaze roamed over the three, resting briefly on their bright fur and weary eyes. "You'll help provide a grand feast for the Dark Ones tonight, I'd wager."

Wisp's eyes widened in horror. "Help to provide a feast? You mean . . . we'll become their servants?"

The mouse's giggle was a quiet, sharp sound, echoing oddly in the chamber. "Servants? Oh, no, little coney. Not servants. You'll be the feast. The food. The main course at the Blackroot table." He said it almost cheerfully as if discussing the weather.

Bracken's breath caught, and he whispered, "Gnash warned us. He said the Crooked Wood was a place for the fast and clever, and that the Dark Ones were always hungry."

At the mention of the name, the mouse's ears perked up, and his eyes grew round. "Gnash? The great cat? You know him?" He scurried closer, his voice dropping to an excited whisper. "He's my friend, don't you know. Most mice fear him, but not me. Not Smig. Not my family."

Sorrel stared at the mouse, incredulous. "How could the cat be your friend? He hunts mice . . . he told us so himself."

Smig puffed out his chest, pride gleaming in his tiny eyes. "Oh, he hunts, all right. Mice, stoats, anything he can catch. But not me, not my kin. Once, the Dark Ones cornered him . . . yes, even a cat can be caught if he's careless. Gnash tried to climb a tree, but he'd been wounded, and his leg wouldn't hold. My family and

I . . . we saw what was happening. We made a racket, scurried and darted, bit tails and nipped ears. Distracted the Dark Ones just long enough for Gnash to haul himself up the tree and into the branches. He never forgot. Swore on his whiskers he'd never harm a mouse of my line. And he hasn't."

Wisp's ears perked with a cautious hope. "Will you tell him about us? About what's happened?"

"You think that will make a difference?" Smig asked.

"We can only hope," Wisp said.

Smig nodded, his whiskers flicking. "I will. Perhaps he will aid you if I speak to him. After all, he owes me more than one." His eyes darted toward the bars and the council gathering beyond. "But I must hurry. The Dark Ones don't like mice in their burrows, and I'd rather not end up as a snack myself."

Sorrel's voice was urgent but grateful. "Thank you, Smig. Tell him we're here. Tell him we need help."

"Yes, anything you can do," added Bracken.

Smig gave a nod, then slipped into the narrow crack between the stones, disappearing as suddenly as he had appeared. For a long moment, the three rabbits stared at the opening, hope and unease pressing against their hearts.

The hush that followed was broken by the low, rumbling voice of Cinder, whose council had now fully assembled in a half-circle behind him. The chamber filled with the scent of old blood and the tension of waiting. Cinder's yellow eyes gleamed in the gloom as he spoke.

"The fire-pelts came here," he said, his teeth clicking softly between each pause. "Trespassers, sniffing at the paths they have no right to walk, daring even the shadow of the Crooked Wood. Let them learn . . . once . . . and not forget."

From the circle stepped Shade, every move like a bow half-drawn. His fur shone darkly in the dim chamber, slick and glossy. His eyes, restless and bright with cunning, narrowed as he spoke.

"A feast will set their teeth on edge more than any snarl at the border," Shade said. "Let the fire-pelts sniff our burrows and find only the stench of marrow and fur. The thought alone will turn them from the Crooked Wood." He gave a thin smile, eyes glinting. "Better than claw or chase, fear is quicker to run ahead of them."

Ashen shifted beside him, broader, his step slower, his hide mapped with scars of many fights. He gave a grunt, heavy in his throat, and nodded toward Cinder. "Shade is right. The fire-pelts that dared to nose our ground . . . let them serve the warren once more. Their bones and fur will tell the tale. Nothing warns better than the taste of an enemy carried on the breath."

The scarred buck's ears leaned forward stiffly, and he added with grim finality, "Better to eat them down to silence than waste the gift they've given us. We'll grow strong on their folly."

Shade's mouth twitched in something close to a laugh, and Cinder's yellow eyes gleamed approval as the others of the council stirred, the chamber thick with the shared hunger of assent.

The council stirred restlessly, voices low, a current of hunger and unease threading through the shadows.

Nightfall shifted then, her scarred flank brushing the earth as she raised her head. Her voice came sharp and cutting as flint. "Let their meat fill the bellies of our kits, and their marrow steel the bones of the next season. A dead foe is no waste to Blackroot Warren. Better we teach our young the taste of strength than let them grow soft on leaf and scrap." She lowered her nose, eyes hard in the dim glow. "If fear is the message we send, let it be carried on our breath, and in the red on our teeth."

No one gave a reply, but ears tipped forward all around, in assent as certain as an oath.

Cinder leaned forward then, voice dropping, almost a growl. "It is decided. The best way is the oldest way. Tonight, we will feast. We shall honor our new guests as only Blackroot knows how. A remembrance . . . of the fire-pelts who thought to nose their way beneath our trees. Their bones will speak for us far clearer than any tale whispered above ground."

A ripple of approval ran through the council. Shade licked his lips, her muzzle stained from an earlier hunt. Ashen's notched ears flicked with anticipation. Nightfall, the scarred doe, watched the prisoners with a cold, hungry gaze. Even Sable and Dusker, standing guard, allowed themselves a smile.

Sorrel pressed closer to Bracken and Wisp, her body trembling with fear and rage. "We're not done yet," she whispered fiercely. "We've come too far to end like this. If Smig finds Gnash . . ."

Bracken shook his head, voice low and tight. "Gnash is a hunter, not a savior. He warned us, but he's no friend to rabbits."

Wisp, though, clung to the hope Smig had offered, her eyes shining in the dim light. "He helped Smig's family. Maybe he'll help us, too."

"He helped them because he owed them a debt," Bracken said. "He owes us nothing."

Wisp lowered her head in sadness.

The council began to disperse, some slipping away into the tunnels to prepare the feast, others remaining to watch the prisoners. The air grew thick with the scent of anticipation and hunger. Cinder remained, his gaze fixed on the three rabbits, his bulk unmoving.

Time passed slowly in the cold, root-strangled chamber. The three prisoners huddled together, sharing warmth and whispered words. Outside, the sounds of the warren grew louder— rabbits moving through the tunnels, the scrape of claws on stone, the low, eager murmurs of those awaiting the feast. Above, the moon struggled to break through the clouds, but its light could not penetrate the Crooked Wood's tangled heart.

At last, the sound of footsteps returned. Pitch appeared at the bars, his eyes unreadable. "Soon, it'll be time," he said, his voice flat. "You'll be brought before Blackroot. A feast in your honor."

Sorrel met his gaze, her own eyes fierce. "We only wanted a home. We never meant harm."

Pitch stared at her for a long moment, then turned away without a word.

Bracken closed his eyes, drawing strength from the closeness of his friends. "If this is the end," he murmured, "let's meet it together."

Sorrel nodded, her voice steady. "Together."

And so they waited, hope flickering in the darkness, as the Crooked Wood prepared for its feast—and somewhere beyond the roots and stone, a small mouse scurried through the tunnels, carrying with him the last, slender thread of rescue.

Smig darted through the twisted corridors of Blackroot and out into the frost-hardened moonlight, his mind racing as swiftly as his paws. He knew that finding Gnash would not be enough; he would have to persuade the great cat to risk himself for three rabbits who mattered little to him. So he thought over the words he might speak as he hurried through the bramble and scattered leaves, rehearsing them in his mind, aware that Gnash's patience was as thin as his hunger was deep, and that the cat's sense of honor was tangled with old debts and instinct.

He found Gnash crouched atop the old yew stump, his fur the color of dried blood, eyes glinting with moonlight and something harder. The cat's tail flicked once, and his ears flattened as Smig approached.

"You come quickly, little mouse," Gnash purred, voice low and dangerous. "Is it hunger, or fear, that drives you tonight?" Smig, breathless but resolute, stood his ground.

"Neither, Gnash. It's a debt . . . and a chance to end Cinder's reign of fear. Three rabbits, strangers, are caged in Blackroot. Cinder means to make a feast of them. They're not like the others. They're lost, and they need help. If Cinder feasts tonight, tomorrow he'll hunt again. Maybe you."

Gnash narrowed his eyes, the memory of his own narrow escape flickering in their depths. "I know those coneys. Met them when they foolishly stumbled into this place. But tell me . . . why should I risk my skin for them? I owe you, Smig, but not them."

Smig's whiskers quivered. "You owe me, and I am asking. But it's not just for them. Cinder grows bolder each season. You know this. He rules by fear . . . your fear, the fear of every creature in the Crooked Wood. If you help now, you show him that not all prey are helpless, that the Crooked Wood is not his alone. Others will see. The stoats, the crows, those of my kind, and even the old badger . . . they're tired of Cinder's law. If you move, I know they'll move. We can end this together."

Gnash regarded Smig for a long, tense moment, his tail lashing in the gloom. At last, he nodded. "You are clever, mouse. Perhaps too clever. But you are right . . . the Crooked Wood is not his to rule. I grow weary of Blackroot. I will help, and I will call in old debts of my own. Those I've accumulated." He stretched, muscles rippling beneath his pelt, and let out a low, rumbling yowl that rolled through the trees like distant thunder.

Later, as the Crooked Wood sank into a hush of true blackness, Smig crouched beneath hawthorn roots, watching the clearing beyond. The last light bled out of the sky like the yolk of a broken egg. He saw the crows arrive first—many of them, dark as burnt stubble, wings whispering like silk as they settled on the low boughs. A stoat followed—thin and mean-looking, his back striped with old scars. Even the old badger came, slow and stiff from years, his muzzle gray and his eyes like damp stones, but still, he came.

Smig crept to each of them in turn, trembling with both eagerness and fear. "Cinder means to roast three coneys tonight, coneys not of their warren," he said softly, his breath forming little clouds in the cold. "Who would do such a dreadful thing . . . to feast on your own kind? He has grown bold with hunger. But if we strike just as the fire is lit, when the scent and smoke rise, we can scatter his black-ringed flock and shatter his false rule."

Gnash came last, as he always did—quiet, but with a weight in his tread that made the stoat stiffen and the crows lift their wings in readiness. He sat back on his haunches, the fire in his eyes smoldering low and steady. Around him, the others waited. They did not speak. Even the twisted trees seemed to still.

"The fire will be lit when the sun dips below the ash ridge," Gnash said. "They'll lead three coneys to the fire. Bound, frightened. Cinder will sit at the table with the others, ready to gnaw their bones and pick the meat from their bellies." He spat into the earth. "That's when we move."

He turned his scarred muzzle to the trees. "The crows go first. They will swoop only when the rabbits near the fire. Not before. Let their cries carry across the wood. That will draw the guards . . . heads high, eyes fixed on the sky. Use your claws and beaks to tear."

Several of the crows flapped and cawed.

The stoat licked his lips, nose twitching. "Where shall I help?"

Gnash nodded toward him. "You'll take the hollow under the ivy bank, where the roots hang loose. No scent-trail. No torchlight. You wait there till the crows scream. When the scream comes, you will run at the Dark Ones. They will take chase and follow you. If they press, bite, and claw at them."

"The old badger," Gnash added, glancing to the lumbering figure beside him, "will block the west tunnel. He need only sit. Nothing gets past him . . . not a council-hare, not a whimpering coward. If they attack, use your claws and teeth to drive them back."

The old badger gave a nod.

Smig's ears flicked. He knew his turn was next. Gnash looked at him.

"You'll go to the spit. You and your runners. The old root-path still holds. Slide down it like wind down a hollow log. Get to Sorrel and the others before the first fire's bite. The cords of bark will burn quickly if the fire catches. Cut them fast. Once loosed, you'll guide the three coneys through the crumbling burrows. Take the paths no longer used, no longer patrolled. Back into the Crooked Wood, away from Blackroot. Back to freedom."

Gnash lowered his muzzle close to Smig and barred his teeth.

"But mind me, Smig," the cat said. "Listen to my howl. That means they've seen me, and I'll draw them to me. All of them. And if I must bleed for it, I will. That is your signal. Not before. Not after."

Smig swallowed. His fur felt too tight against his skin. "We'll be ready," he said. "For the coneys. For their warren. For the ones still waiting."

Gnash did not reply. His eyes turned eastward, where the faintest silver teased the hill-edges. Dawn, cautious and cold, creeping toward the day of fire and false feast.

But perhaps—just perhaps—this time the fire would not devour the innocent. Perhaps it would light the way home.

Gnash said nothing more. He looked toward the east, where the first pale edge of the sun lay like a dull knife behind the hills. The night of the feast would come, and with it fire and song. But this time, perhaps, the fire would not consume the innocent.

As the conspirators melted into the darkness, Smig felt the first stirrings of hope ripple through the tangled roots of the Crooked Wood. For the first time in many seasons, the law of fear was about to be challenged—not by strength alone, but by the courage and cunning of those who refused to be ruled by it.

# Chapter 5
## Bound for the Feast

As the Crooked Wood surrendered itself to the deepening dark, the warren of Blackroot stirred with a feverish, hungry anticipation. In the heart of the warren, where the roots hung thick as the manes of old lions and the air was heavy with the scent of damp earth and old blood, Cinder's council gathered. Their black pelts shimmered in the sickly light of fungus, eyes gleaming with a cold, predatory light. The feast had been decided. Tonight, Blackroot would taste the flesh of strangers.

Sorrel, Bracken, and Wisp were dragged from their cage, their bonds tight and slick with sap, their limbs aching from the long hours of confinement. They were herded through twisting tunnels, the walls pressing close, the air thick with the musk of too many bodies. The sound of the warren—scrapes, shuffles, the low, eager murmurs of rabbits awaiting the feast—echoed around them, a chorus of hunger and anticipation. The three stumbled, half-blinded by the sudden flare of torchlight as they were brought into the great hollow where a fire had been kindled.

Yet, it was no ordinary fire. It rose like some ancient hunger, stacked high with the bones of storm-felled trees and broken thorn-branches, spitting sparks into the dark like wild bees. The flames danced and snapped, casting long, jittering shadows across the hollow. Smoke twisted up into the branches overhead, and the air itself seemed to lean away.

The Blackroot rabbits sat in a wide circle around it, silent, unmoving, as if the heat alone held them fixed. In the center, the three captives huddled—young, trembling things with their fur matted and their eyes wide as frost. They said nothing. There was nothing left to say.

At the head of the ring crouched Cinder, sunk into the ash-thick earth like an old root left to rot. One ear in tatters, the other twitching now and then at the pop of the fire. His eyes, a dull, sickly yellow, never shifted from the captives. Not once. Around him, Shade, Ashen, Nightfall, Sable, Dusker, and grim Pitch sat like stones—still, tight-muscled, and waiting. Their breath came fast through their noses, and some of them licked their teeth without meaning to.

Behind them, the rest of the warren crowded near, their faces glinting with firelight. They made no sound, but their bodies leaned forward in hunger and heat. You could feel it in the soil: the want of a hundred bellies, the tremor of something ancient rising in their throats.

The fire burned on. Its flames crackled and spat, casting long, writhing shadows across the clearing. Its flames snapped and hissed, throwing long shadows that twisted across the clearing. The heat was fierce, and Bracken, thrust to the front, felt it prickle through his fur, drawing sweat from his skin and sending his heart racing. The cords bit into his legs and belly, and every breath tasted of smoke and fear. Sorrel and Wisp were behind him, pressed close, their eyes wide and shining in the firelight.

Cinder rose, his voice low and rough as gravel. "Tonight, we honor the old law. Tonight, we feast as our fathers feasted, and their fathers before them. The Crooked Wood is not a place for hope or mercy. It is a place for those who endure." His gaze swept the assembly, and a murmur of approval ran through the crowd. "Bring the first," he commanded, and Sable and Dusker seized Bracken, dragging him toward the fire.

Bracken struggled, but the cords held fast. The heat was unbearable now, the flames so close he could feel his whiskers curling, his fur beginning to singe. The roar of the fire filled his ears, and the smell of burning fur made his stomach twist. Pain gnawed at every thought, sharp as thorns pressed into the mind. He looked back at Sorrel and Wisp, saw the terror in their faces, and felt a wave of despair so deep it nearly drowned him.

He was lifted, roughly, and placed on a crude spit fashioned from a thick branch, the bark stripped away to reveal the pale, smooth wood beneath. The spit was set above the fire, and Bracken felt the searing heat on one of his hind legs, the crackle of flame beneath him. He closed his eyes, bracing for agony, for the end.

But before the fire could claim him, a screech split the air, sharp and wild, as a murder of crows descended from the trees, their wings beating the air into a frenzy. They swooped and dived, pecking at the faces of the Blackroot rabbits, scattering them in all directions. The guards at the edge of the clearing cried out in alarm, their attention drawn skyward as the crows screamed and wheeled above.

Elsewhere, the stoat struck—a streak of brown and white, tearing through the Blackroot guards with a rush of claws and teeth. The warren shook with the thud and scrabble of rabbits scattering in panic, their screams smothered by the press of running bodies and earth.

Into this tumult lumbered the old badger. Slow but unstoppable, he forced his way through the crush, sides dragging along the walls as he drove toward the western run. There he dropped low, blocking the passage with his great form. From the chamber ahead rose a shrill tide of terror—the council penned tight in the dark with no way through. The badger's jaws snapped at any who dared come near, his growl booming in the dark earth, daring them to run against him.

Behind this din came Gnash. With a roar, he plunged after the Dark Ones, his forepaws gouging furrows in the soil as he bore down the tunnel. He seized one by the haunch, lifted it high in his jaws, shook it, and flung the limp body against the wall, where it struck and lay still. Another he tore open, claws ripping through fur in ragged clumps, the rabbit spinning and squealing as it tumbled across the packed floor. Gnash's eyes burned in the half-light, and he struck again, rending without pause, each blow leaving dark trails behind in the dust until nothing stirred beneath him.

In the confusion, a thin, quick shape darted through the shadows—Smig, his fur bristling with fear and determination. He scurried to the spit, his tiny teeth working furiously at the cords that bound Bracken.

"Hold still, coney," he hissed, his voice barely audible above the din. "I'll have you free in a blink."

Bracken felt the cords loosen, then fall away. He tumbled from the spit, landing hard on the packed earth. Smig was already at Sorrel, his teeth working furiously at her bindings. "Go!" he urged Bracken. "Help the little ones!"

Bracken hauled himself upright, the scorch of the fire still searing along his skin. He lurched toward Wisp and set his teeth to the cords at her forepaws, tugging and raking with all his strength. Wisp trembled beneath him, but she struck out with her hind legs, snapping loose the last of the bindings. Her eyes shone wide and fierce, caught between fear and the chance of freedom.

Cinder roared, his voice cutting through the chaos like a blade. "Stop them! Stop the thieves!" But the crows screamed louder, and the stoat darted between the rabbits, sowing panic and confusion. The badger held the tunnel, and Gnash—silent until now—emerged from the shadows, his eyes blazing, his claws unsheathed.

He moved with terrifying grace, a shadow among shadows, striking down any who dared challenge him. The Blackroot rabbits, so fearsome in their own dark world, shrank before him, their courage crumbling in the face of true predation. Gnash's roar echoed through the night, a sound of ancient hunger and wild justice.

But it was Smig's kin who delivered the final blow to Cinder's reign. As the chaos peaked and the council scattered, a tide of mice—scores upon scores, their tiny bodies darting from every crack and hollow—surged forward. Smig led them, his eyes bright with a wild, vengeful joy. They swarmed over Cinder, who, stunned by the collapse of his order, barely had time to react.

They bit and gnawed, their teeth sharp as thorns, burrowing into his fur, tearing at the skin beneath. Cinder thrashed and bellowed, rolling in the ashes, but the mice clung fast, their numbers overwhelming. The great rabbit, who had ruled by fear and tooth, was brought low by the smallest creatures of the wood. The council, seeing their Chief beset, faltered and fled, their courage lost in the face of the writhing, relentless tide.

Cinder's roars faded to whimpers as the mice did their work, and at last he lay still, his power broken, his body marked by the hunger and fury of those he had long scorned.

"Run!" Smig cried. "This way!"

Bracken, Sorrel, and Wisp bounded after him into the dark, the chaos of the feast behind them. Smig slipped through a narrow cleft in the roots, quick as a mouse, and the others pressed after, trusting his knowledge of the warren's hidden runs as their one chance.

They raced through twisting tunnels, the sounds of pursuit growing fainter as the chaos behind them deepened. The roots seemed to reach for them, the earth itself shifting to block their way, but Smig was quick and clever, always finding a path, always urging them on.

Behind them, the fire raged, the crows screamed, and the old law of the Crooked Wood was shattered. Cinder, his pride and power broken, could only watch as his feast dissolved into ruin, his council scattered by the fury of the night—and the gnawing vengeance of the mice.

At last, the fugitives broke from the warren into the chill of open air. The moon stood high above, its light thin and half-lost among the trees, yet to Bracken, Sorrel, and Wisp it shone with promise. They dropped to the ground, flanks heaving, their limbs quivering with the strain of the run and the release that followed.

Gnash soon appeared beside them, his fur streaked with blood and ash, his eyes still burning with the fire of battle. "You're safe now," he said, his voice low and rough. "But you must go. The Crooked Wood will not forgive this night."

Smig, his whiskers twitching with pride and fear, nodded. "There's a path through the old brambles. Follow it east, then to the north. It'll take you beyond the wood . . . to the open fields."

Sorrel, her voice shaking, managed a word of thanks. Bracken, still dazed, looked at Gnash and Smig, gratitude and awe mingling in his eyes. Wisp, silent, pressed close to her friends, her heart pounding with the memory of fire and flight.

They did not linger. With a last look at their rescuers, the three rabbits slipped into the brambles, the promise of freedom ahead, the nightmare of Blackroot behind.

As they vanished into the dark, the Crooked Wood was left in turmoil. The old law had been broken, the reign of fear challenged by the courage of a mouse, the cunning of a cat, and the desperate hope of three strangers. In the heart of the wood, the fire burned low, its light flickering on the faces of those who remained.

Cinder, defeated, sat in the ashes of his power, his council scattered, his warren forever changed. The Crooked Wood would remember this night—the night the fire-pelts escaped, the night the law of fear was broken, the night hope returned to the shadows.

And somewhere in the tangled roots, Smig watched the moon rise, his heart full of pride and wonder. He had kept his promise and proved that even the smallest creature could change the world.

For Bracken, Sorrel, and Wisp, the journey was not over. The world beyond the Crooked Wood awaited, full of danger and promise. But they carried with them the memory of the fire, the courage of friends, and the hope that had saved their lives.

The moon dangled above the tangled trees, but for the first time in many seasons, its light seemed to promise something more than fear. It promised freedom and the chance to begin again.

The moon rode high above the Crooked Wood, its light thin and uncertain, filtering through the last ragged branches like a blessing withheld. The world was hushed, and the only sound was the soft, uneven thumping of three rabbits—Sorrel, Bracken, and Wisp—making their way through the tangled roots and bramble. Their flanks heaved with exhaustion, their paws raw and stinging from the night's desperate flight. The scent of smoke and blood still clung to their fur, and the memory of fire and chaos haunted every step.

Sorrel led, her ears tall, her eyes narrowed against the dark, her body trembling with fatigue, but her spirit unbroken.

"Keep going," she whispered, voice hoarse but urgent. "We're nearly through. We can't stop now."

She pressed ahead, nose close to the ground, searching for the faintest hint of open air, of grass not choked by the wood's bitter roots.

Bracken stumbled, his hind leg dragging with every step, the pain of his near-burning throbbing through his bones. "Sorrel, I can't . . ." he gasped, but she turned on him fiercely.

"Yes, you can. You must. It's only a little farther. For all of us. Please, Bracken, don't stop."

Wisp, shaken by it all, trailed behind, her eyes wide and haunted. She said nothing, but her breath came in short, panicked bursts, and she pressed close to Bracken's side as if afraid she might vanish if she let go.

The Crooked Wood pressed on all sides, the roots arching overhead like the ribs of some ancient beast, the ground beneath their paws slick with dew and the last traces of ash. Every shadow seemed to move, every whisper of wind a threat. Yet Sorrel would not let them pause.

"We're almost out," she murmured, more to herself than to the others. "Just a little farther. Just a little farther."

The hours dragged. The moon slipped behind clouds and reappeared, casting the world in a shifting, silvery gloom. The rabbits moved in silence, each step a battle against the weight of their bodies and the terror in their hearts. At times, Bracken's mind drifted, and he saw again the fire, the crows, the writhing mass of mice swarming over Cinder's black body. He shuddered and pressed on.

At last, the trees began to thin. The undergrowth grew sparser, and the air lost its heavy, cloying scent. Ahead, a faint line of pale grass glimmered in the moonlight—the edge of the Crooked Wood, the promise of open country.

"We're there," Sorrel breathed, her voice trembling with relief and disbelief. "We're out. We're . . ."

But then from the shadows ahead, something stirred. The rabbits froze, every muscle taut, ears stiff and straining. Out of the dark staggered a shape they knew—Cinder.

He was scarcely the buck they remembered. His pelt hung in clotted tangles, torn open in streaks where blood had dried black. Great swathes of skin were raw and chewed, as though a teeming horde had taken their fill. One eye was swollen shut like a fist pressed beneath the fur, and the lone ear that remained dangled in tatters at his side.

Step by step, he dragged himself on, steady yet dreadful, as if nothing short of death itself would bar his path. Each breath scraped out of him like stone against stone in a dry burrow, rattling deep in his chest. Every sound and every stumble carried with it a sense of relentless hunger and hurt, and yet he pressed forward still, eyes burning through the ruin of him.

The three rabbits shrank back, terror rooting them to the spot. Cinder's yellow eye fixed on them, burning with a madness that was equal parts hunger and hate.

"Come closer," he rasped, his voice raw and broken. "Come, little fire-pelts. You've cost me everything. My warren. My law. My flesh. But I'll have you yet. I'll eat you raw, right here, beneath the sky. Your bones will be my last feast."

Bracken tried to speak, but his throat closed with fear. Wisp whimpered, pressing herself to the ground. Sorrel, trembling, forced herself to stand tall.

"You're finished, Cinder," she said, though her breath caught as she spoke. "The Crooked Wood has no hold on us now. Let us pass."

Cinder laughed—a harsh scrape, like stone dragged over stone in some buried place. "Let you pass? After this?" His teeth showed in the half-light. "Do you think the world beyond is any kinder? You think you'll find peace? There is no peace, not for rabbits such as you. Out there waits only teeth and hunger. Out there waits the tearing mouth. And when it comes, it will be quick, and it will take all."

He drew nearer, his steps darkened by the trail of blood that marked his going. His muzzle twisted as he set back his ears. "I can smell what runs through you. I can taste it on the air. Come close, then. Let me have you. Let me . . ."

He lunged, sudden and desperate, his ruined body moving with the last strength of hatred. The three rabbits shrieked, frozen by terror, unable to flee.

Then the night was torn open. A vast shadow crossed the moon—a crow, older than memory, black as the spaces between constellations, stooped with a cry that raked the silence raw. Its wings swept wider than a fox's spring, each quill lined with the chill shine of midnight. The air trembled under its flight, the grass pressed flat as it sank.

With a single, dreadful motion, the crow's talons—thick as bramble roots and sharp as flint—struck Cinder's back, closing around his shoulders like the jaws of some nameless god out of the dark.

The great black rabbit screamed, a sound torn from him, harsh and failing, twisting and snapping in fury against the hold upon him. Yet the crow's wings only hammered the air, tireless, remorseless, and the ground fell away under them. Up and up it carried him, into the wide, indifferent sky.

For a breath, Cinder's legs flailed in the air, his mouth working in silent rage. The crow climbed higher still, the moon striking every line of its dark wings. Then, with a cry that split the night, it let him go.

Cinder fell, a dark, twisting shape against the moonlit sky, his limbs flailing in a last, desperate reach for earth. The air seemed to hold its breath as he plummeted, the silence stretching thin and sharp. Then, with a sickening, thunderous crack, his body struck the crown of a great stone that jutted from the earth like the knuckle of some buried giant. The sound was dreadful—a hollow, final note that rang out through the clearing, echoing off the trunks and roots, sending a shudder through the very ground beneath the rabbits' paws.

Nothing moved. Cinder's body sprawled grotesquely atop the rock, limbs bent at unnatural angles, black fur matted and torn, blood seeping between the cracks in the stone. His bloodied head lolled to one side, the one yellow eye staring sightlessly at the sky, his jaw slack, a thin thread of red trailing from his mouth. Around him, the grass was flattened and stained, and the sharp tang of iron filled the air.

For a long while, there was only the hush of the ground and the faint drift of wind curling through the cruel branches. Then Cinder drew breath—ragged, tearing, as if each lungful scraped against stone within his chest. A tremor ran across his frame; his chest rose once more. He turned his head, his one good eye fixing on the three rabbits. His voice was little more than a whisper, but it carried in the stillness.

"Run, then," he rasped. "Run as far as you can. The world will find you. The world will eat you. There is no safety. There is no end to its hunger."

His breath rasped once, then again, and at the third it failed. The moon slid free of a passing cloud and spread its cold silver over the rock. In the branches above, crows perched close together, stone-silent, their black eyes fixed on the still form below.

The three rabbits did not stir. Even the night itself seemed caught, as though it held back its own pulse. Then all at once the crows fell, a tangle of wings and hooked beaks, and tore at Cinder's body in a frenzy. The three turned away from the scene.

"He's gone," she said. "It's over."

Bracken shuddered, his body wracked with exhaustion and relief. Wisp pressed close to him, her eyes wide and shining with tears.

"Will it ever be over?" Bracken whispered. "Will we ever be safe?"

Sorrel looked to the east, where the first faint hint of dawn touched the sky. "I don't know," she said. "But we're free. For now, we're free."

They moved past the stone, past the broken body of Cinder, and into the open country beyond. The grass was wet with dew, and the air was sharp and clean. Behind them, the Crooked Wood stood silent, its shadows broken, its law undone.

The three rabbits paused on a rise, looking back one last time. The moon hung uncertain above the tangled trees, but its light seemed gentler now, less burdened by the weight of old fear.

Sorrel turned to her companions, her eyes bright with hope and sorrow. "Come on," she said. "There's a new day waiting."

They set off together, side by side, into the unknown.

Beyond the last gnarled roots and brambles, the open fields stretched wide and free, bathed in silver and shadow. There, at the boundary between wild and warren, Gnash sat—silent, watchful, a dark shape crouched beneath the boughs of an ancient hawthorn.

Beside him, Smig's small form twitched with nervous energy, his whiskers flicking as he peered toward the clearing where Sorrel, Bracken, and Wisp emerged from the shadows. The three rabbits moved slowly, their bodies weary and marked by the fire and flight, but their eyes held something fierce—hope, and the stubborn will to live.

"They made it," Smig whispered, barely daring to breathe. "They're free."

Gnash's eyes gleamed, reflecting the moonlight and the distant flicker of the dying fire behind them. "For now," he said, his voice low and rough like gravel. "The Crooked Wood won't forget this night. Cinder's shadow still lingers, even broken. They'll watch for them, hunt for them."

Smig nodded, his small face set with determination. "But they have a chance now. A chance to find a home beyond the wood's claws. You did well, cat. You kept your promise."

Gnash turned his gaze toward the horizon, where the first hints of dawn softened the edges of the hills. "I keep my debts,

Smig. But debts are heavy things. And the world beyond the Crooked Wood is no kinder than within. They'll need more than luck to survive, I'm afraid."

Smig's tail twitched anxiously. "Then we'll watch. We'll warn them. The crows, the stoats, even the old badger . . . whatever creature is out there. Maybe all old laws can be broken."

Gnash's lips twitched in something like a smile, sharp and fleeting. "Perhaps. But it will take more than courage and cunning. It will take time, and the strength to face what waits in the open fields."

The rabbits paused, looking back once at the dark woods that had held them captive, then turned their faces toward the rising sun. Their steps grew steadier, their breaths less ragged, as they moved into the promise of dawn.

Gnash rose, stretching his powerful limbs, the muscles rippling beneath his dark fur. "Come, Smig. The night is ending, and with it, the old fears. But the day will bring new trials."

The mouse scurried up beside him, small but fierce. "Then we face them together. For Sorrel, for Bracken, for Wisp . . . and for all who dare to dream of freedom."

Together, they watched the three rabbits disappear into the world beyond the Crooked Wood, the first true steps of a journey that would test the courage of all who walked beneath the sky. The moon faded, and a new day began.

# Chapter 6
# The White River

The dawn after their escape from Blackroot came thin and pale, the sky washed in pearl and fading blue, streaked with the last bruises of night. The land ahead, once a promise, now seemed a riddle—open, wild, and haunted by the memory of pursuit. Bracken led the way, his paws heavy with exhaustion, his mind still echoing with the cries and chaos of the Crooked Wood. Yet the world beyond the trees was not the world he expected. The air was sharp and cold, carrying the scent of wet earth and the distant, ceaseless roar of water.

Wisp trotted beside Bracken, her white-patched fur muddied, ears twitching at every stir of the undergrowth. She moved with a nervous energy, as though the land pressed upon her, urging her forward even as it pulled her back. Ahead, Sorrel's steady tread brought a measure of calm—a sign of order and resolve amid the wild country, as she kept her gaze fixed on the paths where enemies might appear.

They crested a low rise, where the grass lay pressed flat by the recent rain, streaked with the muddy tracks of deer and fox. The sun, pale and feeble, struggled to bring any warmth to the land. Sorrel halted at the crown of the slope, her breath misting in the chill, and looked ahead. The sound of water had grown louder, a steady, muffled thunder that seemed to stir from deep within the earth itself. Before long, they came upon it.

Bracken came to her side, ears flattened against the gusts. "Well now," he said softly, a trace of unease in his tone. "I had been hoping for a gently meandering stream. One easily crossed. This . . . this is something else entirely."

Sorrel's voice seemed rough. "A white river. Running high. A killer this time of year. Meltwater from the hills. Fast and cold as death."

Wisp shivered, drawing closer to Bracken. "Do we have to cross it?"

Bracken didn't answer at once. He felt the river's presence in his bones, a deep, insistent pull that was both warning and invitation. In his dreams, water had always meant passage—a crossing from one world to another, from safety to danger, from memory to fate. He glanced at Sorrel, searching her face for certainty.

"We can't go back," Sorrel said as if reading his thoughts. "The Crooked Wood's behind us, and there's nothing for us in Glenmere. If we're to find a new home for us, for the others, we have to cross."

"There's no easy way," Bracken said. "Whatever crossing is likely gone, washed out with the spring floods. We'll have to find our own way."

They moved down the slope, the grass giving way to reeds and mud. The ground grew soft and treacherous, sucking at their paws. Bracken felt the world narrowing around them, the open sky shrinking as the roar of the river grew louder. The trees here were stunted and bent, their roots exposed and tangled, as if clutching at the earth in fear of being swept away.

Just beyond a tumble of flat stones, a shallow pool edged out from the main current. The water lay still as glass, laced with rippling light, broken only where a root dipped in from the mud and sent tiny rings drifting.

Wisp paused at the edge, peering down as her own reflection shivered among the drifting patterns. "It's so loud," she whispered. "Like it's angry."

Sorrel pressed on, her body low and tense. "Keep together. Watch your footing."

They pushed through a stand of willows, their branches trailing in the water, and emerged onto a narrow strip of stony shore. The river was before them at last—a white, churning torrent, swollen with meltwater, its surface broken by foam and the twisted limbs of drowned trees. The current moved with a terrible purpose, dragging everything in its path toward some distant, unseen end.

Bracken stared at the river, his heart pounding. It was beautiful and frightening, alive with the memory of storms and the promise of new beginnings. He felt small before its power, a single rabbit on the edge of something vast and unknowable.

Wisp gently stepped to the water's edge and sniffed. "No easy crossing here," she muttered. "Too deep, too fast. Maybe upstream."

"Maybe there's a place where the bank narrows," Bracken said.

Sorrel nodded. "We'll follow the bank. Keep close."

They moved along the river, the ground slippery with moss and mud. The noise was deafening, drowning out all other sounds. Bracken felt the world shrink to the press of bodies, the slap of water, the cold bite of wind. Every so often, he glanced at the far bank, searching for a sign—a fallen tree, a shallows, anything that might offer passage.

Wisp kept close, her eyes wide. "Do you think the Hollowkin ever crossed here?" she asked, her voice barely audible above the roar.

Sorrel turned to her. "If they did, they left no trace. The river takes what it wants. It slowly removes time."

Bracken said nothing. The wind stirred the grass at his feet, and the hush between the trees deepened as if the world itself were pausing to listen. In his mind, clear as moonlight on still water, he saw the White Buck once more—standing upon the far shore of a river that had no name, its form unmoving, its eyes filled with something brighter than firelight. A light not of this world, but of memory, or meaning. The image struck him so sharply, he faltered mid-step, one paw catching against a root hidden beneath the moss.

"We're heading in the right direction," he said quietly, his voice low but sure as if speaking might scatter the vision. "He's been here. I can feel it. Ash Hollow waits ahead."

Sorrel glanced his way, though she said nothing. Her ears turned slightly, just enough to show she'd heard. Wisp didn't lift her head, but her breath came quick and alert. Neither of them asked who he meant. There was no need.

The White Buck.

They knew. Not with words, nor whispers, nor signs in the dust. It was something older—known in the blood, in the soft pads of their paws, in the marrow hidden behind ribs and fur. They knew it like a wind that changes just before the storm breaks, like a scent half-remembered from a burrow long lost to root and rot. It was the knowledge of things unspoken: that something was moving through the land, old as stone, quiet as frost. Not quite of their world, but bound to it still. A creature of hollows and bramble, of forgotten glades where the leaves fall differently and the moss grows in spirals no wind has drawn. It moved by paths rabbits no longer trod—paths the earth remembered even when they did not.

They said nothing. They only moved faster.

The river stretched before them as if it had risen from the earth itself to greet their gaze, bending sharply around a cluster of jagged rocks, its current hissing and restless with cold anger. The air smelled sharp and wet, and the bank beneath their paws was dark with recent rain. Across the water, a tree had fallen—stripped bare of bark, sun-bleached and worn smooth by seasons. It lay half-submerged, bridging the torrent with a pale and fragile spine.

Sorrel's eyes tightened. Her ears lifted, turning toward the current.

"It's risky," she said at last, her voice clipped. "But I don't see another way. The log won't hold us all at once. Lightest first. Go slow."

Wisp stared at the log, her limbs tight and trembling.

"I . . . I'm not sure I can," she said. Her voice was barely more than a breath.

Bracken edged closer, not crowding her, only close enough for his scent to carry a quiet reassurance.

"You can do it," he said, soft as thistledown. "I'll follow, just behind."

Sorrel dipped her head, ears flicking. "Go on, Wisp . . . easy now. Let the river say what it will, but don't give it a word in return."

Wisp drew a thin, trembling breath, her sides quivering as she edged closer. She pressed her forepaws onto the pale surface of the fallen tree, where the bark had been stripped smooth by sun and rain. The log shifted at her touch—a low groan, a shaky lurch, the soft sound of river water nosing at its underside.

Fright sat sharp in her chest, but she made no sound.

Bit by bit, she eased herself forward, sinking close to the wood, tail clamped tight against her hind legs, nose pointed toward the distant, safe tangle of grass on the opposite bank. The river sent up sharp flecks of spray that stung her whiskers and blurred her vision. Beneath, the water rushed pale and wild over hidden stones, swirling with a restless hunger for anything that slipped.

Bracken hesitated until Wisp had made it halfway, then set his paws on the mossy curve of the fallen log. The bark was slick with river sweat, colder than he'd thought, and every step wobbled beneath him, as though the water itself pressed for his attention— a soft murmur in the hush below, tempting him toward journeys he might not choose.

He kept his gaze lifted, fixed on Wisp's narrow back as she edged forward, her body taut with the careful hope of reaching the far bank.

Behind, Sorrel stood rooted among nettles and stone, ears canted forward, eyes glinting with a steady concern. Not a muscle moved; even her breath gathered itself and waited for the crossing to end.

Wisp neared the far bank. She gathered herself, her small frame tensed. Then—swift as a grasshopper startled from the grass—she pushed off, leaving behind the final, slender sliver of bark. Her feet met not soft earth, but cold stone, and the sound that followed was sudden and clear—a flat thud, as if an acorn had fallen fast upon rock.

She lay there, dazed, her chest heaving. Then she gave a little shiver, came to herself for a moment, and looked back toward the others. Her eyes were wide, her breath fast and shallow, but she said nothing—just watched, waiting, ears tilted to catch the rustle of their coming.

Bracken faltered. Only for a heartbeat. His hindpaw lost its grip, slid back on the slick bark, and for a breathless moment he hung there—legs stretched wide, the white rush of the river beneath him like the cry of some ancient hunter.

"Bracken!" cried Wisp, her voice thin over the roar.

Then his paws found the log once more, slick and cold beneath the curl of his claws. He held himself steady for a breath, muscles coiled like springs, and with a sudden, sure motion, he sprang forward—landing beyond with a splash and a shiver, fur plastered and breath sharp in the quiet air.

Sorrel was the last to step forward. She moved with the calm surety of one who had learned the language of water and stone, each footfall steady where the river sprayed up in gentle arches.

Her eyes never wavered from the far bank, steady and knowing. There was no hint of fear in her, only the quiet memory of crossings past.

When she reached them, they collapsed together—a tangle of limbs and panting breath, wet fur pressed close, the cold of the stones seeping into them. The river thundered on behind, louder now somehow, as though it resented their escape.

None of them spoke. Not yet. They lay still and listened.

Bracken looked back, ears low. His breath was rough, but the echo of the fall still shivered in his limbs.

"It's done," Sorrel said.

But Bracken shook his head.

"No," he whispered. "It's only begun."

And somewhere beyond the bend, in the thickets of shadow and silence, something stirred. The White Buck waited. Not chasing, not fleeing. Just watching. Always watching.

The far bank was a world apart, a place of mud and silence and the slow, heavy drip of water from sodden fur. Bracken, Sorrel, and Wisp lay crumbled on the shore, coughing and shuddering, their bodies weary from the river's unyielding chill. For a time, none of them spoke. The only sound was the rasp of their breath and the distant, ceaseless roar of the White River, now behind them—a force survived but not forgotten.

Bracken was sprawled on his side, the world spinning gently around him. His limbs felt hollow as if the river had washed something vital from his bones. Every breath was a struggle, sharp with the taste of silt and fear. He blinked, trying to clear the blur from his eyes, and saw Wisp curled beside him, her small body trembling, her eyes half-shut. Sorrel, ever the anchor, was upright now, scanning the bank with wary eyes.

The land here was raw and unwelcoming. The grass was flattened and streaked with mud, the earth gouged by the river's recent fury. Tangled roots and broken branches littered the shore, and everywhere was the scent of rot and old water. The sky above was a low, pewter dome, pressing the world flat and close.

Sorrel shook herself, sending a spray of droplets into the air. "We need to move," she said, her voice hoarse but steady. "We can't stay in the open."

Bracken tried to rise, but his legs betrayed him. He managed only to roll onto his belly, panting. Wisp made a faint, whimpering sound, her breath rattling in her chest.

Sorrel hesitated, torn between urgency and care. She nudged Wisp gently. "Come on, little one. Have to keep moving."

Wisp's eyes fluttered open, wide and glassy. "We made it," she whispered.

"We did," Sorrel replied, softer now. "We're safe. For the moment."

Bracken forced himself upright, every muscle stiff with protest. One of his hind legs throbbed dully—a stubborn ache from the fierce struggle in Blackroot, reminding him with each step of the price he had paid. He looked back at the river, its surface still wild and white, and felt a shiver run through him—not from cold, but from the memory of what they had crossed. The river was a boundary, a line drawn in water and fear. On this side, everything felt changed.

Along the bank, where the river curved beneath a leaning alder, there lay a scatter of debris—stones smoothed by the current, bits of bark stripped from upstream trees, and shattered branches tossed like forgotten bones. The water, brown and restless, murmured against the shore, tugging now and again at the tangle of reeds that swayed in the shallows.

Sorrel moved among the debris with the deliberate care of one who has known what it is to find danger hiding in the common shapes of things. Her nose worked steadily, whiskers twitching, as she traced the outlines of stones and root-lumps, sniffing and pausing, always listening.

She stopped beside a cluster of grass, its blades muddied and bent low with silt. A hush seemed to fall around her, broken only by the slap of water against rock and the distant call of a wren.

Gently, Sorrel brushed the grass aside with a careful forepaw. There, half-buried in the thick mud of the riverbank, lay a length of pale wood—swollen with water and worn nearly smooth. Yet this was no river-worn branch; faint, deliberate lines marked its surface, carved long ago by hands now lost to memory, shaped for some purpose that had drifted away with time.

She leaned close, nose almost touching, and sniffed. The scent was old, waterlogged, and masked by earth, but there was something beneath it—something sharper. Unnatural.

"Bracken," she called, her voice low. "There's something here."

She didn't wait for an answer. Her paws began to dig, sending up thick clods of earth that slapped wetly against the reeds. She dug with urgency, not frenzy—like a rabbit who knows the difference between a threat and a warning.

"What is it?" Bracken asked as he padded to her side, his ears twitching at the sound of her digging.

"Here," she said. "Look."

He peered down. "Wood?"

"Not just wood," Sorrel said.

She scraped away the last crusted layer of mud, her paws trembling, the damp earth reluctant to yield its secret. Bit by bit, the pale length beneath emerged—rounded at one end, flattened at the other, and etched with faint, deliberate grooves. Not the doing of water or wind, nor the careless scarring of falling stones. These were marks left with intention, by claw or claw-like tool. It lay half-buried like a memory not yet ready to be spoken aloud. And along its side, there was something stranger still—an impression no flood could leave, no creature's tread could shape.

Wisp, drawn by the soft scratching of claw on mud, crept forward on her belly, her eyes flicking to the shape. She froze. Then, slowly, she inched closer, her breath caught in her throat like a leaf tangled in thorns.

Carved into the surface—rough but unmistakable—was the image of something. Twisting lines that curled like roots and branched off as though grown from the earth itself and coaxed into shape by memory. The patterns were too deliberate for chance, yet too wild, too old, for any rabbit's paw to claim them. They wound through the bark like thoughts through the mind of an elder—

fractured, uncertain, but real. The carving was crude, yes, but not childish. It held a kind of grave purpose, shaped not for beauty but for remembering. It spoke, not in sound, but in a silence too loud to ignore, the sort that settles deep in the bones and lingers there, whispering in dreams.

For a long while, silence held them tight. Sorrel's gaze remained fixed on the carving, her brow drawn low as if it bent beneath some quiet weight. "What does it mean?" she muttered, half to herself.

Bracken's chest tightened, a sudden hitch in his breath. The image called to him—a shadow from restless nights and tangled dreams: the White Buck, threading through tunnels spun of bone and thorn, its eyes alight with a sorrow that warned as much as it mourned.

Wisp's voice was a whisper, thin and trembling. "It's the mark of Hollowkin. I saw it . . . what I saw at the circle of stones . . . the same." She reached out a paw, not quite touching the wood.

Sorrel looked at her sharply. "You're sure?"

Wisp nodded, her gaze fixed on the carving. "Yes, when the Hollowkin spoke. The same as I saw. And in my dream, too. It means . . . something. I think it's a warning."

Sorrel's skepticism flickered in her eyes, but she did not dismiss Wisp's words. Instead, she studied the carving, tracing the lines with her nose. "It's old," she said at last. "Older than any of us. Maybe older than Glenmere itself."

Bracken stepped closer, drawn by a sense of inevitability. The sight of the carving filled him with a strange mixture of dread and hope. He remembered the White Buck's eyes, the silent command to remember, to heed the old stories.

"It's not just a warning," he said softly. "It's a sign. The Hollowkin . . . they left these marks, so we'd know where to look . . . where to go."

Sorrel glanced at him, her voice low and uneasy. "Or where not to go."

Bracken shook his head, feeling the weight of destiny settle on his shoulders. "No. Everything has brought us here. The dark woods and the evil that lurks there. The river, the crossing, this mark . . . it's all part of the same path. The Hollowkin want us to follow."

Wisp shivered, pressing close to Bracken. "But what if it's a trap? What if the carvings mean pain, not guidance?"

Bracken hesitated, the question hanging in the cold air. He looked at the carving again, at the twisting and curling lines. "Maybe pain is part of it. Maybe the Hollowkin suffered so we could learn. So we could survive."

Sorrel was silent, her gaze distant. The river behind them, the wild land ahead, and the mark of the Hollowkin between— these were the boundaries of their world now. She shook herself as if to dispel the weight of old fears.

"We'll rest here," she said at last, voice soft but steady, "only for a little while. Then we go on . . . whatever this mark may mean, we face it as one. Just as we faced the darkness left behind."

They gathered close in the shallow hollow Sorrel had scraped with careful paws, the earth soft and yielding beneath them. A slender mist began to swirl about the river's edge, muting the steady thunder where water met stone. Above, the sky sagged low, a heavy gray shawl soaked through with long-forgotten rain. The morning light was no more than a careful creeping, pale and thin, slipping through the mist like threads of water weaving through fractured rock. It was a day that seemed to lose its own sense of being, neither bright nor dark, but slow, damp, and waiting—held in a moment between shadow and light.

Beside them, the river stretched wide and clear, carrying with it the restless song of their journey—a tangled chorus of slapping eddies, the soft uprooting of hidden roots, and the low sigh of currents weaving through stone. Now and then, a spray of foam would lift and drift through the mist before vanishing like a hare slipping through tall grass. The river was no friend to those who traveled near it. It held its secrets deep below the surface, in dark places no paw could ever touch.

Wisp lay close among them, but there was something different about her. Her sides rose and fell unevenly, as if the rhythm inside her faltered. Her ears twitched now and then, though no sound stirred in their midst. When her eyes opened, they seemed to gaze beyond the treeline, past dripping bark and bare branches, toward a shadow none of the others could name.

"She's not herself," Bracken said quietly. "Something's wrong."

"She's tired, is all," Sorrel answered, though her voice lacked its usual firmness. "Too many days with empty bellies, and too many nights spent without rest."

Bracken didn't reply. He knew the look in Wisp's eyes, though he could not yet speak of it. He had seen it once in an elder, seasons past, just before the warren sang his name one final time and sent him into the earth.

Wisp shifted, her breath catching.

"The sun," she murmured. "It's not warm today."

"No," said Bracken, and his voice held something between sorrow and apology. "It isn't."

Bracken and Sorrel watched in silence. Not the startled hush of fear, but the older kind—worn smooth by long seasons and quiet knowing. It was the sort of silence that drapes itself over empty burrows in midwinter, when the last grass is buried under snow and nothing moves but thought.

Neither of them liked this place. The trees were unfamiliar—leaning too close and whispering in a tongue they didn't trust. The air tasted strange, and the soil, though damp, felt wrong beneath their paws. They were far from Glenmere now, and even the Crooked Wood, cruel though it had been, was behind them. But still the land bore the scent of those dark warrens. Sorrel's ears twitched at every shift in the brush, and Bracken's muscles stayed tight, ready.

"We ought to keep moving," Sorrel murmured, not looking at him.

Bracken nodded, but his gaze was on Wisp. Her breath remained shallow. The cold had settled into her limbs like dew into moss, and though she hadn't complained, they both saw how her strength flagged.

"We can't push her," Bracken said, voice low. "She's not made for running."

Sorrel frowned, the worry plain in her eyes.

"I know. But the longer we stay, the more chance something finds us. Something that remembers the Crooked Wood."

The river nearby went on murmuring to itself, heedless of rabbits and old fears. The wind stayed still, and the trees watched without blinking. And Bracken and Sorrel stood in that quiet, caught between the urge to flee and the ache of care.

They would wait—silent and patient—until Wisp showed she was ready. No call would be made, no urging given. The sun had yet to climb with warmth, and the mist lay heavy and low over the meadow, winding through the undergrowth like a restless memory refusing to loosen its grip. Then Wisp rose, stepping forward with quiet certainty. Bracken padded ahead, light-footed and alert, ears lifted to catch the steady murmur of the river. At Wisp's side, Sorrel moved in step—not following the beaten trail, but matching the slow, steady beat of Wisp's breath.

The path ahead ran crooked beside the water, veering now and again where tree roots broke the soil or stones jutted like old bones. They paused often—not from indecision, but out of quiet care. Wisp walked without complaint, though her limbs moved more slowly than they once had, her eyes dimmer beneath the veil of morning. She did not falter, but she no longer chased the wind.

They reached a gentle rise where the trees thinned, and the river stretched wider, free and slow. There, the three paused. Wisp moved between them, her sides heaving with the quiet work of breath. She turned once more toward the river, eyes soft and distant, as if the river whispered a secret long lost—something old and clean, just out of reach, waiting beneath the current's shimmer.

"It's still moving," she said softly.

Bracken nodded. "It always will."

They stood like that for a while, the three of them, held in the hush between breath and breeze. Then Sorrel nudged Wisp gently, and they went on down the path, not hurried, not lost. Just walking.

The sound of the river running never faded. It was a living thing, a relentless, guttural voice that pressed against the rabbits' ears as they crept along the path, the air thick with the scent of churned earth and cold water. The sky hung low, heavy with cloud, and the wind moved in restless fits, stirring the mist in uneasy waves. On this side of the river, the world seemed both wider and more secretive—a place where every shadow might hold a story, and every gust of wind might carry a warning.

Sorrel took the lead while Bracken kept close to Wisp, his flank brushing hers as they picked their way through the tangled grass. She trembled, each step quick and faltering, her breath coming in thin, uneven draws. Sorrel, ever watchful, slowed her pace to match them, her eyes flicking from Wisp's drooping ears to the shifting reeds ahead.

They had not gone far from the place of the carved wood before Wisp stumbled, her legs buckling beneath her. Bracken pressed his nose to her cheek, murmuring, "Rest a moment, Wisp. The ground is softer here."

Wisp blinked, her eyes glassy. "I'm all right. Just tired."

Sorrel circled back, her dark fur bristling in the wind. "We'll go slow. There's no rush now. The path's our guide, and nothing hunts in this wind but the old ghosts."

Bracken glanced at Sorrel, his heart tightening in that quiet way worry always brings—like a cold wind threading its way through fur. She met his look but said nothing, only dipped her head slightly, as if to say: yes, I see it too.

A little way off, among the knotted roots and stony soil, Bracken found a clearing with a patch of sweet grass, green and fresh despite the grayness of the day. He nibbled at a few blades to be certain, then tugged up a small clump and carried it back to Wisp.

"Here," he said gently, laying it before her. "Eat some, Wisp. It'll help. You need your strength."

Wisp looked at the offering, blinked once, and lowered her head. But she did not eat.

Bracken stood still beside her for a moment, then turned back to Sorrel, his voice low.

"She's weaker than before," he told her. "The river took more from her than it did from us."

Sorrel nodded, her gaze never straying from Wisp as the wind moved softly through the clearing, stirring the fur along the small one's flanks like ripples across still water. "Our journey," Sorrel said at last, her voice low and even, like a doe speaking to kits at twilight, "has not come without cost."

She turned her head, ears tilting with thought, and looked out over the land before them. "The earth rises gently here," she said. "There's a kind of shelter in the way the slope leans back from the river. And those willows there . . . old and broken though they are . . . they turn the wind just enough. There's grass. Not much, but enough. She's small, that's true, but there's strength in her. Not the noisy kind. The kind that holds on, even when no one's watching. We'll rest a while longer."

So they did. The three of them curled close beneath the hush of a willow. The river behind them moved like breath, steady and knowing, and the willows whispered their old leaf-songs to the sky. Bracken and Sorrel watched in silence, keeping close to Wisp without crowding her, their presence a kind of shield against whatever shadows might try to creep in.

At length, Wisp stirred. Her ears flicked. She did not speak. But when Bracken nudged a small tuft of grass toward her—fresh-picked from the slope where the sun had just begun to reach—she bent her head and nibbled, slow and careful, like a creature waking from some long sleep.

Sorrel said nothing, only watched, her eyes soft and thoughtful. And Bracken, though he did not smile, let out a breath he hadn't known he was holding. Above them, the sky stayed low and gray, but the moment held a kind of light all its own.

"Sorrel," he said quietly, "what more do you know of the Hollowkin? Not just the stories . . . the truth, if there is any."

Sorrel did not answer at once. She paused, ears pricked to the wind, as if listening for something older than words. Then she settled beside a nearby clump of goldenrods.

"The Hollowkin," she began, her voice low, "weren't just rabbits. That's what the elders always said. They were dreamers . . . rabbits who could see the old ways, who shaped the land as much as it shaped them. The mark they bore . . . thorns and light . . . wasn't just a scar or a sign. It meant they belonged to both worlds: the waking and the dream."

Wisp listened, her eyes wide, her breathing slow and shallow. Bracken felt the old chill stirring in his fur, the sense of standing at the edge of something vast and unseen.

Sorrel continued, her gaze distant. "The Hollowkin could walk in dreams as easily as we walk the grass. Some say they spoke with the earth itself, heard the voices of roots and stone. They kept the balance . . . between the living and the lost, between memory and forgetting."

She paused, the wind tugging at her whiskers. "But their bloodline is gone now . . . scattered to the winds. The last of them vanished before my mother's mother was born. Some say they were betrayed, others that they chose to fade away, to become part of the land they loved."

Bracken's mind drifted to the carving etched deep in the wood—the lines twisting and curling like roots searching for secret water, branching this way and that. And in the quiet moments between waking and sleep, he saw the White Buck—still, watching with eyes that held more than the hours could measure, as though its gaze reached beyond the bounds of time itself.

"Do you believe it?" he asked, his voice barely more than a whisper. "That they could shape the land? That they could walk in dreams?"

Sorrel's eyes met his, steady and sad. "I believe the land remembers. I believe some things are too old to die. The Hollowkin may be gone, but their mark lingers. In the stories. In the places where the grass grows strange and the wind sings of old sorrow."

Wisp shivered, curling into herself. "If they're gone, who watches the land now?"

Sorrel was silent for a moment. Then she said, "Maybe no one. Maybe that's why the world is changing. Or maybe . . . maybe they're not as gone as we think."

Then, the river's roar behind them grew louder as if in answer. The wind shifted, carrying a scent of cold stone and distant rain. Bracken felt the hairs along his spine rise, a prickling sense of being watched—not by predator or prey, but by something deeper, older, and full of sorrow.

The sky darkened, clouds massing overhead. The river, always present, seemed to draw closer, its voice swelling with every gust of wind. The world narrowed to the press of bodies, the slap of water, the hush of grass beneath the storm's breath.

The air now grew heavy, charged with a tension that had nothing to do with weather. Wisp tried to stand but stumbled, her legs giving way. She collapsed in the grass, her body wracked by a sudden, violent cough. Bracken dropped beside her, panic flaring in his chest.

Wisp coughed again, harder this time, and a mouthful of blood from her lips, dark and cold. She shuddered, her whole body trembling, and her eyes flew wide—unfocused, shining with a strange, inner light.

For a moment, the world seemed to hold its breath. The river's sound a distant murmur. The wind stilled, and the grass ceased its restless dance.

"He's watching," Wisp whispered. Her voice was not her own. It was deeper, older, echoing with the tone of Bracken's dreams . . . the voice that haunted the tunnels of bone and ash, that called him to remember.

Bracken felt a chill run through him, as if the river's cold had seeped into his heart. Sorrel drew back, her eyes wide with fear and wonder.

"Wisp?" Bracken whispered, but she did not answer. Her gaze was fixed on something none of them could see, something that hovered just beyond the edge of the waking world.

The silence stretched, thick and trembling. Then, as suddenly as it had come, the moment broke. Wisp sagged against Bracken, her breath coming in ragged gasps. The river's roar returned, the wind stirred the grass, and the world resumed its restless motion.

Bracken cradled Wisp, his heart pounding. Sorrel crouched beside them, her body tense, every muscle poised for flight.

"What did she mean?" Sorrel whispered. "Who's watching?"

Bracken shook his head, unable to speak. He knew, though—the White Buck, the Hollowkin, the watcher in the dream. The presence that lingered at the edge of sight, guiding them, warning them, waiting for them to understand.

The river crossing was not just a trial of survival. It was a passage—a step into a world shaped by old stories and older powers. The mark of the Hollowkin was upon them, and the path ahead was no longer just their own.

They huddled together in the grass, the river's voice a lullaby and a warning, the wind carrying the memory of thorns and light. Above them, the sky pressed low, and somewhere in the hush between heartbeats, the watcher waited—silent, patient, and full of meaning yet to be revealed.

The river's voice was endless, a restless, guttural music that pressed against the rabbits' ears as they crept through the tangled grass. The sky pressed closer, low and gray, the wind moving in uneasy fits, and the world beyond the Crooked Wood seemed both wider and more secretive than any of them remembered. Every shadow held a story, every gust of wind a warning. Bracken kept close to Wisp, watching her. She shivered, kept coughing, her breath shallow and quick. Sorrel, ever watchful, watched their surroundings, her eyes flicking from Wisp's drooping ears to the ever-shifting landscape around them.

Wisp blinked, her eyes glassy. "I'm all right. Really. Just a bit under the weather."

"No," said Bracken. "You are not all right. Just rest. Gather your strength."

Bracken watched Wisp, worry tightening in his chest. He turned to Sorrel, then spoke quietly, "She's hurting inside. Not just tired . . . something deeper. I've seen it before, back in Glenmere. Sometimes, after a hard crossing, or when a sickness gets in the blood. The elders called it 'root-ache.' It eats at the strength from within."

Sorrel's eyes narrowed, her ears pricking with concern. "Is there anything we can do?"

"There's an herb," Bracken said, recalling the old warren's medicine tales. "Elderwort. It grows where the ground is damp and the sun is thin . . . long, narrow leaves, pale green, with a silver line down the center. The elders chewed it for wounds and fevers. It's bitter, but it helps."

Sorrel nodded. "Stay with her. I'll find it." She slipped away, moving low and silent through the grass, her nose working steadily as she searched among the roots and stones.

Bracken settled beside Wisp, offering her a tuft of sweet grass. She sniffed at it but did not eat. He pressed close, sharing his warmth, and whispered stories of Glenmere—of sunlit meadows and the taste of clover, of the old warren's safety. Wisp listened, her eyes half-closed, her body trembling with effort.

Time drifted slowly in the hush of the river's shadow. After a while, Sorrel returned, her mouth full of pale, slender leaves. "Elderwort," she said, dropping the bundle before Bracken. "Found it near a fallen willow, where the mud clings deepest and softest."

Bracken thanked her with a nod and began to chew the leaves, mixing them with a little grass to soften the taste. He nudged the bitter mash toward Wisp. "Eat, little one. It will help."

Wisp hesitated, then took a tentative bite. The flavor made her nose wrinkle, but she chewed and swallowed, trusting Bracken's gentle urging. Slowly, the trembling eased from her limbs. Her breathing grew steadier, and a hint of color returned to her ears.

Sorrel watched, relief softening her features. The wind shifted, carrying the scent of rain and earth, and for a while, the three rabbits simply rested—safe, if only for a moment, in the hush between river and sky.

As the sky dimmed to a dusky gray and the hush of evening settled over the riverbank, Sorrel rose to her haunches and began to scrape at the soil. It was good earth—soft and pliant, damp from the river's breath, and rich with the scent of leafmold and old water. She worked quickly, her paws flicking the dirt behind her in short, practiced strokes. Bracken joined her without a word, his forepaws widening the entrance, tugging away stones and knotting the floor with lengths of dry grass and shed willow-leaf.

When the hollow had grown deep enough to shelter them all, Sorrel began to gather what the land would offer—tall grasses bent soft from rain, brittle twigs from the bramble's edge. She nosed along patiently, pulling free what she could from the tangled fringe, careful not to break more than needed. With quiet persistence, she worked the stems between her teeth, twisting and weaving them into a rough mat. It was crude, but stout enough to hang close to the earth, holding the wind at bay and shading the burrow's mouth from any watchful eyes that might stray from the far bank.

Together, she and Bracken helped Wisp inside, the little rabbit trembling still from the day's flight. The burrow took them in, small and close and damp with the breath of the river, and though the night beyond whispered of things unseen, within it was still.

Night settled in, thick and cool. The burrow was small but snug, the scent of willow and elderwort mingling in the air. Bracken curled himself around Wisp, who breathed easier now, her eyes closing in true sleep for the first time since the river. Sorrel blocked the entrance with a tangle of branches, then slipped inside, pressing close to her companions.

Outside, the river's roar became a distant lullaby. The wind stirred the reeds, setting them to a restless rustle, and slipped like a whisper through the tall grass. But within the quiet earth of the burrow, there was only warmth, and the calm, steady thrum of three hearts keeping time together beneath the dark.

Bracken listened to the quiet, feeling the tension in his body ease. He glanced at Sorrel, who met his gaze with tired gratitude. "Thank you," she whispered. "For knowing what to do."

Bracken shook his head. "We all did what we could. Tomorrow, we'll see how she fares."

He looked down at Wisp, her breathing deep and even, and felt hope stirring in his chest. The journey ahead was uncertain, the world beyond the river wild and strange. But for this night, they were safe. For this night, they belonged to each other and to the land that sheltered them.

Above them, the sky settled into a vast, silent night. The river slipped by beneath the stars, carrying mysteries no ear could catch, while the world held its breath in the stillness before dawn. In the soft dark of their burrow, Bracken, Sorrel, and Wisp lay curled together, wrapped in the calm of shared warmth and trust, asleep without fear.

# Chapter 7
# Dregg

Dawn spread across the land in a pale wash of gold, touching the tangled grass and the dew that clung to every leaf. The world held stillness, broken only by the far-off rise of a lark's song and the low breath of wind moving through wild thyme. Beneath the roots of the willow, the three rabbits roused from uneasy sleep. Bracken stretched his mottled frame and blinked into the light. Sorrel, always sharp to stir, was already awake, her rust-dark fur roughened by the chill, ears tall and listening. Wisp opened her wide eyes and drew a long breath. The pain and fear of the day before had passed into shadow; she rose with a lift to her step that had not been there, her white-marked coat clear against the green.

Bracken watched her closely, a sense of release passing through him as Wisp nosed his shoulder, her whiskers alive with the scents of damp soil and fresh sunlight. Sorrel flicked her ears and looked across the edge of the meadow before them. What she saw there made her still a moment, for it seemed the morning itself carried promise.

"Are you better? Enough to travel?" Sorrel asked, her voice gentle but searching.

Wisp managed a small smile that shone quick and true. "Yes." She lifted her eyes toward Bracken. "Thank you for helping me get well."

He nudged her with his nose, warmth in his eyes. "You're most welcome, my friend. We stand together."

"We should move," Sorrel said, her words threaded with both caution and hope. "The sky is clear, and the land waits for us."

Together, they slipped from the shelter of the burrow, paws sinking into the cool, forgiving grass. The meadow opened before them, rolling away in gentle swells toward the distant, shadowed line of trees. The sky above was a thin, endless blue, streaked with the first warmth of morning. Behind lay the burrow, the white river, and the days already passed—left for whatever lay ahead on the open path.

Wisp moved with new energy, her steps light and eager as she pressed close to Bracken's side. Sorrel led, her form lean and sure, ears pricked for any sign of danger. The three rabbits moved out into the waking world, hunger and memory close upon them, while hope and doubt pressed at their paws with every step into the day.

The sun rested low along the rim of the earth, and the air at the meadow's edge carried the damp sweetness of dew and the sharp tang of wild thyme. Bracken halted, his paws pressed into the cool grass, and turned to the others. Sorrel, lean and rust-red, held herself a little apart, her ears raised and watchful. Wisp, white-patched and wide-eyed, stayed close by Bracken's flank, her nose working at every stray breath of wind.

The land here was open, rolling away in a gentle swell toward the dark line of distant trees. The sky above stretched pale and blue, streaked with the last gold of evening. It might have been a place of rest, even a place to linger, had it not been for the hollow in their bellies and the thought of their Glenmere left behind.

Bracken's heart thudded as he looked out over the meadow. He had dreamed of this place—of grass that glowed with an inner light, of voices whispering beneath the soil, of a White Buck who would watch from the edge of vision. Now, in the hush of the meadow, he felt those dreams upon him again, as if the land itself remembered.

Then something caught his eye. A shape moved ahead, lightly as a leaf on still water, without effort, parting the grass with the ease of something half-remembered from a dream. It paused as though it had stepped out from a season all its own. The rabbits froze—Bracken stiffening first, then Sorrel and Wisp, their ears flattening—but the figure did not press forward. Instead, it settled atop a smooth rise and turned toward them.

"A buck," whispered Bracken.

"Who is he?" asked Sorrel.

There was no reply.

The day's light touched the fine silver of the buck's fur, but not merely silver—his coat caught and held the dusk like it meant to keep it. His form was lean, elegant, ageless in the way of things that do not quite belong. His eyes, pale and hard to read, held the cool gleam of moonlit shallows. There was a scent about him, not of rabbit nor of any earthborn creature, but of fern rot and stone, of hollows where wind never reached. A rabbit, yes, but not of any warren Bracken had ever known.

There was a quiet poise about him, a charm spun like web across the clearing. Every movement seemed measured, deliberate, as though he understood the land and its paths better than any of the others. Yet beneath that grace was something older, something that spoke of seasons counted and storms endured, a mind that held more knowledge than any rabbit had cause to know. When he paused, the air seemed to listen with him, and the leaves stilled as if aware that he carried more than the day's simple doings.

His voice, when it came, was quiet and melodious, the kind of voice a young rabbit might follow and never quite know why.

"Travelers," he said, and the breeze shifted as though it carried his voice, "and not of these fields, unless I am mistaken."

Bracken's shoulders rose. His legs were set, tight as thistle stems in wind. He stepped forward. "We bring no harm," he said. "We're only passing through."

The stranger's smile was languid, the curve of his mouth both kindly and knowing. His teeth, too white, too even, gave no warmth. "Passing through?" he asked. "Or are you searching for something you've left behind?"

At this, Sorrel moved beside Bracken, steady as frost beneath fallen oak leaves. "Our warren is dying," she said. "We're looking for a place to settle. Somewhere quiet. Somewhere safe. A place where we can belong."

"A place called Ash Hollow," Bracken interjected.

The silver buck tilted his head with delicate amusement. "Ah . . . Ash Hollow," he said, the words rolling gently from his tongue like a pebble dropped into deep water. "Yes, it's not far from here. But the fields have changed. So have the woods. What's safe now may not be tomorrow."

Wisp crept forward, more drawn than driven, her eyes wide with cautious wonder. "What is your name?" she asked, her voice nearly lost beneath the sighing grass.

The buck gave a small, courtly bow, as though rehearsed. "I am called Dregg," he said. "I know this meadow, and the wood beyond, and the places that came before either. I remember names spoken before your mothers were kindled, and places walked by those long left to the ground. But names change, and so do rivers."

Bracken exchanged a glance with Sorrel. "We're following a sign," he said quietly. "A dream, maybe. The Hollowkin . . ."

Dregg laughed, a soft, musical sound that seemed to ripple through the grass. "The Hollowkin! Old stories for frightened kits. I've heard them all: rabbits who sleep beneath the earth, who whisper in roots and ride the wind. You believe such tales?"

Bracken's ears flattened. "I've seen them. Not with my eyes, maybe, but—"

"—but in dreams," Dregg finished, his smile lingering. "Dreams are a kind of hunger, Bracken. They feed on what we wish and what we fear. But they do not build warrens. They do not keep you safe from fox or stoat."

Sorrel's ears twitched as she regarded Dregg, her gaze sharpening with suspicion. "You know our names."

Dregg's gaze flicked to her, untroubled. "Names travel on the wind. Or perhaps I'm a dream myself, sent to test your courage."

Wisp trembled, yet her eyes stayed locked on Dregg, full of intent. "Do you know which way we should travel? Toward Ash Hollow?"

Dregg's eyes softened. "It's a place deep and old, cut into the side of the hill where the grass grows thin and the stones remember rain. It's a haven. A place to begin anew. Yet, few go there now. It's said to be haunted by the Hollowkin, if you believe such things."

Bracken's heart leapt. "The Ash Hollow of my dreams?"

Dregg's smile deepened, but his eyes were unreadable. "Dreams are strange visitors," he said, his whiskers twitching with each word. "They slip in through the cracks of sleep, soft as moss along a tree's root, and linger even after the light finds you. Sometimes, I think they carry more than a rabbit can carry in its thoughts."

Sorrel stepped forward, ears flat against her head, body coiled. "You speak in riddles. Ways that trouble me."

Dregg tilted his head, a soft exhalation stirring through the fur along his shoulders. "Perhaps," he said, his voice low and even, "it is not the riddles themselves that confound, but the hurry with which we press to untangle them. Some answers are meant to be followed like a scent drifting on the wind, not seized with eager paws. Yet, even with the questions that linger, I am willing to guide you, if you care to follow."

Bracken blinked, unsure what to make of the words, and Wisp shivered, her paws drawn close.

"Why help us? You do not know us," Sorrel asked.

Dregg's tail flicked. "Maybe I like you. Or maybe I like the company. Or maybe I'm bored. The world is full of reasons, Sorrel. Some truer than others."

Bracken said, his voice uncertain. "Is it nice? Safe? This Ash Hollow we speak of?"

Dregg's gaze flickered to him, then away. "Nice enough. Safe enough, if you know how to listen. The land speaks, if you're quiet. The stones remember old feet. And the Hollowkin . . . if they exist. . . are but dreamers now."

Wisp's eyes were wide. "I want to see it," she whispered.

Sorrel hesitated, her gaze hard on Dregg. "Dreams and stories are well enough, but we need shelter, a home. If you're leading us into a trap . . ."

Dregg bowed again, almost mockingly. "You're wise to doubt, Sorrel. The world is full of teeth. But I have no hunger for your blood."

Bracken stepped forward, his voice quiet but sure. "We'll go. If there's a chance . . . if there's even a memory of safety. . ."

Dregg nodded, his silver fur catching the last light. "Then follow. The night is soon to come, and the grass grows cold."

He turned, moving through the meadow with a grace that was almost unnatural. The others followed, Sorrel last, her eyes never leaving Dregg's back.

They moved in silence, the grass whispering around their legs. Wisp pressed close to Bracken, her breath quick. "I fear he is not real," she whispered.

Bracken glanced at her, then at the silver shape ahead. "I don't know. But the Hollowkin . . . if they're watching, maybe they sent him."

Sorrel, close behind, muttered, "Or maybe he's a fox in rabbit's fur."

Dregg's voice drifted back as if he'd heard. "No fox here, Sorrel. Only old stories and older paths."

They walked on, the meadow fading into shadow around them, the land opening before them like a story half-remembered. The air grew cooler, the sky deepened to indigo, and the first stars blinked awake above the world.

At the edge of the meadow, Dregg paused, waiting for them to gather. "Ash Hollow lies just ahead," he said softly. "But the way is not straight. You must trust your feet, and your hearts."

Wisp trembled, but Bracken touched her shoulder. "We're together. That's enough."

Sorrel looked to the sky, then to the land ahead. "Lead on, Dregg. But know this . . . I'll be watching."

Dregg's eyes glinted with amusement. "I would expect nothing less."

They slipped into the deepening dusk, the grass closing behind them, the world narrowing to the path ahead. Somewhere, in the hush between heartbeats, Bracken thought he heard a voice—soft, ancient, and full of sorrow—whispering from beneath the earth.

The Hollowkin, he thought. Or only the wind.

But the feeling stayed with him, pressing in his chest, as they followed the silver stranger into the unknown.

As the dusk settled over the meadow, the rabbits set to work, scratching and burrowing into the soft ground beneath a spray of ferns. Together, Bracken, Sorrel, and Wisp shaped a shallow hollow, just wide enough for comfort but obscured from the prowling night. Bracken slipped away and returned with mouthfuls of sweet grass—tender and fragrant from a hidden patch he'd found near the stream—laying it before Sorrel and Wisp with quiet pride. They nibbled gratefully, warmth hollowing out the weariness of the day.

A little apart, Dregg watched from the shadow of a leaning bramble, his silver fur catching starlight, alert and unreadable. Sorrel shifted uneasily, eyes flicking to him.

Bracken caught her glance and murmured, "Let him be. For all we know, he may be the one to lead us to Ash Hollow yet."

The meadow breathed around them, heavy with the promise of sleep and distant sorrow, as the rabbits curled close against the deepening dark.

The morning thickened with scents as they left behind the meadow where the silver stranger had first crossed their path. Mist hung in torn veils along the tall grass, each blade bent under the dew and quivering faintly while the rabbits moved on through it, the land hushed around their passing.

Dregg led, silent as the dawn breeze. His silver coat drifted through the grass, barely touching, yet every living thing seemed to shrink from him. A linnet, bright and lively, fell quiet mid-song as Dregg passed beneath its perch. The air shifted; the sharp, musky trace of fox faded from the wind, though none had glimpsed its shadow. Even so, Sorrel's ears stood sharp.

Bracken followed, eyes thoughtful and distant. Through the night, dreams of white fur, cool water, and tangled roots haunted him—echoes of something deep and old, listening from beneath the earth. Each step now brought uneasy searching, though he did not know what sign he sought.

Wisp moved quietly at Sorrel's side, both at the rear, and Sorrel watched, rust-colored fur flaring in the sea of green, her posture ready and wary. She trusted little that wore a smooth face, and Dregg, gliding with careful stride and polished words, set her fur prickling from the start.

It was Wisp who first spoke of what seemed to linger in the meadow. "They mourn," she said softly.

Bracken tilted his ears toward her. "What do you mean?"

"The flowers," Wisp replied, stopping by a cluster of wood anemone, their pale heads drooping with beads of dew. "They mourn. Even the grasses recoil when he draws close."

Bracken listened with ears moving, but he saw only the land, bowed and slick with moisture. "Perhaps it's only the wind," he suggested, trying for steadiness. "Everything's damp from morning."

Wisp's eyes grew round. "No, there's more to it. I can sense it."

Sorrel soon joined Bracken. "She has the truth of it."

"You noticed?"

Sorrel flicked her whiskers, voice low. "No proof. But I feel it in my teeth, the way you do when a storm draws near and the fur along your jaw bristles."

Ahead, under the spreading limbs of an old ash split by some forgotten lightning, Dregg paused and looked back, his mouth curling in a quiet, knowing smile.

"The morning is beautiful, isn't it?" he said, voice smooth as leafmold warmed by sun. "Ash Hollow lies beyond the ridge ahead. Not far now."

Bracken joined him at the tree. "You've been there before?"

"Oh, many times," Dregg said, as though amused. "Long ago. Before these woods grew tired of remembering. Ash Hollow is hidden from the eyes of men and worse things. Its roots go deep, and the burrows are dry and warm even when winter gnaws at the world's bones."

Sorrel narrowed her eyes. "You speak of it like a poem."

"Is that wrong?" Dregg turned toward her, his ears slanted slightly, unreadable. "Beauty has always needed defending."

"Words don't make warrens," Sorrel said flatly. "Not ones you can raise kits in."

From behind, Wisp, crouched low near a cluster of violets, called softly, "Bracken, come see."

He bounded over. The flowers were crumpled, not just drooped from wet or sun, but bent in on themselves as if twisted by unseen fingers. The scent was wrong too—sour and sweet at once, like berries gone to rot.

"They weren't like this when we came through," Wisp said, her voice almost too quiet to hear.

Bracken glanced toward Dregg, who now waited further uphill, his back turned to them, ears forward as though catching some sound too faint for the rest.

"He didn't touch them," Bracken said. "Not a pawprint."

Wisp trembled a little. "He doesn't need to."

Bracken said nothing. He let his eyes drift shut, surrendering himself to a vision that pressed in from the edges of sense—a pale figure poised on the distant ridge, neither Dregg nor wholly a stranger, yet bound to him by threads older than kinship, as one dark root tangles with another in the secret earth. The presence spoke, but not with words. It was a heaviness, a slow, growing pressure underfoot, like roots thrusting blindly through stone, splitting the world with their insistence. Bracken's eyes blinked open to gray light and wind, troubled by what he'd half-seen and not dared to understand.

They pressed on.

The ground lifted in gentle slopes, shaded by ancient trunks whose bark bore deep cracks and tufts of moss. In the dark folds between roots, stout mushrooms huddled—broad stems topped with caps mottled like old bruises. Ahead, a pale grove of birch trees shimmered in the dusk, their white limbs reaching skyward among the shadows. A vole flickered across the path, its movement barely more than a ripple in the grass, lost to silence in an instant.

Dregg paused at the side of a toppled log, where the soil had slumped aside to show a tight passage, opening in the earth like a mouth clamped shut in fear.

"Here," he said. "We'll rest soon. The hollow lies just beyond the stand of birches. A short climb, and you'll feel the light shift."

"The light?" Bracken asked.

"It's different there," Dregg said. "Like the world forgets itself."

Sorrel's tail twitched. "That's meant to reassure us?"

Dregg only smiled. "Forgetting is sometimes what is required, dear friend."

They passed among the birch, where the pale trunks stood like ghosts in rank. No wind moved here. Even the birdsong had ceased, replaced by the distant ticking of beetles and the faint hiss of sap through trees.

"I don't like this," Wisp murmured. Her eyes were wider than ever. "Everything's watching."

Bracken turned slowly, sweeping the shadowed woods around them. "There's nothing here."

"You don't see it all. It watches us, just beyond sight."

Dregg stopped beneath the tallest birch and turned. For a long moment, he studied them all—the rusted fire of Sorrel, the small and curious Wisp, and Bracken, who stood stiller than most bucks ever could, his eyes pale as misted stone.

"You're not the first," Dregg said softly. "Others have come. Seeking a home. A future. But futures come at a cost, as you'll learn."

Bracken's fur prickled. "What happened to them? The others?"

Dregg's smile sharpened. "They found what they were seeking."

Sorrel stepped forward. "Enough with your riddles. Show us Ash Hollow or be on your way."

"As you wish," Dregg said, bowing again with courtly grace. "But remember, the Hollow does not give without taking. The roots feed as well as shelter."

And he turned once more, leading them up through the silent birches and into the strange light beyond.

The day was drawing on when they followed Dregg through the birch grove and into a swell of grassland. The sky had cleared at last, and the sun—heavy and gold as honeycomb—settled into the west with a slow, stately burn, casting long shadows that swayed with the nodding heads of seed-heavy stalks. Birds called from unseen hollows in the trees beyond, their cries thin and wistful as if recalling some older, forgotten summer. The wind combed gently through the grasses, setting them to rustling like a thousand small paws moving unseen. Clover bloomed low to the earth, and its scent mingled with the musk of dry bark and warm earth. It was a place that might have stirred comfort in a wanderer's heart, had the hour not been so late and their guide so strange.

Sorrel kept her head low and her ears upright, her stride light but her muscles taut, watching the silver-furred buck with eyes that did not blink. Dregg moved as if born to the meadow, silver hide glinting in the late sun, his narrow limbs silent even among the dry leaves and brambles. His lean form was graceful and strangely timeless—neither youthful nor withered, but held in a quiet pause, like a moth pressed beneath glass. Every few steps, he paused—not in hesitation, but in something like reverence. His head tilted toward the distant wind, nose twitching as though listening to a language older than rabbits. His movements suggested grace without fragility, and a kind of practiced poise, like a storyteller who knows the tale before it's told.

"Ash Hollow lies just ahead," he said, and though his voice was soft, it carried with a strange clarity, as though the air itself leaned in to hear him. "The land there is sweet and dark. Burrows shape themselves to the will of those who need them."

Bracken shifted his weight uneasily, ears pivoting at the odd phrasing, but he said nothing.

Wisp followed close, nearly brushing Dregg's flank, her white-spotted ears bouncing with every hop. Her steps had grown slower, the pads of her feet tender from travel, yet something in her manner was lightened by hope, if only by a sliver.

"Is it true?" she asked him, voice low and caught between wonder and weariness. "Do the burrows really . . . shape themselves?"

Dregg glanced at her, and for a moment the sun caught in his eyes and made them unreadable—bright as riverwater in moonlight, yet deeper somehow. "Everything gives way to those who arrive in need," he said. "That is the oldest rule."

He turned without waiting for a reply.

Bracken, trailing behind, caught the edge of Wisp's question but not Dregg's answer. He had paused, nose in the air, testing the wind as instinct demanded. There was something there—something beneath the scent of sweetgrass and dandelion. Not a danger exactly, not fox nor stoat, but a wrongness. Like a bramble bush in leaf with blood on its thorns. His whiskers trembled.

"Are you certain," he muttered, more to himself than to the others, "this is the way?"

There was no answer. Ahead, Dregg was already cresting a ridge, and the sun's last edge clung to his back like the outline of a shadow not yet born.

"Bracken," Sorrel muttered, doubling back to him, "are you lagging on purpose?"

He blinked and shook his head. "No. Just . . . thinking."

She grunted and turned away, but not before casting another narrow-eyed look at the silver buck ahead. "Well, don't think so loud.  The noise hurts my ears."

As they moved deeper through the grassland, the flowers changed. Where earlier there had been buttercup and daisy, now grew tall foxglove and monkshood, their colors rich but strangely dull, as if the light avoided them. Trees rose in clumps, black-barked and ancient, and once Wisp stopped, her ears twitched.

"Did you hear that?"

Bracken tilted his head. "Hear what?"

She lowered her voice to a whisper. "It was like . . . like crying. Not loud. Just soft. The flowers. They're weeping."

Bracken frowned, turning his head to the wind. "We've been through this already. Maybe you're hearing bees? Or wind through the stalks?"

Wisp shook her head, her eyes wide and solemn. "No. The sound is not that of bees or stalks waving in the wind. No. What I hear is more like . . . like sorrow."

Sorrel, just ahead, did not turn. "Don't fill your head with too many sounds, or dreams for that matter. This buck we're following speaks in a strange way. And now you're hearing things. Flowers crying. We must be careful. Get your feet under you and mind your path."

But Wisp looked back once, over her shoulder, and though the air was still, a single petal from a blue flower dropped without a touch.

Dregg led them onward, between the roots of a massive elm, its trunk gnarled and hollowed by storms long past. Here, the ground dipped gently, and the grasses parted to show dark, rich soil. A stream, narrow but swift, ran beside the path, gurgling as if amused.

"We are closer," said Dregg, his silver fur catching the pale light that sifted through the branches. He paused, laying a paw upon the broken earth. "This was once a well-worn path, trodden by more paws than you or I could count. . . more than either of us could imagine. In those days, the world stretched green and vast, and the stars above were young, still shining faintly with the dew of their first dawn. The footsteps that passed here long ago still tread beneath our feet, and will continue to do so, long after your names have faded to little more than scratches in the dust."

"How would you know this?" Sorrel said, coming up beside him. "You speak as if you were alive in the days before we were kindled."

He turned to her, his expression soft as fog. "And how do you know I wasn't?"

Sorrel's ears flicked back, uneasy. For a moment, the old stories of moonlit ghosts and wandering spirits pressed at the edge of her mind, and she found herself searching Dregg's face for any sign of jest or ordinary truth. But his eyes, pale as river stones, gave nothing away.

She gathered her composure as instinct warred with dread. "If you are as old as your tongue would have us think," she said quietly, "then you know what becomes of those who linger too long among dreams and stories. The earth forgets us all, Dregg . . . sooner or later. I trust what I can see and feel: the soil beneath my paws and the breath in my chest. If you remember some other world better than this one, so be it; but don't lead us chasing shadows while there's still real ground underfoot and real dangers on the wind."

Her words were steady, but the fur along her spine would not quite lie flat. She watched Dregg warily, uncertain if she spoke to a fellow traveler in flesh or something far stranger, older, and just out of reach.

He only smiled. "Shadows are everywhere, my dear Sorrel. In every moment. In every time. Come now. We must forge onward."

They came to yet another grove of birches, this one a ring, their trunks pale and peeling, their roots tangled and welcoming. Dregg turned there, motioning with his chin.

"We sleep here," he said. "Tomorrow we will reach Ash Hollow, and you will see for yourselves that I have spoken nothing but truth."

Bracken looked to Sorrel, who gave a reluctant nod. "It's as good a place as any," he muttered.

They settled, scraping shallow hollows into the soil. Wisp tucked herself close to Bracken, her breathing steady, but her ears twitching even in stillness. Dregg, as he had done the night before, lay apart, beneath the arms of a willow, and watched the stars as they brightened one by one.

Bracken, though tired, could not easily sleep. He stared into the darkness beneath his own lids and found it gave way. In the dream, he was not himself. He was taller, stronger, and his fur shone like snow under starlight. He ran without fear through ash trees, the ground cracking with frost beneath him. Ahead, a stream, black as pitch. Beside it, a rabbit, silver-furred and small with youth.

"You don't belong here," Bracken said, though his voice sounded different.

The silver rabbit lifted his head, his eyes bright with something old and knowing. "Nor do you," he said.

When Bracken opened his eyes, the world had returned—the birch trees arching overhead like watchful elders, their white limbs pale in the starlight. The stars themselves had wandered on, rearranged like thoughts in a dreaming mind. Wisp murmured, curled in sleep, her ears twitching at some half-remembered sound.

Sorrel shifted, her muscles still tight, even in slumber, as if chased in dreams. And Dregg?

Dregg lay without motion. His eyes were open, staring at nothing, as though he had gone beyond the need to blink.

Bracken turned his head upward, toward the thinning sky.

"He was young," he whispered to himself. "Once."

No wind came to meet his voice, yet the grass to his side quivered, as if some unseen paw had passed gently through it.

# Chapter 8
# The Hollow Temple

The night slipped softly away, unspooling its dark threads beneath a pale, widening sky, and morning crept in like a cautious breath. Soon, the burdensome warmth of day wrapped itself around them, slow and inevitable. They had been moving since sunrise, through the tangled gloom beneath ancient trees, where the air hung heavy with the scent of damp bark and the faint, lingering musk of old fox dens long abandoned.

It was then, as the hours slid one into the next, that the way beneath their feet began to shift—not in form, for there was no true path to follow, only a plain ancient beneath leaf and root—but in the very fabric of the place. The ground turned uneven, broken as if the earth itself had grown restless, and the scattered rustling of dry leaves grew oddly subdued. Even the birdsong seemed to falter, retreating, as though they had passed unseen beyond some whispered curtain, woven by the forest in secret, where the world held its breath and waited.

"Wait," Bracken murmured, lifting his head. "There's something not as it should be."

But Dregg was already pushing ahead, low and lean, the tip of his ears brushing against hanging bramble.

"Keep on," he told them, though he did not turn back. "The place is near now. I know it."

Bracken hesitated, his brown fur darkened with the damp, and his whiskers trembling. He looked to Sorrel, but she was focused ahead, her eyes narrowed, her breath shallow.

"The undergrowth is wrong," she muttered. "Too thick. No wind."

"It hasn't stopped him," Wisp said, staying close to Bracken's side, her small body pressed nearly to his.

Dregg slipped silently beneath a curtain woven of honeysuckle and dogrose, its blossoms weaving soft shadows across his silver fur. One by one, the others followed, threading through the arch of thorn and twisting vine as if stepping through a hidden gate into another world. The scent of blossom and earth hung thick and sweet, mingling with the faint rustle of leaves stirred by a tentative breeze.

The trees drew back, their limbs giving way as though some old path were opening, and a clearing revealed itself. What met them was no simple meadow, but a wide hollow, sunk deep and sheltered in the earth, as though the land had chosen to fold itself inward. Here, the branches at its rim leaned kindly, spreading in a slow arch, and the sun, tempered by banks of drifting cloud, struck through in shifting patterns that played across the soft green beneath. At the hollow's center lay the quiet ruin of a forgotten place: the cracked stones and moss-clad remnants of a structure built by hands now vanished from memory.

The stones seemed to carry a murmur of old purpose, a temple perhaps, long ago set apart for meanings now buried in silence. They were sunk askew, the walls no more than broken shoulders of masonry pushed up from the moss. Ivy hung thick over the remains of columns that once would have stood like guardians. In the center rose a platform—a slab of stone split by root and frost, blotched with iron-colored stains. Scattered about lay heaps of bones—birds, voles, and something larger—bleached pale by long years of stillness. Even the wind passed it by in silence.

None of the rabbits moved.

Sorrel's ears turned forward, stiff with tension. "What is this place?"

Dregg stepped to the edge of the ruin as though it had called him there.

"They brought gifts here," he said. "Before the Twolegs forgot themselves."

"Gifts?" Bracken asked. "What are you talking about? What sort of gifts?"

Dregg's tone sank, heavy and solemn. "Sacrifices."

The word seemed to glide across the stillness, sharp and chill, like the wing-shadow of a bird of prey passing over the ground. Wisp flinched—not from terror, but as though some hidden nerve had been struck—and crouched low upon her hindquarters. A sudden tremor ran through her head, jerking it aside, and then her eyes turned languid, fluttering half-shut.

Bracken cried out. "What's happening to her?"

Wisp's lips stirred, and out came a voice thinned and wavering, nothing at all like her usual lilting squeak. It rasped from her throat as though something older and wearier had slipped into her body, speaking in her stead.

"She is the bright one," said the presence inside her. "She bears the seed. She knows not . . . but she was shown. Through ash and claw. Through blood and earth."

"Wisp," Sorrel shouted. "Wisp, stop!"

But the little doe only swayed where she stood, her nose flickering quick and sharp.

Still the voice unfurled, spreading like roots. "She walks with the wind-hung dead. Down among stone teeth. She must . . ."

Suddenly, her body shuddered, and she toppled forward. Bracken rushed to her side.

"For a heartbeat," she said, her own voice raw and trembling, "I heard them call me. The Hollowkin. They say the trial is near."

"She's fine," Dregg said. "No need to fret."

Bracken turned his eyes up at him. "You don't seem surprised. You knew this would happen."

"I told you," Dregg answered, quiet as dusk. "We're close now. So close even the old ones stir in their sleep."

"What did you mean by trial?" Sorrel asked Wisp.

The little rabbit shivered, ears pressed back. "I don't know."

Sorrel turned her back to the ruin and looked out over the tree line that hemmed them in. The branches there grew too evenly. Not wild, like normal trees, but as if they had been planted. She sniffed the air. Damp. Stagnant. No wind moved through this hollow. And still—

"Something's watching us," she whispered.

Bracken's head snapped toward her. "You saw something?"

"No. But it's there. Up in the trees, maybe. Or beneath."

"Beneath?"

She glanced again at the flat slab of stone in the center of the ruin. "This place has a belly," she said.

"You feel it too," Wisp said.

Sorrel stiffened. "I don't want to feel it."

Bracken shifted uneasily, nudging Wisp's unconscious form with his paw. "We should move on. This isn't Ash Hollow. This is some cursed thing the Twolegs left behind. If there's a path through, we take it. But I say we don't sleep here."

"Sleep?" Dregg's ears swiveled back. "We are not here to sleep."

"What do you mean?" Bracken narrowed his eyes. "You said Ash Hollow was near."

"It is. This is its gate."

Sorrel stepped forward, voice hard. "You said it was a haven. A place to begin again."

"And it is," Dregg replied. "For those who deserve it."

Bracken rose. "What are you talking about?"

Dregg turned his head with the slow care, letting his eyes rest on each of them in their turn.

"You think it lies open to all," he said. "But Ash Hollow is not a hollow log for any wanderer to crawl into. It holds itself apart. To step within, one must prove the strength of their journey. It is a trial-place, a measure of truth. Only those who shed the pelt of the past and stand renewed may pass its threshold. That is the law."

"No such law exists," Bracken snapped. "I've had enough of your riddles and this madness."

He lunged forward, muscles coiled, his hackles lifting like windblown grass before a storm. Dregg did not move, save to raise one broad paw against the air. At once, a pressure swept the clearing, invisible yet heavy as floodwater, and Bracken's rush faltered. The ground beneath his paws seemed to heave back against him, driving him a few paces away before he stumbled to a halt. Dregg's eyes held him steadily, calm and ancient, as if he were showing not power but the bare truth of the gulf that lay between them. The hush that followed carried no sound of birdsong, only the echo of Bracken's halted challenge.

"Listen to me," Dregg's voice was firm. "I speak the oldest truth. The burrows of Ash Hollow were not carved by tooth and claw. They were shaped by will. The same will that demands sacrifice. This . . ." he gestured with his nose toward the ruin, ". . . is the beginning. The place where the journey either ends or becomes something greater."

Wisp stirred then, groaning, her ears flickering faintly as though roused from a dream. The spell upon her was thinning like mist at sunrise. Sorrel stepped close beside her, planting herself squarely between the youngster and Dregg.

"You brought us here on false pretenses," Sorrel growled.

"No," answered Dregg, his eyes shining in the half-light. "I brought you to the threshold you were bound for all along. Turn back, if that's in you. But I'll not turn. My paws know this ground. I've carried the path inside me since the last burrow sank in on itself and the last warren let its name be lost to silence."

Bracken thrust himself forward, his anger still not cooled. "This trial you speak of. . . what is it truly? And what becomes of us if we see it through?"

"It is never the same," replied Dregg. "Each band that comes to it finds a different task waiting. Should you endure it, then that which was lost returns to us. But we are not the same as before. We come out keener, surer, as though the marrow itself has hardened. You see, a rabbit who has endured does not merely dig for his living. He conquers."

"And if we fall short?" asked Bracken.

Dregg kept silent.

The air held still. Not a twig stirred. Wisp peered blearily at the crumbled stones and said in a low tone, "There are bones set in that place."

"I say we turn back," Bracken said. We sought a place to live, not . . . this."

Dregg kept his eyes on the dark line of trees, where the boughs closed over one another like jaws. "Go, then. I won't hinder you. But if you turn away now, the path you're seeking will never show itself again."

"And if we go on," asked Sorrel, "will you see us safely through it?"

"No," Dregg replied. "I only promise to guide you true."

He turned and stepped onto the first of the mossy stones. His paws made no sound, and his silver pelt seemed to drink the light.

Wisp sat up, still dazed, eyes rimmed with tears. "Something down there is hungry."

Sorrel and Bracken exchanged a look, old as kinship, old as the thump of warning on hard ground.

"What is down there is a reckoning of spirit and flesh," said Dregg, voice low as if the earth itself might overhear. "Those long before us have kept this truth close, older even than memory. Some have called it a blight, some have called it a blessing. But none who stand here will pass through unchanged. Many will fade. A few will rise stronger than before."

Sorrel's tail lashed, bristling with disquiet. "And how are we to know we'll be among that few?"

Dregg moved a pace closer, his eyes catching the dim light like water stirred at dusk. "You do not know. That is the heart of it. Do not look for salvation—see it instead as a trial by flame. What is forged must first meet fire."

Bracken's jaw tightened. "I fear for all of us, and for you as well, Dregg. You speak of parting with the self as though it were a simple coin to spend."

"And you call it fearfulness where others might see the mark of their fate," Dregg said, his tone cold, as steady as old stone. "Mark me well . . . some paths once set upon will never turn aside."

Sorrel stiffened, tension running the length of her frame. She drew in the wind as though scenting the danger carried there. "Then we must weigh each step with care. We will not forfeit more than we must."

Wisp, pale still, yet steadier than before, looked from Bracken to Sorrel with quiet resolve. "Tell us the. . . what is it we must face?" she asked quietly.

Dregg's gaze swept the hollow as if he could read their very thoughts. "It is not a riddle that calls to be unraveled. It is the land itself that will test you. . . your strength, your heart, your spirit. And it will demand a toll. Not all who stand before it will endure the asking."

The hollow seemed to pulse in the gathering dusk, shadows creeping like living things along crumbled stones and skeletal remains. The weight of unseen watchers grew heavier, pressing close, as if the Hollowkin themselves breathed just beyond the veil of the world.

Bracken stepped forward, his voice steady despite the storm within him. "We have little choice but to face whatever it is together. Whatever comes."

Sorrel nodded, fierce and unyielding. "Together."

Wisp trembled as her paw touched a cold stone, her eyes distant yet bright. "If this is our destiny," she whispered, "let it be one we choose, not one chosen for us."

Dregg smiled then, the cruel elegance of a silver fox. "So it begins."

The silence of the hollow closed tightly around them, the future veiled in shadow and thorn.

They followed, silent and watchful, into the belly of the broken shrine. The bones at the edge of the altar shifted slightly, as if disturbed by breath or dream.

And somewhere beneath, something ancient listened.

The hush seemed to fold in about them, thick as the velvet dark that filled a burrow at midnight. For a long moment, none of them moved, and even the wind seemed to draw back to the edges of the sunken ground. Sorrel was the first to step forward. Her rust-dark fur brushed dew-slick moss as she went, eyes locked intently on the silent altar at the heart of the hollow. The feeling of being watched, of history peering through root and stone, grew heavier with every careful step she took. She carried herself like a sentry, shoulders set taut and wary, placing each paw as if the earth beneath might shift or betray her.

Dregg lingered at her flank, his silver coat a glimmer against old stone. There was something in the line of his body—an alertness or perhaps delight—as he crossed the mossy threshold into the ruin proper. The place seemed to welcome him, or at least, to know him in some silent fashion. He said nothing, his eyes tracing the stones half-lost beneath the creeping ivy, nose twitching to the old scents that clung there—loam, damp rot, and the faint echo of long-forgotten things.

Bracken and Wisp brought up the rear, moving slowly beneath the sweeping shadows of the ragged colonnade. The temple, such as it had once been, was ringed by a series of squat stone pilasters, their faces carved with labyrinthine loops and the contorted forms of rabbits winding through thorny thickets. The carvings caught the ever-weakening sunlight, just enough for Bracken to glimpse a faint shimmer that seemed less like light and more like the memory of touch—a flicker on the edge of sight.

"Look closely," Sorrel murmured, halting before a slab thick with moss and lichen. She reached out a trembling paw and traced the ancient lines incised in the rock—spirals and loops that wound around stylized eyes, thorn crowns, and limbs fleeing or leaping through twisted black canes. Where her pad brushed one coil, that resembled a hare, the line pulsed, faintly alive, as if responding to warmth. She gasped.

"These are ancient," she whispered. "Older than any Twoleg scent I've smelled."

Bracken crouched, aware of a strange pressure filling his chest, at once familiar and foreign. Bones scattered in drifts around the altar—both a warning and a call. He read their patterning as he might read the scatter of droppings at a fox's den—sign and portent, layered in meaning he could not decipher. Among the small white ribcages of birds and shrews gleamed the thicker, hollowed skulls of rabbits, bleached and pocked, their sockets empty as storm drains in winter.

He reached out to steady himself on the edge of the altar. The stone was cold—colder than earth should be, colder even than the air that pooled here—yet as soon as his paw touched it, a sudden and intense sensation shot through his whole foreleg, up to his shoulder and heart. With it came swift, stuttering images: tunnels bathed in pearly radiance, rabbits running fleet and mutely purposeful beneath bulging, vaulted roots; faces turning in the dusk, their eyes slick with vision, half-warning, half-invitation.

He drew back with a gasp, blinking and dizzy.

"Bracken! What's wrong?" Wisp whispered, coming to his side with a lightness that was almost reverent.

He glanced at her, words failing him, his tongue thick. "There's . . ." He shook his head. "Nothing. Or everything. It feels

. . . it feels as though something waited in the stone. . . something waiting still."

Behind them, Dregg's voice threaded from the gloom, shivery and coaxing, as if he spoke not to the living, but to the dead or unborn: "This place remembers. What was lost here, what was mourned here, what was willed to endure. None leaves such marks without a debt called due."

Drawn as though tugged by some half-remembered tale, Wisp crept toward the altar. The faint lines of sigils carved into the stone shone with a tremor of light, pulling her step by step. The moss beneath her paws stirred uneasily, as though it knew more than it wished to say. She lowered her body, stretching along the slab, her eyes fixed upon the markings with a hush of reverence. For the span of a breath, she seemed elsewhere, lost to the world around her, her look widening into a dim, star-pale gleam, reflective as a kit's in starlight.

Carefully, she prodded at a leaf-choked groove that wound from the base of the altar to its top. It wrapped a stylized rabbit—thorn-crowned, its paws splayed amidst curling darkness. The pattern was unmistakable.

"Bracken . . ." she called, low and hushed, like grass stirred before daybreak. "Come closer. This. . . this is the same sign . . . I've seen it before. Do you see it now?"

He came up beside her, narrowing his eyes. The sign stood plain, raised from the wood, the same as in his dread-dreams and as the sigils etched into the wood near the White River. He nodded, voice lost, his fear leavened by awe.

"What do you think it means?" he whispered.

"I don't know," she answered.

For a time, the group could only stand or crouch, caught in uneasy reverence, ears swiveling at every creak of tangled root. The silence gathered thickly around them, disturbed only by the dry hiss of wind through brittle grass and, just audible, the staccato tap-tap-tap of a woodpecker at the edge of the wood. No birdsong ventured into the hollow itself.

"This place," Bracken said, "it's like a grave, and yet . . ."

Wisp, still transfixed, whispered, "More than just sorrow. I can feel something moving inside the stone . . . like a song that won't be still." She pressed her paw firm to the altar, and for a fleeting instant, the sigil beneath her pad glowed—a peak of light, quickly doused.

Sorrel gazed warily toward Dregg, whose silence now bristled. "Do you know what any of this means? Is this part of the trial?"

Dregg's mouth twitched, almost a smile, almost a sneer. "I came to bring you to the boundary. What happens now belongs to memory, to will, and to what raven rests in your hearts."

Wisp drew back, shuddering, her paw held before her eyes as if she could still see the rune burned there. "The Hollowkin," she murmured, "they drew these marks . . . so none would forget. To call back those who wandered or warn those who followed."

Bracken glanced at her, then Sorrel, aching with the pain of not-knowing and almost-knowing. He did not speak, for some moments are hollowed out by awe, resistant to words.

A chill breeze ran its fingers over the altar, and the bones at their feet clicked softly, as if in response. The woodpecker fell silent, and the hush returned, heavy and waiting. The ruin pressed secrets on them, thick with patience and expectation.

Beneath Sorrel's paw, the carved rabbit seemed to quiver with possible meaning: a warning, or a command, or some promise buried so deep in time that even the Hollowkin, wherever they were, could barely recall it.

They stayed thus, crouched and mute between day and night, between ignorance and some approaching revelation—caught in the charge of something timeless and potent, wordless and immense, waiting only for the next turn in the story to draw them deeper in.

Night fell quietly over the hollow, draping bramble and stone in bruised velvet. The last of the sunlight sifted out among the twisted birches, and the world drew itself in—small, dark, and close. In the gloom, the ruin seemed to breathe, ancient stones gathering the chill and faintly glimmering with old, half-remembered light. An owl called from beyond the rim, and after, there was only the hush of wind in the moss and the slow, patient rhythm of living hearts.

They settled for the night near the edge of the ruin. Sorrel scraped a shallow hollow beneath an overhang where nettles traced thin, green fingers along the stone. Bracken chose a dip in the grass a little farther off, where he could keep the crumbled walls and altar in his sight. He did not know whether to dread them or to look for some silent guidance in their leaning shapes.

Wisp lay nearest the ruins, her white patches faint in the deepening dusk. She pressed herself into a bed of moss tufted with seedheads and soft with the season's damp, as though some part of her yearned toward the old stone, listening for a memory or a promise the earth might hold.

Dregg did not lie near them. He stayed among the leaning walls and tumbled stones, a silver shadow moving now and again between ivy and broken column. From where they rested, he was only a suggestion, the hush of paws on moss, the faint gleam of his fur when the clouds pulled aside from the moon.

The air smelled of wet stone and distant river. A thrush gave one final call before night claimed the clearing, and all around the ruin, the hush of watching seemed to grow. For a long time, they lay motionless, as if pinned by the gaze of some great, slow-breathing beast. Only their ears flicked at the murmur of wind, the shifting of roots, or the tiny click of beetle against bone. Bracken struggled to let his own mind settle, but something prickled along his whiskers and under his skin—a feeling of anticipation, as if the night itself lay in wait.

It was Wisp who shifted the air.

First came the faintest sound, a change in her breath, deep and uneven, as though the hollow's shadows had drawn her further down than sleep alone could reach. Then, almost softly, her voice slid out—not song, not speech, but a low, trembling sound, no more than the sigh of wind through coarse grass. It coiled among the stones of the ruin, winding through every crack and hollow.

Sorrel startled awake at once, muscles tight, head lifting as she stared into the dark. "Wisp?" she said, her tone quick and sharp. No reply came. Only that curling sound, thickening, taking on a rough rhythm with each breath.

Bracken, still and listening, knew the beat of it; the same measure had followed him through dreams on many strange nights. Wisp's lips shaped the syllables in slow, careful turns—the pulse of roots and briar, the promise of buried earth, the hush of tunnels heavy with memory and loss.

"Hrair, hrair, silflay marli, Narn embleth, u embleth-li; Tharn onlay, ni Frith hrang," she chanted in the old tongue, the sounds rasping, as if pulled from deep burrows where the sun never shone.

The words, if words they were, carried a dark cadence older than the warren itself. Each rise and fall snagged on some unspoken meaning, like claws raking over stone. It was as though the chant circled its own heart, keeping its secret close, while the night around them listened.

Wisp's voice rose and fell, the ancient rhythm thrumming in the hollow's bones, foretelling something the dawn had yet to show. Sorrel's ears trembled, but neither spoke. Bracken felt his fur prickle.

He could not follow the meaning of the sounds, yet he felt their intent all the same. They passed through him like the steady thrum of some heart not his own, stirring shapes and stories behind his eyes.

He let his eyes close, surrendering to the sound, and a pageant of visions rose—images blurred at their edges, like memories told a thousand times and thinned with each telling. He saw rabbits painted white as bone and limned with thorns, running in silence through caverns of living root. Beneath their feet, the ground trembled, pulsing as if alive; above them, the vaults shimmered with patterns of old power—sigils as twisted and ambiguous as bloodlines driven deep into the earth's marrow.

In his mind's eye, these dream-rabbits touched noses, exchanging meaning in silence: sorrow and defiance braided in a single gesture. Between their paws, the stone of the world split, and the past urged itself upward in a slow, relentless pushing, breaking through the dim earth to reach the open, wounding air.

Wisp's chant grew sharper, oddly urgent. Her silvery voice rose, rippling in the hush, spilling unfamiliar syllables that hung in the ruined hall like frost. Sorrel pressed herself low, her hackles lifting, the old wariness in every line of her posture. She scanned the shadows, but saw only the flicker of bramble and the ancient, watchful form of Dregg, silent and motionless by the nearest pillar.

"She's dreaming deep," Bracken whispered, unable to look away. "She's lost to them . . . all the way down."

Wisp's paws fluttered over the moss, drawing invisible lines, her claws tracing out patterns older than any story Bracken or Sorrel had been told. From her lips poured images—now words understood, now music, now pictures painted in pure sound and night. The language was not for their ears but for the hollow itself: a calling, a summoning, perhaps a remembrance.

Her voice slipped lower, lilting, as she began the old rabbit chants, a song of roots and stars:

"Hrair-rah, silflay, tharneth-lah . . . Under root, under sky, stones remember who we are . . . Frith's eye, Inlé's ear . . . shadows running near . . . Owsla of the deep earth, listen, listen here . . .

Hrair-rah, feffer-lah, ni-Frith ni-Inlé . . . Ash to ash, bone to bone, paths that show the way."

The hollow seemed to lean closer as she sang, and the trees above gave a soft rustle, though there was no wind. Bracken something, not from fear but something older stirring, like the memory of running through moonlight in a place he had never seen. Sorrel said nothing, only watched her with his ears turned forward, as though the sound itself were drawing them on.

Bracken's own thoughts blurred at the edges. He felt himself floating between sleep and waking, unsure whether he was listening with ears or something deeper—something of blood and root.

Through the chant, now woven soft and now harsh, there arrived fragments of meaning pitched not at the mind, but at the heart: the sorrow of a line broken, the longing of generations for what had been lost, the terrible, breathless hope of a kind that had once dreamed of harmony with earth and shadow and sky.

Sorrel crept close, her tension shifting slowly to awe. "What does she say?" she breathed.

"I don't know," Bracken replied honestly, his voice husky, "but I can feel it. It's as if she's walking there . . . between the worlds . . . and opening doors for us all."

Wisp's chanting faltered and dwindled until at last it stopped. She trembled once, drew in a sharp breath, and spoke a final line, no louder than the sound of leaves drifting in autumn.

"Hrair elil vethra, silflay marli-tharn . . . Many foes lie at our backs, yet the grass waits for the bold," she said in the old tongue, her voice low and steady.

Then all was still again; the silence seemed to gather about them, as though the ruin itself crouched, listening.

They waited, breathless, as the night grew thicker. At last, Wisp stirred. Her eyes opened, clouded and bright with internal light. When she spoke, her voice was her own, and yet colored with a deeper resonance. "I saw the warren . . . deep, bright . . . roots and bones . . . thorns and light. They said the trial draws near. That we are the echo, and something far older is the voice."

Bracken dipped his head, feeling the heaviness of her words settle over him. Sorrel breathed out, her shoulders easing, while her eyes flicked about, searching the dark for anything that might stir unseen.

The spell had faded, yet the unease lingered. Bracken and Sorrel nestled close to Wisp near the altar, finding warmth in one another against the chill of the old world. Beyond them, the dark deepened. In each heart, the shadows stirred and the ancient tales roused, waiting.

And in the silence of the hollow, beneath root and bone, something watched, waiting for what the dreamer would do next.

The night pressed cold and close about the hollow, the moon laced in tatters of cloud. Bracken twisted in their mossy nest, unable to court rest. The hush of ruined stone and the shadows that pooled about the old altar weighed on him like a second hide. He could hear the breathing of the others—Sorrel's clipped and steady, even in sleep, Wisp still muttering soft, broken echoes of the night's chant. Only Dregg seemed fully awake. He lay quiet as frost, eyes narrowed to glints beneath the silver ruff of his fur, staring out into the bramble-ringed darkness as if he waited for some signal only he could read.

A stray wind gusted, rattling dried nettle stalks, and Bracken's paws twitched. He sat up, heart crowding his chest. Something pressed on him, gentle but insistent—a pull rooted deep in the paws as any warren-bound memory.

He crept from their nest, softly as he could, glancing back at the others. "Sorrel?" he whispered, testing her sleep. Her ears flicked, but she did not stir.

The moon, breaking free for a moment, washed the altar in pale milk and ink, and the carved sigils snaked in and out of the blue darkness. For a moment, Bracken stared, half-afraid and half-entranced.

He moved further into the open, and the stillness grew heavier around him, each step fading as if the earth itself drew it down into silence, like sound swallowed by the deep walls of a buried run.

As he drew close to the altar, he looked about him. "If you are watching," he spoke softly, whether to stone, to root, or to the lingering memory of the Hollowkin, "then know that I am listening."

Taking a steadying breath, he placed his paw upon the cool altar surface. The jolt was immediate—a living cold shot through him, and sight and sound bent beneath an unseen hand.

In a blink, he was elsewhere. The hollow blurred and re-formed—the ruin rebuilt, stones flush and bright, vaults rising overhead painted with looping, thorny sigils. Rabbits moved through the nave—dozens, pale-coated, cloaked in dark garb threaded with briars. They circled the altar, their voices rose and mingled, a low chant like Wisp's dream-language. Bracken could almost taste the words, older than dawn.

The hush of the world seemed to fold around him, fur at his throat rising thick and proud, his eyes drawing the moss-dark hollow into their keeping. In that shimmer of stillness, he beheld himself as a young rabbit once more, standing shy yet steadfast among the elders gathered in the ring beside the altar.

A voice rang out, echoing. "What price do you set upon memory?" a doe asked, her whiskers gray with age.

One by one, the rabbits gave their answers, low and deliberate, as though each word had to climb a long hill before it left the mouth.

"Blood and shadow," murmured one.

"Home and loss," breathed another.

"The hiding of names, until the time of need," said a third, and a shiver ran through the dream.

At the edges of Bracken's sight, darkness thickened—not the gentle dim of evening, but a creeping shadowy presence that made the air quiver with unease. He called into it, his voice barely more than a thread.

"What are you guarding?"

There came a reply, thin as mist, and it seemed to belong to a small rabbit—a young hare, or the echo of one long buried. It spoke in the old tongue, yet Bracken understood:

"The earth keeps its stories. Deeds of kindness do not vanish, but lie as bones beneath the soil. Grief is only a seed, not the finish of the tale."

The little rabbit put him in mind of Wisp.

Then the dream sharpened, and the circle around the altar stirred as if a gust had passed through their very hearts. Some voices wavered, the chanting faltering. Fear bled into the air. Anger followed.

"Sacrifice," whispered a voice at last—a word that felt brittle and ancient, as though it had been waiting seasons to be spoken.

A thin buck at one end of the altar, spectral in the moonlight, spat: "You would bleed us generation upon generation, for a hope undone a thousand times. Why should we not break and scatter, let the world forget?"

A silence fell. Then the oldest among them spoke, "Because the forgetting is the death, and the memory the trial. Those who bear the mark must choose: rebirth must come, or all is lost."

Around Bracken, the stonewalls shook—not with noise but with the force of old pain. He flinched, tried to turn away, but the dream bound him close.

He heard his own voice—older, deeper—cutting through: "Then we bear it, and bind what comes, and leave a trail for those who wake later in dust and hunger. Let the world know we tried."

Something stirred, and the vision came rushing at him, fierce as wind tearing through meadow grass. The rabbits broke from the circle in scattered fright—some plunging nose-first into dark holes as if the ground alone could save them, others crumpling by the stone altar, flanks shuddering, whiskers flicking with the last tremors of dread.

Bracken saw the story in their trembling, in the pain that ran as deep as old roots. Yet, threaded through it, the small, stubborn pulse of perseverance. Most had already sunk into lifeless heaps of bone, but a few still lingered. They dragged their claws across the stone, carving worn sigils that staggered into one another, their voices raw from the endless droning of the rite. Their eyes still held a faint glimmer, though dimmed by toil, until at last each one fell silent in turn, leaving only a scatter of bones upon the floor. It was a chain of memory, he realized—loss passed down, but also the stubborn will to go on, each life a fragile bead strung along the same thread of time.

Shapes wavered and swam; Bracken caught Dregg among the drifting shades, sly and knowing, Sorrel rigid and unbroken at his flank, Wisp watching from behind with her soft glow, shy and quiet as moonlight on dew.

And there, at the edge of it all, Bracken saw him: the White Buck, still and solemn, his face steeped in a sadness that felt older than the hill itself.

The dream settled upon him at last, heavy as a stone in deep water: "The world does not seek out the worthy; it only asks if you will raise your song while the darkness draws near."

And then the vision snapped. Bracken gasped, pulled upright, shivering. The ruins crowded round him again, moss cold beneath his pads, and the moon had veiled herself once more.

He staggered back from the altar, ears ringing, eyes full of afterimages. The world seemed fragile and hollow like the bones around him.

A soft, trembling whisper found him—Wisp, half-awake now, curled beneath fern. "Bracken? The dream didn't take all of you, did it?"

"No," he answered, shaping firmness into each word, though it came with effort. "But I believe it has taken its share, and I will not walk as I once did."

He heard movement to his right. Sorrel, wide-eyed and wary, emerged from the gloom. "What did you see?" she asked, her voice a hush.

He hesitated, then spoke—the words tasting strange and old. "The temple, as it was. Rabbits gathered to bind memory, to bear sorrow forward. A reckoning. They could not forget, nor could they live on without pain. The hollow wind promised both ending and beginning."

"The Hollowkin," Wisp breathed, the word escaping her as though she had stumbled upon it rather than spoken it.

Dregg's voice drifted across to her, calm and steady as a slow stream: "Then your eyes are open. You understand what must be carried forward . . . and what may still come into the world."

Sorrel bristled. "Is this your 'trial,' then? Remembering? Hurting?"

Bracken shook his head. "No. It's not just pain. It's what we'll do with it. Whether we bury it, or share it, or let it shape what lies ahead." He looked at Wisp, then at Sorrel again. "I think the

Hollowkin knew. . . we are always on the edge of rebirth and destruction."

For a moment, none of them spoke. The silence was total but charged with hidden voices. The hollow seemed to steady itself, listening.

Then Wisp said, in her own trembling cadence, "It's not just memory. I think it's a path. We must go onward, together. Or all this is for nothing."

Bracken leaned close against her flank, nodding once. "We'll face what waits. But we remember. That must count for something."

Sorrel gave a curt, grateful nod, her guard never entirely falling. "We keep moving. When day comes, perhaps the ground will open a new door."

Dregg, lit silver where the moon broke the cloud again, met Bracken's gaze. "The trial is all around us. Be careful what you dream. . . these stones are hungry."

Bracken took a long, slow breath, feeling the pulse of the altar inside his chest, steady as the turning of the earth. All was shifted, yet all remained: night, stone, the memory of hope hard-won and hard-kept.

He lowered his head once more, eyes wide to the darkness, and waited for dawn, not as a promise, but as a challenge freshly born.

Dawn stole slowly into the hollow, blue and hesitant, touching the stones with fingers of thin mist and faded silver. It did not chase away the night entirely, but draped it, soft and tattered, over the ruins and the mossy earth. Birdsong, so vigorous in other places, shied from the broken archways; only the faint tick of dew slipping from leaf to stone, and the occasional call of a woodmouse, disturbed the brittle calm.

Bracken was awake before the light strengthened, crouched beside Wisp's curled form where she lay tucked beneath the fern. The fronds arched over them like a roof of green, casting a hush upon the hollow, and he steadied himself in the quiet, watching the slow rise and fall of her breathing.

He had dozed in fits, never truly sinking into the stillness of sleep, for the memory of the vision clung to him like sodden fur after rain. Faces he had never known—old lives, old reckonings, pale eyes beneath thorn-crowned brows—had seemed to pass through the dark about him, silent and reproachful.

The Hollowkin's voices still trembled in his mind, half-warning, half-song, a murmur like the echo of wind moving deep inside roots. Yet when he turned his head, the soft rise and fall of Wisp's sides brought a fragile calm. Her ears flicked once in some gentle dream, and Bracken watched the tip of her nose quiver with each warm breath.

Sorrel rose too, pacing along the edge of the ruin with the slow tread of a watchful sentry, as though both darkness and stone might hold some sly intent against them. Her muscles tensed and loosened with every slow circuit, ears jerking toward the tiniest scuff or sigh of the clearing. She paused often to look toward Wisp, her eyes sharp as flint, counting each little movement of the younger doe's chest as though it were a promise she could not allow the night to steal. The pale streak of dawn had not yet touched her fur, but the cool of the earth seeped through her pads, keeping her wakeful and grim.

Dregg sat apart upon a fallen column, his body drawn in upon itself, still as a stone left long to weather. Around him, the moss climbed over broken edges, clinging close as his silver pelt caught the earliest gray of morning, turning him into a ghost among ruins. He did not blink, nor did he fidget, but stared toward Wisp with a strange, sunken patience, as though pondering some private riddle. When a drift of wind slipped through the clearing, stirring the ivy and the fur along his back, he did not lift his head. He simply watched, quiet as frost before dawn, and the ruin seemed to share his breath.

With a languid shudder, Wisp dragged herself awake. She yawned wide, blinked into the odd hush, and stretched—first one paw, then the other—before slowly rising out of her mossy cocoon. The pads of her paws pressed hard into the soft earth, leaving behind not just the faint depressions of a sleeper but traces—lines, swirls, shapes unmistakable even to unpracticed eyes.

Bracken's attention sharpened. There in the black, rich dirt were marks—sigils, exactly as he had seen carved and worn into the temple stones the day before. Beside him, Wisp drew back sharply, as though the earth itself had jolted beneath her paw. Bracken lowered his head, nosing close to the ground to study the signs.

"Look," he whispered hoarsely, nudging Sorrel with his chin. "There . . . where she slept."

Sorrel came close, her body tense and wary. She crouched, nose to the earth. What they beheld was impossible: delicate patterns—the looping arcs and spiked circles, winding back upon themselves, arranged just so—sigils repeated for centuries in secret places beneath the stones.

There was a glow about them, subtle at first, little more than the damp shine of fresh fungus on a shaded trunk. Yet as the sun climbed higher over the rim of the world, the light caught in the carved lines, filling them with a quicksilver shimmer. Thorn, spiral, the curve of a rabbit's ear, and old rune took on a living gleam before ebbing slowly away, vanishing as the dew was drawn off by the morning's warmth.

Wisp stared down at the marks with wide, startled eyes, her breath trembling. "I . . . I didn't do that. Did I?" she whispered, voice stripped bare of certainty.

"It came from you," Sorrel said softly, her guard still high but her words gentled. "In your sleep, while you dreamed. You traced the very shape of their stories . . . just as the Hollowkin must have, long ago."

Even Dregg seemed shaken. He advanced slowly, nose working sharply, his eyes hungry and dark. For once, he did not hide his keen interest, nor the sliver of unease that haunted his gaze.

"These are blood marks," he said, stooping over the sigils. "Heritage . . . not taught or learned by imitation. It is born in the marrow, as true breath is born in the kit. None have drawn these since the old names failed. Not one has . . . until now."

Bracken glanced at Wisp, caught by a dart of fear. "What does it mean?" he asked, laying a paw gently on her shoulder.

She shook her head, mute with bewilderment, a tremor passing through her as though the soil beneath had turned suddenly cold. "I don't remember. I dreamed . . . or thought I did. I saw a burrow alive with song, tangled roots stretching everywhere, and a darkness filled with watching eyes. Then I was alone . . . yet not alone . . . for voices came from every side. They showed me shapes, signs perhaps, but most of it flows away from me now... its meaning lost. I'm sorry."

She looked from Bracken to Sorrel, then to Dregg, who alone seemed to understand something beyond what was spoken.

Her eyes moved from Bracken to Sorrel, and at last to Dregg, who regarded her with an understanding that seemed to belong to some deeper place than words could reach.

For a long while, none spoke. The hollow itself seemed to wait, still and listening.

At last, Bracken broke the silence, his tone low. "You are of them . . . the Hollowkin . . . kin to their line. I saw it, I think . . . I saw you in the vision crowd. You stood among them, younger, yet with the same patterns swirling round your paws. The old ones set their mark on you . . . but for what purpose, I cannot say."

Wisp's chin quivered. "But why me? Why now?"

Sorrel pressed in tight, the wariness in her stance shifting to protection. "It doesn't matter. We're here together. The old blood can mean hope, or it can mean a curse. But you are Wisp, and that is enough."

Bracken turned to Dregg, sudden fire in his voice. "You knew something of this, didn't you? All your talk . . . nothing but riddles . . . this . . . this was the test all along. Not for us alone, but for the line that wouldn't let the world forget."

Dregg's mask was gone now. The charm and silkiness had drained, leaving his face shadowed, his words sharp as frost.

"The trial is no haven," he said, low, eyes never leaving Wisp. "Ash Hollow is a crucible and grave, a wound that never healed. Only by passing through . . . by giving all that is called for . . . can the kind begin anew. That was always the bargain. Not all will pass. Not all are meant to."

Sorrel bristled. "All your talk of future and hope, and you bring us to a place thirsty for blood?"

"No hope is given without weight," Dregg replied, voice heavy. "The old kin knew . . . the world rebirths itself in pain. Someone must remember . . . someone must let go."

Wisp trembled, lowering her head toward the fading sigils, the trace of light dissolving under her paw. Her voice was a trembling thread: "If it must be me, I'll go where the path leads. But I won't go alone."

Bracken pressed in until his nose touched hers, his resolve quiet, desperate, unyielding. "Wherever you walk, we walk. The story is all of ours now."

Sorrel nodded, war-painted in sun and shadow, fiercely protective. "We choose each other. Not the old laws, not someone else's doom."

Even Dregg seemed struck—his poise shaken, eyes flickering with a rare flicker of self-doubt.

Wisp managed a small, sorrowing smile. "I am afraid," she said softly, "yet I think the Hollowkin knew fear as well. If their voice rests with me, then the words I speak must be chosen with care."

Bracken glanced again at Dregg, who now seemed smaller, less celestial than ever before. "Then let us face what comes as kin, by birth or otherwise."

He looked at the sky, which was brightening, and the ruin behind them. "We will pass through your trial, Dregg. But if the Hollowkin speak through us, they will hear this: we carry not just burden, but all the hope left in the world."

The hollow, sunlit, and strange, watched them. The sigils in the earth faded forever, but what passed between the rabbits had been set—intent, inheritance, and choice—woven, at last, into something even the oldest story could never quite predict.

And somewhere beneath, in the cool deep, a waiting presence nodded, patient and grave, listening to the old world pass and the new begin.

# Chapter 9
## The Bone Warren

The morning light slipped quietly over the broken stones of the temple, casting long, softened shadows that stretched like fingers across the mossy floor. Each ray wove through the tangled branches above, dappling the leaf-strewn earth in a gentle mosaic of gold and green. Bracken moved with slow caution, his pawfalls measured and soft, as if the very ground beneath him were gifted to silence. He felt the age of the place—the years curled inside its stones—like an unseen song thrumming beneath his pads.

Beside him, Sorrel lifted her nose to the air, muscles strung taut as a bow drawn to its fullest. Her ears twitched, and she gave a soft, warning chuff.

"Something's been here," she whispered, her voice like the rustle of leaves. "Close . . . but I can't catch the trail."

Bracken's ears rose, catching the faint drip of water somewhere deep in the stone, and the restless wind that wound itself through the temple's broken arches. "Then keep to the moss," he said softly. "If the stones still hold our scent, they'll tell whatever hunts us."

Wisp slipped between them, her pale fur flickering with light and shadow, eyes wide and glistening. "I don't like it," she said, crouching low to the earth. "This place . . . it listens. I can hear it breathing."

"Quiet," Sorrel snapped softly, though not unkindly. "Fear makes noise of its own."

At the rear, Dregg came like a silver ghost, each step measured, fur catching threads of sunlight that broke upon him in thin, shivering bands. Dust clung to his coat as if the temple itself had tried to claim him. His voice drifted forward, calm and low.

"I have walked through many ruins," he said. "This one knows the past. The stones keep their dead close."

Bracken pressed his nose to the mossy ground. The smell of damp earth and old stone rose like something breathing beneath him. A crow called once from the window's broken mouth, and the ruined temple seemed to answer in silence.

Beyond the crumbled walls of stone, the land bent and split as if torn by claws long gone. "Look there," Bracken muttered. "Ahead of us. Hills now. . . rough-backed, studded with thorns and black cracks, and dark forests. Even the sky hangs swollen, ready to collapse upon us."

No wind stirred, not even a small stirring among the stones. The air pressed close, thick as water. Bracken shuddered, drawing in every smell that rose from soil and moss, and felt the place send its coldness into him like a shiver of history. "This ground's older than any warren I've known," he said. "Older than roots clinging to the hill, older even than the oldest tales whispered in the burrows at night."

"The winds carry talk of Twolegs and their cruel ways," said Wisp.

"I feel something," Bracken murmured at last, his voice little more than a thread of sound, hardly daring to stir the quiet.

"What? What is it?" Sorrel asked.

He hesitated at first, then said, "The ground here . . . it remembers . . . remembers something we let slip from our hearts."

Sorrel flicked an ear, uneasy, and even Wisp stilled, her wide eyes roaming the shadows as though the earth might speak again.

She glanced around, the sharpness of her gaze cutting through the gloom. "The silence is heavy. Too heavy for something simply empty."

Wisp, crouched low, her breath shallow and rapid, whispered, "I don't like it. It feels as if we've crossed some thin veil . . . as though we walk not on earth but on a resting heart."

Before another word could fall between them, the snap of a dry twig shattered the quiet like a winter frost cracking underfoot.

Sorrel's whole body shifted in an instant, a blazing ember of alertness. "Others are here," she breathed, eyes fierce with ice and flame.

From shadowed gullies, figures began to emerge—rabbits unlike any the three had seen. They were ghosts given shape, gaunt and pale as moonlight stretched thin over bone. Their fur was bleached white, patched with the dusty gray of earth turned to ash. Ragged scraps of cloth hung from their thin frames like remnants of old dreams, and a fine dust of bone powder settled softly on their brows and whiskers.

Their eyes were hollows of dark fire—wild, fevered, haunted by some grim certainty. They moved with deliberate menace, their ragged breath a rasping chorus of whispered curses, half-torn prayers, and ancient oaths meant to bind themselves beyond death.

Bracken's heart hammered in his chest a wild, urgent drumbeat. "Sorrel," he hissed, barely moving his lips. "Ashfur. We must be careful. Watch close. Watch all."

Sorrel's ears strained forward, then flicked back, catching whispers of movement that Bracken could not hear. Her nostrils flared wide, drinking in the damp scent of rot and stone.

"There's a sourness about them, of long-buried fur and something sharp beneath it," she growled, a low and quivering sound, and her teeth bared in a silent snarl that lived only in the pale fire of her eyes.

"The stench of old bones and fierce iron . . ." she continued, her voice a rough rasp meant only for the earth and those close enough to hear. Her tail twitched once. "That is their mark. The Ashfur." She glanced sideways, the whites of her eyes showing. "I've heard the stories since I could run. They're the cursed children of these hills. . . born in darkness, raised on fear. My dam told me they eat the marrow of their own dead to remember who they are. And if they catch us here . . ." She swallowed, her voice thinning. "No one sees the sun again."

She lowered her head further, ears trembling. "I can feel them, Bracken. The hill itself listens for them."

Wisp crouched beside them, her small frame trembling, yet her eyes alight with stubborn fire. "We cannot be taken," she whispered fiercely. "We will not walk into shadow without a fight."

Dregg's voice cut through the rising tension, calm and dark as a winter brook under ice. "This ground is theirs. Their roots run deep in ash and blood." His silver coat flickered in the low light, a calm banner amidst a storm's wind. "No dance of shadows can outpace the silence beneath."

Before their breath could settle, the Ashfur struck.

Metallic traps, camouflaged beneath leaf and dust, snapped tight with harsh, bone-breaking clicks. Steel gnawed at flesh and fur alike, a sudden web woven in cold efficiency. The pale ones swarmed around them like crows drawn to carrion—swift, ruthless, relentless. Their numbers overwhelmed the four, born of grim discipline and fanatical hunger.

Sorrel became a tempest—sharp teeth flashed, claws raked, a wild force of nature contained only by the limits of her body. She fought with a fierce wrath, a storm rebelling against the coming night. Wisp was nimble as the wind itself, weaving and darting, shrieking defiance between snarls and bites, a flicker of silver lightning amongst the gloom.

But the Ashfur were tireless. Cold patience wound tighter, their hunger swallowing the brave in waves like creeping frost. Bracken felt a cruel bite as a trap fastened around his hind leg— sudden, brutal pain like winter's thorn stabbing at his marrow. He twisted in vain, dark shapes closing in, and the cold cage sang a death song.

At the edges of vision, darkness pooled, swallowing light and thought. Ancient voices in Bracken's mind stirred—long-remembered warnings haunting him now like ghostly bells tolling a fearful reckoning. The echo was old and sharp, braided with sacrifice and blood owed.

Bracken turned, and for a moment, his eyes found Dregg among the Ashfur. One of them—no mistaking it now. Then the light went from the ground as a shadow passed over, steady and deliberate. The cold that followed was not the kind that stings and soon passes, but the still, creeping kind that seeps into root and marrow alike. It was the silence of a creature that had long since shed all trace of kindness, watching with the slow patience of frost upon a hare's last trail.

His breath came ragged, each inhale a question clawing at his bones.

Why did we trust him?

The thought burned hotter than any wound.

Now bound, the three were ensnared in the tangled web of Bone Warren's cruel covenant. The ghostly rabbits whispering voices wound around them like iron chains—talking of trials, of fire that must cleanse, of laws old as time that would soon be etched again in flesh and bone.

Sorrel's eyes blazed, defiant even in defeat. "We did not come here to be prey," her voice cracked, but never faltered.

Wisp's breath came quick, her limbs quivering with fear and resolve together. "The trial is close upon us," she said softly. "Yet our hearts will not be claimed."

Bracken felt old terror rise once more, colder now and more biting. His thoughts swirled.

The price whispered in dreams. The sacrifice foretold.

Under the fading sky, amidst the clatter of bones and whispered oaths, the captives were pulled from their snares and driven onward—side by side yet apart; hope and dread knotted together as firmly as their tied limbs.

The paths they followed were nothing like the open tracks of daylight, where leaves told their soft secrets and the hedgerow wind played its quiet songs. Those bright paths were behind them now. Here, everything had aged into gloom; the air was damp, and the light had grown tired, little more than a dim trickle slipping through a forest canopy. Their paws found the earth slick with moss, and every step carried the cold memory of rain long past. The scent of rot and stone rose around them.

Around them moved the Ashfur—hard-eyed, hollow-flanked rabbits, their movements stiff and ritualistic, as though each step obeyed some old law of the hill. Their eyes never softened, not even in the dim light. One among them, known as Rude, seemed to relish the march with a sour sort of pride. He paced alongside like a thorn-backed stoat, his nose twitching with scorn. Every few strides, he drove a sharp jab into Bracken's side or rapped Sorrel's haunch with a sudden, punishing shoulder.

"Keep your heads down, leaf-eaters," he snarled, his voice a rough rasp that cut through the stillness. "This isn't your gentle burrow-ground. You're in the hills now. . . our hills. . . and they hold no welcome for the likes of you."

Wisp flinched at his touch, stumbling on the slick ground. Rude gave a short, ugly laugh. "Small one shakes like a leaf," he jeered, leaning close enough that his breath stirred the fur along her ear. "The hills like the frightened ones best. Sweet meat, tender bones."

Sorrel's lip twitched back in a silent snarl, but she said nothing. Her pale eyes flashed, catching the dim trickle of light like splinters of ice. Bracken felt her trembling with the same fierce tension that thrummed in his own chest, but he kept his head down, ears low, listening to the uneven thud of paws behind and the soft, wet sigh of the trail ahead.

Through the dripping canopy and the breath of the damp earth, the forest seemed to close in around them, a tunnel of old roots and watchful silence. The procession wound forward, each step carrying them deeper into the hill's waiting mouth until the entrance to the warren appeared suddenly ahead.

It was a shadowy, open mouth set in the hill's flank, half-choked by roots like the tangled veins of the world itself. Cold air breathed from its depths, a low, persistent sigh, carrying with it a scatter of whispering tones—as if the wind had been taught the language of the dead and recited their murmurs softly.

Bracken halted at the threshold, his ears rising high and stiff, and sniffed the chill that crept from below. A hard knot tightened in his belly.

"I smell it," he whispered, voice no more than a trembling thread. "The ground remembers . . . something we forgot long ago."

Sorrel crouched low beside him, her wiry frame quivering like a coiled spring. Her eyes darted over the roots that framed the opening, up into the hollow blackness beyond. "I smell it too," she muttered, voice taut. "This is no friendly warren. This hill keeps old company, and it doesn't welcome strangers."

Wisp huddled against Bracken's side, her small body trembling in the cool air. Her wide eyes caught the faint light filtering through the trees, two pools of apprehension. "Do we have to go in?" she asked, her voice sharp and thin.

"We have little choice, I'm afraid," Bracken said at last, the words tasting bitter on his tongue. He set one paw forward, then another, until the darkness curled around his whiskers as if it were alive. "Stay close. Move quietly. Let the hill know our presence, not our fear."

From behind came a sudden, sharp jab at Bracken's haunch. He flinched, teeth set hard, and swung his head just far enough to see Rude looming with a scowl. The buck's fur was mottled and coarse, his shoulders hunched and heavy as stones, and in his eyes burned two hard lanterns, offering no light but a kind of cold watching.

"Move," Rude spat, his voice low and scraping, the sort of sound that seemed to thin the air around them. He drove his nose hard into Wisp's flank, knocking her forward so she stumbled, moss scattering under her paws. "Keep on, all of you. Talking's for rabbits who don't mind being bones. The ground here listens close, and it remembers voices longer than it remembers fur. If you chatter, it'll set you in its depths before sun-up, staring out from it with empty eyes. So walk, and keep those mouths shut, unless you fancy joining the hills as another tale for hungry kits."

Bracken's ears flicked back. "There's no call to shove her," he said, though his voice carried more restraint than fire. "We can walk without your thumps and prods."

Rude gave a snort—half laugh, half snarl. "Soft words and kind looks, is that it? You'd not last a night under the barrows. Prey that argues ends up meat faster."

Bracken's muscles bunched, but he forced another step forward, head low. "If you reckon shoving makes you strong, then you've never stood against real fear. I've walked places that remember the dead. Your nose at my flank is nothing beside that."

At this, Sorrel gave a sharp side-look, ears twitching uneasily, but said nothing.

Every few paces, Rude drove his shoulder or nose into one of them—Bracken, Sorrel, Wisp—each rough nudge a wordless reminder: in the Bone Warren, you were no rabbit at all until the warren itself called you one.

At last, they reached the mouth of the warren.

The descent unfolded slowly, twisting beneath the earth. The path curled downward, and with every turn the light thinned until the world became a maze of shadow and the faint glow of fungi clinging stubbornly to the walls. The tunnel sides, worn smooth by countless years, seemed to bend around them like the ribs of a giant long passed. Roots wove through the stone and soil, coiling about one another—some thick as a rabbit's leg, others fine and quivering. Drops of water clung to their ends and fell in a steady rhythm, like some distant pulse, the hill's quiet breath itself.

As Bracken looked around, he hesitated at the shapes before him. To the eye, they looked little more than scattered remains—here a rabbit's skull, half-buried in the soil, there the pale arc of a bird's wingbone bleaching slowly under the open air, left behind like tokens of stories long faded. But the further the tunnel reached, the more the bones appeared, until they stood in silence of their own making. They lined the passage walls, some stacked with harsh tidiness, like a harvest turned cruel, others leaned against each other in careful, deliberate arcs. The oldest were thinned to the likeness of parchment, friable with age, while farther along lay heavier remains—broad ribs and long limbs that once belonged to deer, to fox, and to something else more shadowed, whose hollow sockets seemed to follow them, watching without eyes.

Wisp gave a stifled squeak and pressed her nose to Bracken's shoulder. "It's . . . it's a tomb," she whispered. "Every step we take, it watches us."

"Hush," Sorrel hissed gently, though her own eyes darted from skull to skull. "If this place remembers the dead, let's not rouse them with chatter."

In places, the faint glow of mushrooms bled across the walls, pale green like the memory of moonlight. Their soft sway in the underground air currents made them seem alive, breathing in time with the hill's slow exhalations. Among the glow, Bracken caught sight of carvings—lines and circles, spirals and jagged runes etched deep into the stone. They were the same shapes they'd seen in the ruins above: sigils that spoke of worship and warning, of fear hardened into ritual.

His ears flicked back. He could hear something now, beneath the drip of water and the soft tremor of their own movements. It was a chant, low and steady, threading through the earth like the voice of a river flowing in darkness. The words were indistinct, yet the rhythm carried the pull of something ancient and relentless. He felt it in his chest more than in his ears—a summons no living creature wished to answer.

"We are no longer in the world we know," Sorrel said, her voice almost swallowed by the hum. "This is not a place of safety and warmth."

"No," Wisp murmured, eyes glassy with fear. "This is a prison that feeds. It swallows the living and speaks with their bones."

Bracken kept still, his forepaws pressed hard into the soil so that the grit worked between his claws. The smell of crushed grass and cold earth filled his nose, and under his ribs, a slow, knotted fear turned over. Yet somewhere in the tangle, a firmer thing had taken root. If the hill, this warren, was a beast with a great, dark maw, it would not swallow him without a fight.

"Look at it," he said, voice hushed but clear. "Roots and stone above, twisted together like an old net. You can't even see where it ends. . . only faint sparks, like water hiding far off in the dark."

The walls curved around them, bone upon bone, worked into strange designs: spirals of skulls, lattices of ribs and long legs set one over another, as though some dark paw had woven death into patterns.

Bracken's ears drew back as his eyes fixed on the center. "There . . . see it? A great slab, rough cut, scarred with claw-lines. The stone's stained dark, as if with old blood. And there. . . by its base." He flicked a paw toward the mounded offerings. "Feathers, cracked shells, all tossed down layer on layer, like autumn woods forgotten underground."

Sorrel's fur bristled along her spine. "An altar," she breathed. "They bring life here to feed the dark."

"The Bone Warren feeds," came a voice from the edge of the light.

All three froze.

From the shadows, Dregg emerged, his silver fur ghostly in the glow. He moved without haste, as if the cavern itself permitted his steps. His eyes were grave, reflecting the chamber's terrible beauty.

"It takes what it must," he continued, tone low and even. "It demands a toll from all who enter its belly."

Bracken's voice was steady, though he felt the tremor in his chest. "You have seen what that toll is."

Dregg nodded once. "I have. It is the sacrifice. The part that none of us can run from."

Sorrel stepped forward, her nose nearly touching Bracken's shoulder. "Then we don't run," she said. "We endure. We gather strength. We watch and wait. Even a shadow like this cannot last forever."

Wisp's breath trembled, but she lifted her chin. "I fear what happens next," she whispered, "but we cannot turn away. If we must face it—"

"—we face it together," Bracken broke in, his voice quiet but firm, the way an old oak answers the wind.

Dregg said nothing, only studied them with the stillness of a rabbit who had seen the seasons turn too many times, his eyes carrying a knowledge he did not yet share.

Chanting rose around them, first a distant hum like wind in hollow stones, then a low, thrumming murmur that settled in their bones. It seemed to come from everywhere and nowhere—the walls, the roots, the very soil beneath their pads. Soon their hearts took up its rhythm, thudding in time with that grim, crawling song.

The Ashfur were hidden at first, only shadows among roots and stone, yet their voices wound together into a single, quavering note. It was not music as the open hills would know it, but a broken litany of hunger and remembrance, syllables chewed as much as spoken:

"The Bone Warren takes,
the Bone Warren keeps,
feed the dark, feed the deep."

The walls seemed to pulse with it. Bracken felt it through his paws, a slow tremor moving up his legs, into his chest. Sorrel's ears twitched, and her eyes rolled white for a moment. "They're calling to something," she whispered, voice like a frayed reed in the wind.

The air thickened with the smell of damp fur and buried earth. Roots hung like the ribs of some long-dead giant, brushing their ears, while from the shadows came another rise of the chant, this time sharper, faster, like teeth clacking together in hunger:

"Bone to bone, blood to root,
The Bone Warren waits,
the Bone Warren eats."

Wisp whimpered softly, pressing against Bracken's side. Her eyes reflected the dim green glow of the fungi along the walls, wide and wet with fear. Each word of the chant seemed to crawl into her pelt, pricking her skin like nettles.

The hunger was no longer imagination. Bracken could feel it now—a silent pull, as if the tunnels themselves leaned closer with each verse, eager to taste, eager to know the heat of living flesh.

He lowered his head in silent pledge. Whatever this place demanded, it would not take his spirit. He looked at Sorrtel, then to Wisp.

"We are not for them," Bracken said, low but steady, his ears set firm. "Hear me now. . . we keep on. Let the bones sing their hunger; they shall not feast on us while I still draw air."

The slab rose from the damp floor like a tooth of the Bone Warren itself, its surface smeared with ocher that caught the dim glow in dull gleams. Along the edges lay dark streaks of dried blood, brown-black, cracked like old bark—signs of offerings long past, heavy with fear and finality. From a shallow hollow at the rim of the altar, smoke drifted upward, spiraling from briar twigs half burnt through. The scent was sharp and bitter, clawing at the throat with a taste that carried memory better left behind. Bracken's eyes smarted, Wisp coughed and held it down, yet the harsher flame-smell could not hide the deeper reek beneath—the sodden stink of soil steeped in rot and bone through years uncounted.

Bracken blinked, startled, and stepped back from the smoke. "Fire?" he said, ears rigid. "Rabbits keeping fire here? Since when does any warren dare such a thing? That's for Twolegs . . . snaring and burning what they please. Not for us. Not for rabbits."

The faint glow of mushrooms crept along the chamber, dull and steady, painting its light over pale skulls strewn like fallen fruit, and the long, clean arches of ribs that seemed to bend inward, as though the walls themselves were looking on. Beyond the altar, the rabbits of the Bone Warren had gathered in a ring. They were hushed, still as roots sunk deep under frozen earth, their shapes half-hidden, half-shown, the gleam of their eyes flickering in the hollows of fur and shadow. Each carried signs upon them—roots twisted and knotted across their chests, bird skulls dangling from string, scraps of hide and clotted feather, all hung in grim remembrance of prey that had come before and been taken.

None of them moved or made a sound. The captives stood ringed by their watchful keepers, rooted to the ground as if the Bone Warren itself had grown paws to bind them. Thin smoke uncoiled in slow strands between their bodies and the stone slab, drifting upward to vanish against the chamber's dark roof. All about them, the earth lay still, listening, patient, as though waiting for the moment when silence itself would speak.

"Keep close," Sorrel breathed through her teeth, eyes rolling white as she took in the circle. "There are too many to charge. Not yet, not now."

Wisp gave a tiny whimper, pressing flat to the moss. "It doesn't matter how quietly I move. This place hears everything."

"Quiet, hush now, little one," Bracken soothed, placing his paw gently across her. Even so, his gaze flicked to Dregg, who stepped into the light with a curious authority, as if he'd always known this was waiting.

At the far end, beneath a knotted arc of animal skulls, sat one of the Ashfur named Fang. He seemed impossibly old, his pelt mottled and yellowed, ears folded and scarred by a long life. The black of his eyes was ancient midnight; his whole attention bore down on the captives as the hush deepened.

Fang raised his head, slow as frost creeping up a log. "Children of the Bone Warren!" His voice cracked like a breaking branch, yet the sound traveled clear. "The Bone Warren remembers! The Bone Warren is hungry!"

A chorus of voices rippled around the chamber: "The Bone Warren remembers! The Bone Warren is hungry!"

Fang continued, words brittle and grave: "In every season, the debt renews. The Bone Warren is flesh and root by pacts known and pacts kept. Tonight, as forever, the earth calls its price. To deny that toll is death for all."

Rude, the lean, bitter one who had driven them so roughly here, now strutted at Dregg's side, lifting his chin high. "Let them see the altar! Let them see what's sustained us these many winters."

Dregg stood, proud and restless, tail flicking. "These three were led here by old dreams and old debts. All who walk the roots are marked by forgetfulness and fear. . . who is innocent?"

Sorrel's voice, low and sharp, sliced through the tension. "You know nothing of us, nor of what's just. You talk of debts, but who counts the tally of lives spent buying a single thaw?"

Dregg's eyes flickered. "It isn't justice, Sorrel," he replied almost gently. "It is the world as it's always been."

Fang's cold gaze turned on them. "Step forward, one who dares meet the Hill's demand. The sun will not rise for the faithless."

A cold fear took Wisp. "Bracken . . ." she whimpered, shuddering.

"Don't volunteer!" Sorrel hissed, fur bristling, voice fierce as iron. "Let them do their own dirty choosing."

A hush-like breath withheld settled. Bracken swallowed, heart thumping a sick flutter in his chest. He remembered old tales—of the one that steps forward to shield the warren, of luck and cunning that could turn dark law to dawn.

Bracken looked back at his friends, then, sucking in a breath scented of moss and grief, said, "I'll go. If one must be given, let the burden be mine."

Wisp let out a thin, frightened squeak, and Sorrel's head snapped up. "No!" she cried, the sound raw in the hollow chamber. "No, Bracken . . . don't. This is not for you. I won't . . ." She tore free as an Ashfur tried to hold her back, her fur bristling. "If you step forward, I step with you!"

Bracken kept his voice soft but would not look away. "Sorrel, listen. It's not the first to step forward who is lost . . . sometimes it's the only way to see where the paths truly run."

Fang fixed him with those tar-black eyes. "Enough! Do you know the laws, buck?"

Bracken nodded, summoning calm. "I do. I offer not for glory or despair, but because your warren asks. I offer to keep my kin whole if the law must be paid."

Rude snorted, scuffing the bones with a careless kick. "Always one for the big words, eh? The Bone Warren likes brave talk. Makes the biting easier."

"It is harder to glory in death when the one bound for it chooses to walk," one of the Ashfur muttered, its face betrayed something less than surety.

"It is done," Fang pronounced, slow and heavy. "Let the altar judge. We will see if the Bone Warren will keep what is given."

A hard touch to his flank from Rude pushed Bracken to the altar. The stone was jagged—sharp enough to bite his paws as he stood atop it, staring out over skulls and shadows.

Behind him, Sorrel turned, speaking softly yet firmly to Wisp. "We don't let him go, not truly. If there's a break, we make it. Understand? Watch for my tail."

Wisp's eyes shone, wide and tear-bright, but she nodded. "I'll stay near. If there's a hole, I'll dart through."

Dregg's voice was soft, barely audible. "Sometimes, the stone's coldest edge can cut the snare. Keep your hearts knotted close."

"Hill of the earth, pit of dusk, send your sign," Fang said. "Take the gift, let the root remember."

A chant rose around them, echoing from stone, bone, and root:

"The Bone Warren takes,
the Bone Warren keeps,
bathes in dark, buries deep.
Give the blood, mark the way,
Let the dawning fight the clay."

Bracken braced against the chill, kneeling as if he might listen for a hidden drumbeat through the altar stone. He fixed Sorrel and Wisp with a look—steady, insistent. "Wait. Rules are never the whole tale. Watch for an opening."

Suddenly, Sorrel reared, struggling with new fury against an Ashfur's grasp. "He's not a lamb for the knife!" she barked. "Dregg . . . you owed us more than this!"

Dregg met her with a flare of anger. "Hold steady! Steady! This is not your final test."

Fang's voice cut short. "Enough. . . a sign!"

As if on cue, a thin thread of dust fell from the roots above, followed by a tremble. All eyes looked up; the chamber itself seemed to shudder, ancient and dissatisfied. For a heartbeat, the Ashfur broke their rigid ring.

Bracken seized the moment. "Your warren waits for true worth!" he cried, leaping down, scattering bone like leaves. Sorrel launched herself into the confusion, bowling Rude aside with a glancing blow. Wisp skittered quick and light beneath their legs, her small form almost vanishing amidst the moss and bones.

Chaos splintered the ritual's gravity. Fang bellowed, "Hold them! The law is the root. . . do not let it loosen!"

Bracken skidded beside Sorrel, both panting, braced for the counter-assault.

Wisp darted to his flank, whispering, "Now, Bracken! Lead, we'll follow."

Bracken looked at Sorrel, whose body quaked but whose eyes were fierce as fire at midnight. "Together! That's all this place ever needed from us."

Dregg lingered, voice a dusk-laden hush: "Run for the root passage," he told Bracken. "There, beneath the hornbeam skull."

Rude shouted curses, but tumbled in the bones as Wisp darted underpaw.

Within moments, the three captives had burst past the altar, ducking beneath the piled trophies of the Ashfur. Bracken's heart thundered—a drum in the dark.

As the Ashfur regrouped, their chanting scattered, their law shaken, and the darkness itself seemed to sigh—deep, uncertain. Fang's cry of outrage became a memory, fading behind the fleeing rabbits.

"Together!" Bracken urged.

They plunged into the tunnels, paws drumming the cold soil, ears laid flat to the rushing wind of their own speed. Roots scraped along their backs as the passages narrowed, twisting like the guts of the hill itself. Faint threads of fungal light streaked by, then were swallowed in darkness. The scent of damp and old death clung to their fur, and behind them, the echoes of shouts and scrabbling claws chased like hungry ghosts.

"Left!" Bracken gasped, veering into a low crawlspace where the stone roof nearly grazed his ears. He felt Wisp brush against his flank, quick and trembling, while Sorrel's heavier panting followed close. Pebbles and old bones clattered under their paws, the whispers of the warren rising and fading with each bound.

"I can smell fresh air!" Wisp squeaked suddenly, a flash of hope breaking through the dark. Her whiskers twitched toward the promise of open sky.

Bracken said nothing, but his chest swelled with a fierce pulse—survival, kinship, defiance against the Bone Warren's gnawing hunger. He leapt a narrow gully where water trickled, cold as fear, and then they were climbing, the earth sloping upward, slick with moss. Sorrel grunted behind him, claws scratching for grip.

With a final wrench and scramble, they burst from the Hill's dark mouth into the cool night. The forest loomed about them, the trees black and brooding, their branches whispering together as if sharing secrets with the restless wind. No moon shone to lead them—only the soft murmur of leaves and the occasional gleam of damp bark where a thread of starlight caught and clung. The air was alive with the scents of moss, wet earth, and running water. Beneath it all, faint but unmistakable, came a scent that made every hair along their backs prickle.

"Do you smell him?" Sorrel whispered, her voice tight.

"Yes," said Bracken, his nose twitching.

"Me too," breathed Wisp, ears flat to her skull.

Ahead, where the shadows thickened into something more than darkness, crouched Gnash—his paws struck the earth with a dull thud that carried through the ground like the start of an earthquake. Upon his broad back perched a small ball of rough, straw-colored fur, its fiery eyes bright with mischief—Smig, grinning as the night seemed to hold its breath around them.

"Gnash!" Bracken rasped, his chest heaving. "It was you who helped us break free."

Gnash rose in a single fluid motion, a ripple of predatory grace. He padded toward them, each pawfall soundless, a living shadow against the twisted roots. When he reached them, his breath was the soft rasp of the forest's own whisper.

"I smelled your fear," he said, voice low, a growl braided with amusement. "And theirs. The darkness spat you out."

"Leave those wicked coneys to us," Smig spat, his voice cracking with glee. "We'll see what's left of 'em when we're done talking."

Sorrel shook dirt from her pelt, ears still quivering. "They'll come," she said. "There are too many. The Bone Warren doesn't forgive."

Gnash's eyes narrowed to dark slits. "Then let them come. This world has its own laws." He circled them once, brushing his flank against Bracken in a quiet benediction, then settled into the shadows, a living omen among the thorns.

Wisp pressed close to Bracken, her fur trembling. "You'll help us?" she asked.

Gnash's ears flicked. "Help?" he murmured, voice like a claw along bark. "Of course. I've missed my coney friends. Me and the little Smig here. I hunt, I kill. That's my way, keeping the land clean of those who forget the old ways. Lead on, and we'll keep up and stay near, my little coneys. May the dark favor you tonight."

The three rabbits pushed on, every muscle drawn tight as a set bow, ears flicking and lifting at the smallest sound. Behind them came Gnash, sliding from the shadows as though the darkness clung to his hide. Smig rode low between his shoulder-fur, small and still. The cat's heavy paws struck the earth with a dull thud, and though he made no haste, the sound carried through the ground like a warning to anything watching, a sign of the trouble that would follow. Far behind, the Bone Warren moaned with distant, broken cries—the Ashfur howling for law and blood.

# Chapter 10
# Ash Hollow

The rabbits reached a low rise as the night spread cool and clear across a hidden valley below. The moon, thin and sharp as a sliver of bone, drifted above black cliffs that circled the hollow, spilling its pale light into the bowl of green lying still beneath. Their noses quivered, fur lifting with an unspoken knowing. They felt it in the roots of themselves—this was the place foretold, the shelter they had sought through dream and fear alike. This was Ash Hollow.

At first sight, the hollow seemed an untouched sanctum: silvered grasses waving in quiet breezes, mossy stones dappled with dew, a slow chorus of frogs and night crickets weaving soft patterns at the edges. Not far off, a trickle of clear water wound between the rocks, bright in starlight.

Gnash shifted, ears high, and Smig jumped from the cat and stood close at his side. They both simply stood there, their eyes wide. None needed to speak. The hollow waited, patient and alive, and the new day would find them here.

The silence between felt too thick—a quiet that blanketed every rustle, that choked off birdsong and stole the breath from the world. Even the wind skirted the hollow, never daring to linger too long beneath those brooding cliffs. The place looked restful, magical even, but the sense of something unresolved hung in the air—something dreamlike and unready to welcome. Not a warren, nor a burial ground, but a world awaiting judgment.

The three rabbits moved on to a gentle slope just at the hollow's rim, where they settled among bracken and wild thyme. Gnash, burly and battered, hunched close to the moss, his ears low, nose twitching for any trace of enemies. Beside him, his small companion Smig kept vigil with wary, rolling eyes. Sorrel, her rust-colored fur streaked with old mud and new sorrow, paused to smooth a patch of fur behind her ear with a distracted lick, her posture alert, listening beyond the hush. Wisp, half-hidden by fern, sobbed softly. She gazed out at the ghostly trees, her eyes shining with fear and some deeper ache.

Bracken crouched a little apart, torn between exhaustion and the wild, strange certainty the land inspired in him. He had wandered many nights beneath moon and thorn, but never had his dreams moved so close to waking. The hollow called to him—not as a beckoning home, nor a place of safety, but as something half-recalled, as if his paws knew each patch of grass though his mind had never mapped it.

Sorrel flicked her ears, uneasy. "We should move on, find a true hiding burrow deeper within. This place looks lovely, but it smells like a trap. Even the crickets keep their peace now."

Gnash snorted, "I'd rather rest in a fox's den, Sorrel, than sit out in the open with those coney-rats behind. This valley's too neat by half. You may think it home, but I don't like it."

Smig sniffed. "Nothing natural about this quiet. It's as if the field itself listens, waiting for us to slip."

Suddenly, a sharp crack—like the snap of a dry twig—echoed faintly beyond camp. Five pairs of eyes found the darkness together; whiskers stood out, and claws gripped earth. Sorrel darted forward, and Bracken braced himself.

A silver-gray shadow glided out of the gloom, thinner than moonlight but moving with a limp. Dregg. His side glistened wetly, and he dropped to his knees at the base of a gnarled maple, drawing shuddered breaths.

Sorrel was first to recover. She leapt, landing squarely before him, her teeth bared. "You snake!" she spat. "After everything, you follow us here? Give me one reason I shouldn't claw your nose to the bone."

Wisp cried out, hiding behind Bracken. Gnash rumbled low, moving to block Dregg's retreat, while Smig flanked the other side, ears flattened.

Bracken's voice was soft but iron-shod: "We trusted you, Dregg. Accepted your trial. But that . . . what we went through . . . remember . . . warrens don't forget so quickly . . . I ought to—"

"—what? Tear me open?" Dregg fixed them with eyes like deep hollows of pain and resolve. "You cannot. But listen. You need to know what's coming, or you'll never get beyond this place . . . as I have not."

"Talk," Sorrel snarled. "But keep your tricks."

Dregg bowed his head, the mask he had worn since the beginning finally slipping away. "I . . ." His voice wavered. "I was once like you . . . looking for a new home. My warren was slowly destroyed by the Twolegs. Years ago, I happened upon the Ashfurs and was offered to it, same as any prey caught by its law. It's what they do: pick ones with the least to lose, dress it as duty."

Smig curled a lip, "So you ran?"

Dregg shook his head. "No. I was given. I stood at the altar . . . just as Bracken did . . . and felt the dark root of the Bone Warren reach for me. I wasn't afraid of death . . . I embraced it. I felt that only comfort would come after. And I awoke . . . changed. Not by luck, but by the old law renewing itself through me. This place, the Hollow, left me arise, but it set a bargain in my bones: guide others to the test, be gatekeeper for a higher purpose. I lost everything. My kin. My loves. I gained only this vision . . . a purpose none can discard."

Bracken's voice was low, uncertain. "You . . . died?"

Dregg's eyes glimmered. "As much as any soul does and finds a way back. Since then, I have spent every season among those of the Bone Warren and shadows. I led you there not for malice, but because I know the truth. The Hollow isn't a refuge . . . it judges." He gestured to the pale moonlit bowl. "It tests those who would belong, twisted to the heart's shadow. If you're found wanting, you disappear. If not, you might yet remake fate. Find your new home here."

A dreadful silence spun through the camp. Sorrel looked as though every old fear had come true at once. "So, this is a ghost's great wisdom? You drag us to a haunted vale to feed the earth again? You filthy, traitorous . . . "

Dregg winced, spreading his paws. "No words clear my treachery. But neither was there ever a choice. Listen, all of you . . . the Ashfurs are not far behind. Fang's gathering them, Rude at his side. They'll cross the land, coming closer, and fan out like stoats in spring. This is your final trial."

Wisp's breath came in little gasps. "I . . . I can't . . . face them again . . . hear their chants . . . witness that altar."

Bracken turned to her, forced calm into his voice. "You won't. I won't let that ever happen to you. We have been brought to this place for a reason. I don't know why, but I feel it. Somehow, we shape the road ahead."

Gnash sneered at Dregg, "If this is truly a trial, old one, how do we pass it? What must be done?"

Dregg shook his head, fur matted with blood and dew. "You must meet the place as it meets you. If you wish harm, harm returns. If you walk with open heart, it may yet let you through. But if you turn on each other, or let fear rule you, it will eat your hope just as it eats bones. I . . . I have failed it once before."

Smig bristled. "So, we're meant to bare our souls to dirt and moss, show we're worthy, or else vanish?"

Dregg let out a breath that seemed both a surrender and plea. "You are not powerless. You shape the Hollow as much as it shapes you. You can choose . . . courage or cruelty, faith or despair."

Sorrel's anger found a new shape. "I'll never forgive you, Dregg. You led us on a wild run and called it fate. But perhaps . . . perhaps even stones can be turned, if we choose."

She moved back and nudged Wisp, who stared into the uncanny trees beyond. A gentle shudder ran through the silver-lit valley. The wind, such as it was, shifted ever so slightly—almost curious, almost kind.

The camp, a loose circle of wary souls and difficult truths, settled into uneasy rest. The cliffs loomed, silent and implacable, pinning the moonlight in shifting mosaics across stone and grass. From somewhere unseen, a solitary bird called out—a shrill, plaintive note, uncomforted by the green bowl below.

Bracken looked at the Hollow and at his ragged companions. "It's true, I feel something deep here. As if I've walked this grass in dreams, or my paws have fashioned these paths before sky and burrow had names. I do not know how this trial ends. But I mean to face it . . . as I am, not what the world would make of me. If any hope remains, it is because we hold it together."

Gnash bared his teeth in the smallest of smiles. "You talk like the elders, Bracken. I'll stand with you, trial or not."

Smig pressed his nose to the earth. "We'll need luck . . . more than any band of fighters ever had. But perhaps luck is just hope that refuses to die."

Sorrel, gathering strength, looked at her friends and then at Dregg. "If there's a choice, we'll find it. Let Ash Hollow judge us if it must. But we'll give no ground to fear."

"I'm sorry," Dregg whispered, head low. "May the Hollow forgive . . . and may you outwit it . . ."

The old rabbit watched them with a worn, knowing look, his mouth opening as though to shape one last word—yet nothing stirred the air. His fur began to thin and unravel, turning to trails of silver mist that curled into the night, widening and spreading until his shape was lost. For a heartbeat, only his eyes remained, shining like twin drops of dew in the moonlight. Then they, too, slipped away, and he was gone.

A hush fell over them. The cliffs and the trees seemed to lean nearer, as if the Hollow itself was listening to the emptiness he left behind. A faint breeze ran across the grass, rustling through stalks and roots, and Wisp pressed her face into Bracken's flank, trembling.

"Gone," she whispered. "He's truly gone."

Bracken lowered his head, feeling the absence like a hole in the world. "No," he said quietly, though his own voice shook. "He is part of this place now. Part of the Hollow, same as the wind and the stones. He hasn't left us . . . only changed."

Sorrel's claws dug into the earth, a low growl rising in her throat, born of grief and fierce resolve. "Then let the Hollow hear me," she said. "Whatever comes, we will stand. We will not fade as he did."

Gnash gave a single, sharp nod, and even Smig, for all his bluster, glanced about the darkened grass with unsteady eyes. None of them spoke after that, and the wind died to stillness. The valley seemed to hold its breath, as if waiting to see whether the little band of survivors would keep the promise they had yet to speak aloud.

They settled at last, each one curling into the uneasy hollows of the grass. But Bracken did not sleep with any ease, only with the bone-deep weariness of a creature flung too far, too fast, across the rough face of the world. The night's stillness pressed close, the cold dew collecting along his spine, his heart thumping slow and certain in his chest.

His head sank toward the earth, his eyelids sinking with it. And then the meadow fell away, fur and bone loosened, and he slid softly into dream.

He was standing, somehow, at the very lip of Ash Hollow. The night in his dream was high and clear, the moon not thin but great and round—a kingly lantern bathing every blade with silver. The silence was not foreboding now but bright, prickling, as if every leaf and stem bristled with meaning.

On the far side of the hollow, where the cliffs sloped down into darkness, a company of rabbits began to assemble—strange and wild, their fur rough as brushwood, pelts every shade of cold ash and battered stone. Their eyes gleamed red and hostile, and their teeth flashed like broken flint as they spread in a restless line, snorting and stamping, eager for spoil.

Bracken watched them in fear and in awe—to see so many—more than any warren's muster, more than the blackthorn could hold. They began to move as a flood, gray as hunger, shoving one another for place at the front. Their cursing reached Bracken's ears, harsh and jeering.

"Run, little bones! The Hollow is for the strong!" they snarled. "Let the old hope rot! We claim what's owed!"

Panic leapt in Bracken's chest—he could smell their old anger, the rankness of old wounds unhealed. He twitched, looking desperately for his own kin, but the grass seemed to have emptied; the valley waited wide and naked for the storm.

But then, standing where the heart of the hollow dipped lowest, a form appeared—so white that the moonlight was drawn into him, not repelled. The White Buck. He stood tall and unbowed upon the stone, ears high, one great hind paw resting on a mound of moss, his fur luminous as milk in shadow. Every whisker trembled with strength, eyes deep as sunrise over frost. When he turned, Bracken saw not only power but kindness, a surety that ran deeper than dread.

The gray horde hesitated. One, larger than the rest, slashed his teeth in derision. "Show us your trick, ghost-king! The Hollow makes no kings, only meals!"

The White Buck neither cowered nor bristled. He lifted his head, and the air rippled around him as if made soft by a forgotten song. He spoke—not with words, but with a timbre that carried through fur and stone, a command deeper than memory:

"This place was bought with courage, not anger. You take nothing that was not freely offered. If you would shatter peace, you must answer for it."

The gray rabbits howled and threw themselves forward. They came on in a wave—dozens, scores, bounding with claws and cruel laughter, the hollow shuddering beneath their stampede.

But the White Buck set his hind legs firm, as though the earth itself had claimed him like an oak fastening deep below the soil. He lifted his head, proud and still, and out of his eyes burst a pale fire, cold yet fierce, the color of frost lit by moonrise. The light cut across the meadow in fine, weaving lines, like the work of spiders spun in air, flashing quick and sharp against the shadows. Wherever the fire traced its mark, the ground stirred and swelled with sudden growth: grass shot high and supple, thyme pushed through in fragrant clusters, its sharp scent rolling over the clearing. The plants curled about the paws of those standing nearest, climbing gently as though the earth itself wished to hold them in its green embrace.

Half the gray ruffians faltered, their charge broken. Others leapt and tumbled, but each time, the White Buck spun, dodging and dazzling with light. He slipped through their ranks like wind through reeds, leaving confusion behind. When the boldest enemy rushed him, he stamped the earth—thrice, then again—and a ring of brambles shot up, living and sharp, barring their path.

"To stand here is to be tested," the White Buck thundered. "Will you raise one another, or drag the world into hunger?"

A hush fell suddenly. The gray rabbits wavered, their bravado cooling. Some bolted for the cliffs, while the rest, hearts exposed, wilted before the shining of peace.

Bracken, watching, felt his fear bleed away, replaced by hope as strong and bitter as blackthorn in bloom. He stepped forward—and the White Buck turned to him with a gentle nod.

"Remember," came the voice, "the Hollow bends beneath the strong and humble both. Let yours be the story of healing, not hurt. Shape it well, little one."

Bracken's vision blurred, the white and silver world sprawling wider. And as dawn's first breath touched his whiskers, he felt as if he had touched something far greater—a power born not only of strength, but of softness and memory, stretched wide across the waiting earth.

He woke with the White Buck's blessing ringing, faint but sure, in his chest, and for a moment, all the hollowed world seemed possible again.

Dawn crept in thin and gray, trailing its light over the jagged teeth of the cliffs. It was no true morning yet, more the ghost of one, and the land seemed to wait, listening. Below, the sea muttered and coughed against the rocks, turning in its sleep like some old spirit too tired to stir. The air ran sharp with salt and damp, stinging their noses, setting their fur on edge.

Bracken stirred first, dragging himself to his paws, and nosed along the rough ground. His pads were gnawed sore by the flight of the night before. He sniffed at a patch of moss, damp and bitter with gull droppings, then lifted his head. "It smells of strangers here," he said. "Stones and salt. I'd sooner have the good stink of thyme in my mouth."

Wisp stumbled after him, her sides fluttering. A shadow slipped across her, and she started, turning her head quick. "Strange place. Too many sounds. Even the water sounds thick, as if it's hiding teeth. And the gulls. They cry."

"You think they cry because they're hungry?" Sorrel said as she prowled the ledge, her ears laid flat against her skull. "No . . . they cry to tell the cliffs they own them. Every corner here is claimed, and we've no story in it."

From behind came a low rustle, and Gnash rose from the hollow where he had lain. He stretched his long back, jaws gaping wide, teeth flashing white in the dimness. The smell of him rode the damp air, cat-thick and strong. "Rabbit-talk, rabbit-fears," he said. "The night's gone, the day comes. What more d'you want than ground underfoot and sky above?"

"Sky's nothing to a gull," Smig laughed, hopping up, scattering loose gravel over the ledge. "They'll take an eye if you give them the chance. But ground's good enough for me."

The gulls wheeled overhead, their cries cracked and sharp as hunger, answered by the hush and crash of the sea below. Along the cliff face, the wind prowled steady and sure, chasing the last rags of night back into the water.

The valley of Ash Hollow seemed a place drawn from some other story—one whispered by dew and wind, meant for quiet spirits rather than living rabbits. Pale cliffs of charcoal stone loomed above, facing inward as though guarding a secret. Below, the bowl of green lay hushed, its grasses silvered with morning damp, bending in slow ripples where the faintest breeze wandered. Ancient stumps and moss-hung boulders lay scattered across the hollow, as though the land itself had once paused, caught between bursting into thicket and sinking into silence for all time.

Dawn laid a soft, blue veil over the hidden field. At its rim, where mist pooled beneath the thorned briars, Bracken crouched with Sorrel and Wisp, their fur beaded with cold droplets. The world smelled of wet stone and crushed leaves, sharp with the promise of a new day. Even Smig, usually restless and full of mutters, kept low near a curtain of lush ferns, his bristling fur slicked by the morning damp, his nose twitching at every shifting scent.

Bracken gazed out across the hush. "Have you ever known grass to be so green?" he said, his voice barely louder than a beetle's step. "It's brighter here than anywhere I've been."

"Brighter," Sorrel replied softly, ears set back. "Yet nothing sings in it . . . not insect or night-hopper. It feels wrong, Bracken. As if sunlight itself recoils from what's underneath."

Wisp sniffled, wiping her nose with a trembling paw. "I can hear the trees thinking," she whispered, voice catching and quivering. "But their thoughts are all remembering. It's like . . . all the good stories in the world have ended, and only old songs are left."

Sorrel padded quietly to the edge of a shallow dip, peering down into the grassy bowl. Roots rose here and there, knotted like old paws gripping the memories beneath. She glanced back, tail twitching in warning. The sense of being watched was relentless, as though Ash Hollow itself waited, gauging the hearts perched upon its lip.

Above, crows circled—midnight shadows, wing to wing, watching and bickering in the gathering dark. Their eyes caught every twitch, every tentative movement. There was a sharp, uncertain note to their calls, as if they, too, were wary of stepping down into such a silence.

On a thistle-crowned rise, Gnash emerged like some old tale come to life, his hulking shape blotting out the strip of pale sky beyond. His great head swayed from side to side, nose lifting to taste the scents that rolled through the hollow—damp leafmold, the musk of frightened rabbits, the faint tang of far-off rain. His fur was rough and coarse, thick in some places, worn thin in others, with tufts along his spine that lifted and fell in the restless breeze. He stood solid and immovable, jaws square and grim, every slow breath leaving him in a visible puff that stirred the thistles at his feet.

Smig bounded up to Gnash and pressed himself close to the cat's flank, burrowing against the thick, untidy pelt until he was swallowed by its warmth. The smell of earth and brushwood clung to Gnash like a mantle, and in that living shelter, Smig's shiver eased a little. He craned his neck, peering up past Gnash's shoulder toward the sky, where clouds chased one another in uneasy swirls. A stray gust rattled the dry stems around them, and Smig flattened his ears. Here, in the shadow of Gnash's great bulk, the world lost some of its edge, and the hollow below seemed far away.

Gnash grunted, settling onto his haunches with a weary sigh. "Not used to such an easy place for sleeping," he rumbled. "Still, better to huddle here than wait for those bone-hearted coneys crawling up our tails. I'd wager my longest claw they won't be far behind by first light."

Sorrel shook her head slowly, her ears tilting back as though the very air pressed against them. "Every shadow's long in this place," she said. Her nose twitched, tasting the damp that clung to the air. "Why does it feel so . . . lonely?"

She crept a few steps forward, paws sinking into the spongy turf. The grass stood stiff as old whiskers, springing back only when she pushed it aside with her nose. Droplets of dew clung to every blade, round and heavy, so large they quivered before sliding free, darkening the soil where they fell.

"This place is so . . . different," she whispered, her eyes sweeping over the hollow. The trees stood apart, as though they'd quarreled and refused to lean together, their branches held like wary paws. No birds sang, no beetles clicked, and the air itself seemed to be listening. Sorrel's fur rippled along her spine. "As if it doesn't know we're alive. Or doesn't care."

Before Bracken could answer, a slim figure slid from the shadows: a fox, vixen, her coat the ruddy hue of dusk's fading fire. Long in limb and light on her paws, she moved with the ease of one born to the hunt, and though her lips drew back to bare her teeth, a glint of mirth shone in her golden eyes. The crows fell still at once, unsettled by her noiseless coming.

Gnash rose stiffly, the fur along his shoulders standing high. "Easy there, toothy," he warned. "This camp's under my watch."

The fox's ears tipped back, not in refusal but as if in jest. "Name's Ginger, Mr. Cat," she drawled, circling at the edge of his reach. "Why stand guard for coneys? Not many with your bite would trouble with such small fry."

Sorrel glared. "Take your teeth elsewhere, vixen."

Wisp, shivering, huddled behind Bracken. "She'll eat us," she whispered into the tommy's ear.

But Gnash only huffed, a deep, chesty sound. "These aren't fry. They're my friends, and friendship holds its own oath."

Smig poked his twitching nose out from within Gnash's pelt. "Everyone needs friends," he chirped, almost brightly. "Rabbit, fox, even badger."

"Even stoats?" Ginger asked with a chuckle.

Smig hesitated. "I suppose so. What's a burrow for if you can't share it at least once in the moon's turning?"

Ginger's tail twined, her head cocked with quick intelligence. Her nose twitched as she peered into the dim hollow, whiskers trembling like fine wire. "Hmf," she said. "You mice and your brave words. So, this is the snug little refuge of Ash Hollow." Her bright eyes slid to Bracken, gleaming like dew in moonlight.

"What's it to you, fox?" Bracken asked.

"No great matter," Ginger replied. "Makes no odds to me. Still, I'd say you're not here because you want to be. Looks to me as though some great shadow is snapping at your downy tails."

Bracken held her stare, though a hard knot pulled tight inside him, as though the roots underpaw had drawn in. "I don't know what you know or how you've come by it," he said, his voice steady but low. "We're hiding from other rabbits. Those of the Bone Warren. Those of the Bone Warren. They hunt us for a ceremony none of us care to join." He let his ears tip forward, a small defiance in the close dark. "If your curiosity's so keen, Ginger, perhaps for once you might do more than chatter and watch. Perhaps you'd help."

The fox licked the corner of her mouth, appraising him. "Help?" She lowered her voice, all taunt. "Against those coneys that worship death?"

"You know of them?" Sorrel asked.

"Oh my dear, every creature in these parts knows the Ashfurs," Ginger replied. "They stink of old bones and promises no honest soil will take. I've crossed their paths before. . . seen their stone tokens wedged in burrows, heard their grim chants running through empty air. You rabbits think yourselves prey to them, but there are others they've hunted, too. They fancy themselves keepers of an old law, yet everything they touch grows haunted. So, tell me, then. . . why should I stand between coney and coney, when a hungry night might fill my own belly nicely? I've two cubs in my den, and they chew my ears for something fresh every morning."

Smig grumbled. "Noble work, nipping the weak and hiding the spoils. I'd think a fox could aspire to more."

"Foxes do what foxes must," Ginger snapped back, eyes bleak as flint, then paused. "But sometimes a clever tale outshines an easy meal. Little mouse . . . what makes these creatures here your friends?"

Smig left the warmth of Gnash's fur and shuffled closer, unafraid. "Friends?" he said, with a quick flick of his ears. "Not the kind that share nests or roots. But they run. They fight. They don't turn hollow when the dark closes in. And they carry kindness. That's enough for me. I'd sooner face a badger's snarl than tread through a world where kindness has gone out of it."

"Hmf . . . good words, mouse-friend," Ginger said as she turned to Bracken. "You're not as foolish as you look, buck," she told him. "What would you have me do? Bite your pursuers? Stand tooth-to-tooth with rabbits who make a religion of old bones?"

Bracken's tone was quick, earnest. "Help us watch the edges. If the ones called Fang and Rude come this way, even a little warning could mean the difference between another tale buried in the hollow and our chance to make it out."

Gnash added, "And bare your teeth for the bone-hearted ones, vixen. There's more meat on their bones than you'll ever pull from these little scraps."

Ginger's vulpine grin widened, sly and unsettling. "A feast of religious coneys, eh? Perhaps I'll be remembered as the one who dined on the priests of the Hollow."

Wisp found her courage then, soft as it was. "Your cubs . . . they must miss you. We all want to get back home," she whispered, almost pleading.

For a long moment, Ginger seemed neither fox, nor hunter, nor killer, but merely a tired mother with too much to lose and too many debts to count. Her tail drooped.

"They do miss me," Ginger answered at last, her voice low and rough with weariness. "Every time I leave the den, I feel their waiting, sharp as hunger in the belly. But hunger does not pity, and neither does the world. A mother feeds her cubs; however, she must . . . or they lie still, and she carries nothing back but silence."

Then the crows stirred uneasily on their roosts, wings rasping like dry reeds before rain. The air seemed to sour with their movement, a thick stillness rising as if the day itself resented their presence. Their feathers, once sleek, sagged dully in the heavy light, catching no shine, only a grayness that clung to them. All heads turned upward, eyes following the black forms above. It was as though the birds had heard something older than sound, something carried deep in the ground beneath their claws, and now the watching silence pressed that knowledge into the hearts below.

"Something's about," said Ginger, flicking her ears. "Tonight, at least, I'll leave you your ears. But don't trust that every moon will spare you the same mercy." She turned, tail flicking back over one slender shoulder. "Call out if your enemies come, cat. I'll be in the thicket. No promises except this . . . you give me a story worth the telling, and I'll give your pursuers a night to remember."

Gnash nodded, gruff and satisfied. "That's all anyone can ask."

The clouds above parted ever so slightly, sending a shaft of purest sunlight into Ash Hollow. It bathed the grass in an unnatural glow, silvering every blade and stone. Sorrel watched as the luminance slid over Bracken's face; he looked both older and strangely at peace, the shadows of memory flitting over his eyes.

"I know this place," Bracken said, his voice low, half to himself. "I've seen it, or dreamed it, in nights long before I woke beneath the first thorn."

Sorrel said nothing but watched him closely. The hollow seemed strange indeed now, as if shaped by the dreams of every creature that entered it, reshuffling fate to fit the wish or wound in each heart. Wisp trembled, but whether from fear or hope, even she could not say.

Somewhere deep in the day, a crow flapped down and called out harshly. And in that valley, beneath the uneasy truce of fox and rabbit, a test awaited—one that would measure not claws nor teeth, but the shape of memory and the weight of longing, and whether those present could shape their own ending within the heart of Ash Hollow.

The sun crept slowly higher, spilling golden dashes upon the softened greens of Ash Hollow. The quiet in the valley was brittle beneath the thin song of the dawn birds and the distant murmur of running water. The rabbits—Bracken, Sorrel, Wisp—and their unlikely companions, Gnash the cat and Smig the mouse, moved cautiously among the mossy hills and scattered standing stones, preparing for a trial none wished to meet, yet all knew would come.

Bracken pawed at the earth near a crouch of nettles, setting a simple snare made of twisted vines and thorns. "We need eyes and ears," he muttered to Sorrel, who circled like a tall, lithe flame, ears pricked for sound. "Those who hunt us come with shadows on their breath."

Sorrel glanced toward the bracken thicket, amber eyes sharp as tacks. "Here, between root and stone, we have some shelter. But the Bone Warren is patient. They come for slow hunger. We must be swifter."

Wisp, trembling but determined, helped Gnash gather fallen branches and brittle sticks. "We need traps. . . traps can buy us time," she said softly. "But we need more than that . . . we need a plan."

Gnash chuckled, his great form lumbering closer, the sunlight catching the colors of his thick fur. "It's been a long time since I planned for anything but a winter's sleep," he said, low and rumbling. "But I smell the sickness in the air. These bone-coneys . . . they're worse than fox or stoat."

Smig, perched uncertainly atop a fallen log, twitching whiskers in every direction, piped up. "Quiet. We must not have our new friend hear you talk this way."

"Ahhh . . ." Gnash said. "I care not what a fox hears or doesn't hear."

"Well, you should," Smig said. "Foxes and stoats hunt with teeth and quick feet. But those zealot-coneys . . . they hunt with old fears and older bones. I don't like the sound of that one bit."

Gnash looked away from his little friend and gave a deep sigh.

"Wisp is right," Bracken said. "We need traps and a plan." He started gathering bundles of thornvine to string between saplings as the others watched. "We'll make the hollow itself into a snare," he continued, looping the vine between two young ash stems. "It needn't be iron or wire . . . only enough to turn their own malice back upon them. Hatred is like a briar in the dark; push hard enough through it, and you'll soon be tangled fast."

Sorrel stopped and faced Bracken. "And what if they come prepared? With others like Dregg? What if the hunt is not for food, but for souls?"

A shadow passed over Bracken's face as he considered her words. "Then we fight not just with claws but with the fire in our hearts."

Wisp pressed close to Sorrel's side and whispered, "And with the friends who stand beside us."

The plan unfolded slowly, each setting of trap and marking of trail threaded with whispered counsel. All worked steadily, weaving branches into snares, stacking loose stones into precarious piles, and hollowing out places for cover beneath the tangled roots. Their movements were careful music in the underbrush; their breaths held in time with the slow beating of the hidden land.

Deep within the shadows of the thorn-thicket at the far side of the hollow, Ginger the fox lay curled, eyes half-closed but attentive. Her lithe body was coiled with the readiness of a spring-wound predator, muscles flexing even in rest. Nearby, just beyond

Ash Hollow, in her den, two cubs huddled close, small and warm, breathing softly like the soil around them.

Ginger's eyes flicked toward the valley where the rabbits busied themselves. "I think I may feast well tonight," she said quietly to herself. "The bones of zealots will satisfy more fully than timid prey."

A low rustle near her brought a flash of movement as a small shadow—a vole—darted past, unaware of the silent teeth watching nearby. It skittered past, with its own small purpose, and in the same instant, her jaws closed upon it. The squeak was cut short, and the grass grew still again.

Gnash came close to Ginger, his breath forming small clouds in the cold dawn. "My little mouse friend spoke rightly," he said, his voice low and steady. "We need cunning as much as strength. Like us cats, foxes notice what hides in shadow, hear what the wind forgets."

Ginger's lips curved in a small, bright smile. "Even the smallest can make a mighty difference. It takes more than teeth to topple a wall of bone."

Gnash gave a slow nod and moved back to join the others, settling among them with quiet patience.

Later, Bracken approached Ginger's thicket cautiously, his ears flicking in greeting. "Will you hold watch and warn if the Bone Warren comes?"

Ginger raised her head, nostrils flaring as she scented sunrise and danger both. "Watch and warn," she agreed, tail flicking with promise. "But tread with care. I fear these zealous ones carry more than teeth. They bring the cold hunger of old gods, the darkness of past Twolegs."

Sorrel, joining Bracken, raised a brow. "So, you do care about the quarrels of rabbits?"

"Even the cleverest fox," Ginger replied, eyes narrowing, "knows where the scent leads. This is not only your fight. The land whispers its tales to all who listen . . . fox, cat, mouse, and buck. I will stay . . . for my cubs, and for the story."

As the light crept toward mid-morning, the camp began to stir with quiet industry. Rabbits slipped among the ferns and nettles, their paws careful and sure, arranging snares along well-worn paths and patting down the earth above pits set with sharpened stakes. The air was thick with the smell of trampled grass and the faint tang of fur warmed by sun. Somewhere, a thrush called sharply from a branch, and a beetle skittered across the moss, pausing as if to study the movements of the rabbits. Even the soil seemed to hold its breath, carrying the rhythm of paws over roots and stone, carrying the tension that clung to the morning as tightly as dew to the leaves.

"Then we bring them in close. To the traps and snares, to the pits," Bracken said, crouching with Sorrel beside an old hemlock stump, tracing patterns in the loose soil.

"We run, they follow," Sorrel replied, ears flicking toward the far edge of the camp. "They'll think it their own choice."

"Ash Hollow is a trial," Bracken said, low. "It answers not just to those who tread, but to what they carry inside. Fear or hope, courage or cruelty . . . it knows."

Sorrel met his gaze, fierce and tender all at once. "Then let us bring only what we can bear. I will not let them swallow us whole."

Wisp crept close, shy but steady. "And when they do come, we will be ready. We carry our ancestors' strength . . . and each other."

From the forest's edge, a whisper of wind stirred ginger leaves and lifted the scent of rain to come. Somewhere distant, the first cry of the Ashfurs reached their ears—a rising wail, equal parts chant and challenge.

Gnash growled low. "They gather, as the hawk calls before the dive."

Smig's nose twitched. "They crawl like creeping ice, waiting for the thaw that breaks the earth."

"We will meet them here," Bracken drew a long, steady breath and stood. "They will find no easy prey. The land will remember the ones who dared to stand."

"And if they come with fire," Sorrel said, stretching her limbs, flexing claws in the clearing, "we will be the storm."

The shadows lengthened. The air thickened. Beneath the watchful moon and moonlit trees, the quiet valley prepared to become a battlefield—not just of teeth and claw, but of wills entwined like the roots beneath their feet.

# Chapter 11
# The Hollow Remembers

By the following day, the sun climbed fast, and before long it stood high and unyielding, dry and keen as a hawk's wing cutting across the sky. It glared down on Ash Hollow, where the trees bent back just enough for light to pour through, silver-bright upon the open ground. This was not a kindly warmth, but the sort that lays everything bare. Each tuft of grass showed itself for what it was—green and strong or shriveled and fading, sprigs pushing new shoots beside stalks rotting where they stood.

The trees kept their silence, branches locked tight above. Their shadows lay drawn out and straight, like old scars baked into the soil. A hush hung over the hollow, empty of any flutter or trill. No thrush called, no wren stirred. Even the wind seemed to hold away from that place.

Bracken lingered in the half-shade beneath the great ash, its black roots thrusting up through the loam like the knuckles of some hidden giant. The air there was cool and smelled of damp bark and moss. His eyes, pale and intent, followed the southern path where the grass lay bent, the blades flattened by more than wind or rain. The day stretched long and thin, the sort of day when the sun feels far off and the ground carries its own secret restlessness. Bracken thought he could sense old tales stirring faintly in the soil, curling around his paws like unseen threads, as though the earth itself sighed with memory.

He had dreamed of this turning before, though not with any wish to see it. The dream had come stark and hard-edged: rabbits with faces sharp from long suffering, ears torn and coats roughened with the marks of hard living. They belonged to harsher places—hares of the world's edges, with eyes bright as thistle-spines and a hunger that no meal could quiet, a hunger that gnawed inward more than out.

Yet with that darkness had come another vision, clear and cold as the first frost on autumn grass. The White Buck had appeared—aloof, shining in the mind's night—driving away the shadow-things of nightmare with a fierce, steady strength. He ran before the coming sun, and where his hooves struck, he left behind a glimmer of hope, like dew caught in morning light.

Sorrel sat apart from the rest, ears tilted half-back, tending her forepaw with slow, deliberate strokes of her tongue. The fine rust-red of her coat was streaked with dust and specks of old leaves, faded now but carried with the quiet pride of one who bore her trials openly. Around her, the afternoon lay close and stifling; when the breeze shifted, it brought with it the bitter tang of nettles, the sweetly sick edge of old blood, and the musk of distant bucks grown sharp and sour with time.

She paused mid-groom, paw held motionless. Rising onto her haunches, she peered between the tree trunks, every muscle drawn taut. "They're close," she said, her voice scarcely more than the stir of air through grass. Her dark eyes moved from one companion to the other. "Have you set the snares? The traps? Are you ready?"

Bracken dipped his head, the motion so small it hardly stirred a stem. The clearing felt drawn in on itself—the trees clutching their shadows close, the grass stilled as if afraid, and even the soft dust hung in the air, refusing to lift. At such times, the world seemed to hang between one heartbeat and the next, waiting to see which way chance might tilt.

Under a loose fringe of roots, Wisp huddled with her paws tucked beneath her. Her white-splashed flanks rose and fell, ears folded tight, her nose twitching to some secret dream. In slumber, she looked younger, as though she were back among milk-scented nests. Bracken had heard her talk in the nights of strange sounds beneath the earth, of shudders through the soil at sundown, of warmth turning to sudden chill. He had never scoffed; the Hollow carried old memories in root and bone. It remembered, in ways rabbits did not always understand.

A soft rustle came from nearby. Gnash flicked an ear and muttered, "She'll be out there. You know she will. Fox's never far when the light runs thin."

Smig, crouched beside him in the ripening grass, kept his head low, eyes narrowed to slits. "Aye," he answered. "And she has cubs. I've smelt them near. Hungry mouths have no mercy for the likes of Ashfurs."

Bracken shifted, glancing toward the shadowed edge. "Or us," he said quietly. "When this is over, we must be clever with her."

Gnash gave a dry snort. "You don't trust her, then?"

"My trust wavers, all the same," Bracken said, shaking his head. "As Smig said, she has small bellies to feed and they hunger constantly."

From beneath the roots, Wisp stirred, blinking awake. "She's out there," the small rabbit said, her voice no more than a thin breath. "I heard her steps in the dream."

Smig's fur bristled. "Dreams won't save us either if her cubs' bellies call."

Bracken kept his voice steady. "Dreams or not, let us worry about what comes first."

Gnash snarled. "The bone-rats."

"We'll move when it's time," Bracken said. "Stick to our plan. Till then, keep your bellies to the earth. The land sees all."

At that, no one spoke. Beyond their circle, the Hollow held its silence, and the earth seemed to listen.

Bracken stepped closer to Sorrel. "They'll take the low path," he said quietly. "Where the brambles thin out near the old stones. That's where they'll try to come through—"

Sorrel looked at him with her dark, unflinching eyes. "—to try to kill us?"

"Yes."

She didn't flinch. "Then, let them try."

Wisp stirred then, lifting her head. She blinked at the clearing, then stood and came toward them, brushing lightly against Bracken's side.

"It's time, isn't it?" she asked, her voice still tangled with dream.

He looked down at her. "Yes. Time to end all this, I fear."

She didn't question him further.

A rustling came from the southern bramble.

One by one, the Ashfurs came out, as if the hollow ground itself was releasing slow, reluctant shadows. They did not swarm; there was no thunder of feet nor the reckless surge of an army, but rather a somber procession—shapes drawing themselves upright from the tangle of roots and bramble. Their fur was torn and roughened by thorns and hard seasons, ears bitten and notched by old fights, backs drawn thin by lean times that stretched too long. Their eyes, sharp with a wary brightness, shone out from faces haunted by hunger and the memory of too many miles traversed without reward. There was no parade, no call to order. Instead, a troubled menace lingered about them—the kind that settles on creatures with nothing more to lose, those who have left their hopes behind with the turning earth.

At their head shuffled Fang and Rude.

Fang was a patchwork of the long seasons—his pelt faded to the yellow of dead straw and the ash of old fires, age sagging heavy in every step. His ears, bent and torn as old leaves, carried a map of a hard-won life, and in the depths of his dark eyes glimmered a midnight older than this soil, steady and fathomless. When he settled his gaze on the Bracken and Sorrel and Wkisp, the hush thickened—as if the very roots were listening.

Beside him loomed Rude, whose fur was coarse as bramble and whose heavy shoulders spoke of burdens carried through stone and snow alike. He huddled into himself, a living boulder, and his eyes burned small and sharp in the dusk, like lanterns left too long in the cold—brilliant but giving out no warmth to friend or stranger.

"Bracken," Fang growled, scanning the three of them. "We've come for you. And for the others. No games. You're done."

Wisp stiffened beside Bracken.

Sorrel took a single step forward. "You will leave now," she said flatly. "There is nothing for you here. This is our place. Our home."

Fang sneered. "We weren't asking."

Behind him and Rude, the other Bone Warren ruffians fanned out—half-circle, watching, shifting on their paws. They did not look eager, only tired. Yet tiredness can be deadly when it stops fearing consequence.

Bracken stepped forward slowly.

"I saw you coming," he said. "Before I opened my eyes this morning. You think you're chasing us. You're not. You're chasing the Hollow."

Fang spat. "You think this patch of dirt is something sacred? It's just another hole in the ground, same as the rest. You put names on wind and think it will protect you."

Bracken looked at the grass, then at the trees. "It's not the name that protects," he said. "It's the remembering."

Fang laughed—sharp, ugly. "You talk like Dregg. Full of riddles and rot. Where is he, then? Where's that silver-tongued ghost? He was supposed to lead us."

"He did," Sorrel said. "He led you to ruin. Same as he always has."

"Don't pretend you're better."

Wisp raised her head. "We're not pretending."

Fang stepped forward, just a little. Enough to show his teeth. "You want to die standing up, is that it?"

The wind changed.

Something shifted beneath the grass. Not sound exactly, not movement either, but a presence—deep and old. The air grew heavy, but not with heat. The Hollow had taken notice.

Bracken closed his eyes. "You shouldn't have come."

For a long moment, the world seemed to hold its breath. The gathered rabbits—the Ashfurs and the three—stood braced in the long grass, ears pricked and hearts pounding, each waiting for the other to loosen their grip on fear. Sunlight slanted through the thorn-tangled hedge, heavy with dust and drifting pollen, and every pulse of the breeze smelt of root and old, unsettled earth. Somewhere above, a blackbird let out a ragged alarm and fell silent.

Bracken met Fang's gaze; there was no hate in his heart, only a kind of sorrow for what necessity had made of all of them. The old buck's nose quivered, as if he might scent the warning stirring beneath the soil.

"Go back," Bracken said quietly. "Take the younger ones, the moth-bitten and the lame. There's nothing here for you."

Fang's only answer was to shift his weight, flanks trembling with the effort of holding so much age, so much anger, in his bones. Rude growled—a low, grinding sound, not made for show but forged to frighten off hungry stoats in lean seasons.

Sorrel flattened her ears and stood her ground, fur bristling, blazing rust-red as she turned herself half-sideways, half-shield to Wisp behind. "We're done with running."

"Running?" Rude barked, spittle licking his lips. "We've crawled through brambles and thorns for this. To come here. We've lost many along the way. To wolves, hawks, owls, and dogs. All that's left is here."

The Ashfurs shuffled restlessly, eyes flitting to the shadows under the trees, to the cliffs around them, to the tall grasses. They pressed forward—not brave, not cruel, but driven by the bitter logic of animals cornered too often, too long.

Fang's jaw quivered; when he spoke, it was not a shout, but a tired, hollow tone that seemed to come from under the hill itself. "You'd have us go hungry? Scratch about with no place of our own? Fade away for the sake of your treasured Hollow?"

"This place . . ." Bracken said, voice soft but steady, " . . . it belongs to those who remember. Those who choose."

Wisp, trembling but with the shine of her strange blood showing suddenly, stood up straighter. The light in her eyes was not defiance, but something deeper. "Maybe we could share it. You only have to stop taking." Her voice was thin as the last thread in a winter nest, but some of the Ashfur looked away, uncertain. A soft murmur flickered through the ranks.

Rude snorted, setting his feet. "Easy to say, little one. Hungry mouths can't eat dreams."

"Dreams are what kept you alive till now," Sorrel answered, her eyes sharp, cold as the river in spring. "You sleep too long in the dark, you start to believe the sun isn't real."

At that, the hush grew unbearable. A draught swept through the grass—no ordinary wind, but a shiver felt in bone and whisker alike, as if the ground itself were remembering old promises.

Then, as if answering some signal only the oldest heart could hear, a hush passed through the Bone Warren ranks. Several lagged, shifting uneasily, eyes darting between Fang and Bracken, between hunger and hope.

Fang let his gaze fall to the earth. The midnight in him faltered, just for a heartbeat, replaced by something that smelled of dust and old nettle beds. "You will fight us, then," he croaked.

Bracken glanced at Sorrel and Wisp, his voice no louder than the summer wind. "If you make us."

But before Fang or Rude could close the gap, the air thickened—a low, thrumming pulse, as though the hollow beneath the grass had woken and remembered what it meant to hold so many lives at once. Roots trembled, and the earth itself seemed to lean closer.

Wisp looked down, her paws stirring the grass. "Do you feel that?" she whispered.

Sorrel nodded, voice gone unsteady. "It's the Hollow. It knows."

Fang shuddered, and beneath his ancient paws, a fissure opened in the moss, thin and black as the memory of an old wound. The cold hush that swept outwards seemed to rise from somewhere deeper than the Hollow itself—a warning, perhaps, spoken ages ago, that not all fights are finished with tooth and claw, but with the aching weight of what can't be forgotten.

Bracken stood silent for a heartbeat, his breath drawing long and slow. "This is your last chance," he said, his voice carrying like rain on the dry leaf. "Leave now, before something wakes that none of us can put back to sleep."

Stillness pressed tight over the clearing; each rabbit poised in its own hunger and fear, every tuft of grass bristling with expectation.

Fang's ears, battered and furrowed, lifted a little at the edges. "You talk of sleep and waking," he rasped, voice thick as blackthorn bark. "But some of us have never slept. We remember things—the old shadows, when times were good, and then, the taste of loss. You think words and warnings will protect you?"

He drew himself to his full height, muscles tense beneath his fur, eyes glowing like coals in the dimming light. "I've come too far for empty talk. If the Hollow stirs, let it judge us all!"

Rude, bunched thick beside him, spat into the grass at Bracken's feet. "We're not afraid of stories, nor of you. There's no safety left . . . only what we take. Step aside, or you'll find out what running costs when there's nowhere else to run."

The Ashfurs that lined their flanks took heart from these words, shoulders knotting, eyes burning with tired desperation. They pressed forward, mouths tight with resolve and bellies pinched by a season too long.

The old air trembled, and then, with a scrambling rush, the circle of Ashfurs surged together—Fang bounding first, teeth bared in a wild grimace, Rude low and fast at his side, their voices tangled in a ragged cry. Behind them, the rest followed—no order, no rallying cry but the primal song of hunger and loss, the living storm of a clan with nothing but this moment left to claim.

The Hollow watched, silent and unmoved. Roots shivered underpaw. The battle, when it came, broke not upon a field, but within the tangled lives of rabbits and the long shadow of history.

The moment split open like a seed under fire.

Bracken turned, not to run but to lead—and Sorrel and Wisp were with him, darting into the gorse-thick underbrush where the Hollow's body narrowed and bristled with every secret they had laid for this day. Behind them came the Bone Warren—a mass of gaunt ruffians, snarling and stumbling, their ragged coats whipped into the wind, limbs wild with a hunger sharpened by frost and ash.

Bracken did not glance over his shoulder. The pulse of the Hollow thrummed through him more surely than the beat of his own heart. Every curve of root, every thinning patch of bramble, each ribbon of grass where the wind whispered sideways—all these were familiar.

"They're behind us!" panted Sorrel, her breath harsh in the still air.

"Let them think themselves hunters," Bracken replied. "These paths will turn on them soon enough."

Wisp gasped as she labored to keep up. "The Hollow shows no kindness to those who come seeking to tear it apart."

At a bend where three small trails diverged, Bracken slowed, his ears lifting. Without a word, the three separated, each following a different path that wound between the trees and tangled roots. The Ashfurs followed each in silent pursuit, the sound of paw against soil swallowed quickly by the Hollow, leaving only the sighing of the wind through the branches.

The snares lay hidden, waiting with the careful artistry of a blackbird's song, each set with patient paws and sharp minds. Bracken had traced these paths with Sorrel beneath the cool silver of the moon, and Wisp too, moving softly where they had woven the strong, pliant ropes from long grasses gathered painstakingly. They knew where the bramble-snares waited, where the small, pointed stakes leaned like silent sentinels against the earth, tipped with the cruel poison of thorn. They had prepared; every step was memory, every breath a promise.

And now, their work would speak.

The first of the Ashfur fell near the bramble-laced ditch—a broad-shouldered doe with a torn ear and haunted eyes. Her leap carried her cleanly through the narrow pass, but her hind leg caught in the slip-noose of twine they'd made from old grass stems soaked and knotted hard. She screamed once—a brief, bitter sound—and vanished from the chase, kicking wildly as thorns drew blood.

A second crashed down into a pit Wisp had dug with her own paws, hidden with wind-blown leaves and the curling tendrils of fern. A bone-crack. Then silence.

Still, they came. They always came.

Smig and Gnash struck like flint and steel.

They rose not from cover but from the very sides of the Hollow, moving with the fury of things too long held in shadow. Smig flung himself at a buck a hundred times his size, his teeth finding the soft place under the jaw and clamping down. The ruffian shrieked, thrashing in blind panic. Smig did not let go. Blood bubbled. Fur flew. They rolled, a blur of claws and bite, until the ruffian stilled and Smig, limping now, spat and lunged again into the crush.

Gnash tore into two more with a swift, fluid grace born of countless hunts; his body was sinewy and lean, each muscle rippling beneath bristled fur. His ears flattened close to his skull, narrowing his senses as teeth—sharp and gleaming with fresh intent—found their marks. He moved like a shadow scattering dry autumn leaves, paws soft and soundless as whispers, swift as a sudden gust racing through the grass. His eyes burned bright and cold, fierce with deliberate purpose. The bone-thin rabbits barely caught a flicker of his approach before claws slashed and teeth snapped with merciless precision. A sudden storm of panic erupted—Ashfurs scattered like startled crows, breaths ragged, hearts hammering wild and raw. Yet Gnash flowed through the chaos like a secret wind—silent, inevitable—a fierce, untamed spirit born to hunt and unleash quiet reckoning.

Ahead, Bracken, Sorrel, and Wisp pressed on, deliberate and steady, luring their pursuers further into the narrowing grasp of the Hollow, where roots and thorns tangled thicker and snares waited like patient sentinels weaving shadows into steel. The tension of the dark earth seemed to pulse beneath their paws, the weight of old magic threading the air around them.

But Sorrel faltered.

She'd taken a blow in the flank—a cruel rake from an Ashfur who had lunged before being crushed by falling bramble, one of the spiked traps tied high and loosed with a careful tug. The gash was deep, fur peeled back, blood dark and thick on her side.

Bracken saw her slow, her breathing ragged.

"Go!" she rasped, teeth bared. "Lead them in. Finish it!"

But he turned, catching her with his shoulder, pressing close. "You can't fall here," he murmured. "Not where they can find you."

"You can't carry me and win," she hissed. "Think of Wisp. Think of the Hollow."

"I am," Bracken said.

They stumbled together through a low crack in the cliffside—a place marked by white stones and the dry breath of dead leaves. A hidden burrow lay beyond, choked with ivy and hollowed with old claw-work. Bracken eased her inside, licking once at her wound, the taste bitter as nettle and dirt.

"Stay quiet," he said, voice barely more than the wind. "If I don't come back . . . "

"You will."

Outside, the world had come alive with the ragged music of battle. Thumps, shrieks, the scrape of claws against stone, and the heavy thud of bodies meeting earth. The Bone Warren, fierce though they were, were bleeding. The Hollow had teeth.

Wisp was at the heart of it now, darting between shadows, her small body nearly invisible in the tall grass and sun-slashed earth. She had little strength to meet the bucks head-on, but she was swift and strange and full of a courage deeper than blood. She darted before one of the larger ruffians—a brutish doe with scabbed shoulders and broken whiskers—leading her directly into a snare of thorns and sharpened wood. The scream that followed was short and ugly.

Then Wisp vanished again into the grass.

One of the Ashfur bucks—gray-eyed, his sides sunken with famine—saw her and gave chase, snarling. She ran faster than she ever had, ears flat, eyes stinging. Her paws found the path just as the buck lunged, and she twisted, slipping through a hollow under a root. He crashed after her, only to trigger a lever hidden in the dirt. A crude mechanism, but deadly—a net of briar vines dropped from above, smothering him in barbs and tangled green.

Across the clearing, Gnash faced Rude.

The great Ashfur buck was bleeding, his sides torn and slick, but his eyes were mad with rage. He charged, low and brutal, and Gnash barely dodged in time, catching a blow to his ribs that sent him skidding across the stones.

"Come on, Hollow-worm!" Rude bellowed, his teeth bared. "Come and die like the rest of your friends!"

Gnash rose slowly, his mouth tight, pain lacing every breath. But his eyes burned. He stepped forward.

"I don't die for friends," he whispered. "I die for the memory that endures beyond us all."

And then they clashed—not with ceremony, but the brutal, snarling violence of creatures long hardened by wind and war. The Hollow stilled, even the leaves ceasing their murmurs, as if the place itself recognized something final at hand. They fought with low growls and slashing paws, the air sour with blood and panic. Gnash, broad-shouldered and heavier by far, moved not with grace but with grim certainty. Rude, wiry, and quick, darted like any cornered rabbit would—until one misstep spelled his end.

With a dreadful sound—part shriek, part bark—Rude staggered, and Gnash seized him, sinking teeth into flank and tearing downward with a force that stripped bark from bone. Rude kicked and spat, even as the ground slid beneath him.

"You'll not see me trembling!" Rude hissed, teeth bared, eyes blazing with defiance. "I've faced worse than you, gnawing brute!"

Gnash's amber eyes narrowed, a low rumble rolling through his throat. "I tire of your words," he growled. "Soon you will learn how brief the end is."

Rude laughed, sharp and raw, even as Gnash's claws scraped closer to the edge. "Brief? You? Ha! You'll make it last long enough for me to enjoy the taste of your fur!"

A single sweep of Gnash's paw sent Rude spinning outward. For a moment, his claws scrabbled at the stones, but the bluff offered nothing to hold. He struck with a muffled crunch against the cliffside and did not rise.

Gnash lingered for a heartbeat, ears flicking, as the wind carried the echo of defiance fading into the hollow below. "Where are your words now?" he chuckled, running off to help the others.

The Hollow watched, silent and knowing. Somewhere, beneath the scrub and brush, the ragged rabbits of the Bone Warren kept low and still, their eyes round and shining—not with grief, but something like reverence.

The battle lingered long into the light of day and stretched further even as the shadows lengthened with the approach of evening. The clearing—the broken earth beside the Hollow—was a patchwork of trampling, blood-stained grass, and scattered leaves darkened by the struggle of the Bone Warren and the small band they sought to crush. The air hung heavy, not just with the musk of fur and fear, but with the heavy breathing of those who knew the fragility of life as vividly as the sharpness of claws.

Bracken and his companions fought with desperate courage. Gnash moved like a silver whisper through the maelstrom, silent and poised, every sinew taut, his muscles lashing with a fierce, restrained power. The fox, Ginger, soon emerged, darting and twisting like a curling flame, teeth bared, bright eyes burning with wild resolve. Smig, small but fierce, fought with all the fury of a creature who carries his world on his shoulders, claws scraping the earth beneath him, every movement sharpened by the sharp edge of survival.

Yet, despite their courage and skill, the Bone Warren pressed on, closer. Their numbers were like a tide, weary but relentless, muscle and hunger combining to form a dark flood that threatened to wash the small company away—earth-marked and worn though they were. One by one, the space around Bracken narrowed, and the bright hope of victory dimmed beneath the weight of growing odds.

Then, in a sudden flurry of motion—quick as the flicking tail of a startled kit—a pair of Ashfurs broke from the scattered fighting. Silent and swift, they seized Wisp. Her small form, pale and trembling, was yanked away before the others could reach her. The ruffians hauled her forward, thrusting her high into the air, small, fragile.

"Bracken!" shouted Fang. "Bracken! Where are you? We have something here that might interest you."

Bracken froze. He could see Wisp in the distance, being held above the tall grasses. His breath drew deep and tight in his chest. Wisp's wide eyes searched his face, reflecting a fragile flicker of fear, but also something else—defiance, slender as the thinnest thread of dawn.

Fang stepped closer to Wisp and her captors, voice low and brutal like the grinding of stones. "Give up, Bracken. Surrender what you hold here, or she dies."

The threat hung between them, cold and cruel as winter frost. But Bracken's spirit was untouched by fear. His gaze locked on Wisp's brave, quaking figure, and he stood taller; the sway of the clearing felt beneath his paws like the slow beating of ancient drums.

Bracken held his words close before releasing them, his gaze lingering on Wisp with a sorrow softened by something like gentle resolve—as if seeking pardon for the pain their stance might bring.

"No." His voice was quiet, bearing the steady force of the earth itself. "We do not surrender."

Wisp met his eyes, a faint, knowing smile playing at her lips—small, tender, and full of quiet courage.

At Bracken's side, a rustle stirred—a shift of motion that brought Gnash and Smig forward, moving to stand with Bracken, muscles coiled, eyes unyielding. Ginger slipped from the edges of the skirmish, padding silently beside the trio, her fiery gaze brightening like a sudden flare in the growing dim.

Together, they formed a line drawn not in sand, but in the fierce certainty of kinship and unbreakable will. The Ashfurs glanced uneasily, the bitter edge of hunger mixed now with something older—a hesitation born of respect, or perhaps of fear.

But the moment held no surrender.

By now, night had settled fully over Ash Hollow, and the moon hung high, spilling cold light across the tangled roots and fractured stones. Shadows stretched long and wavering, silvered and trembling in the stirring wind. The air was still yet full of something—an expectancy that brushed along fur and feather alike. Beneath the dark canopy, the last desperate struggle unfolded in soft sounds and strained breaths, in the faint rustle of fur against stone.

Wisp lay on the uneven earth, the rough soil chilling her side, a cruel reminder of the bone-weathered ruffians who had thrown her down without hesitation. Her breaths were shallow, mingling with the sharp tang of crushed leaves and the metallic bite of fresh injury. Each thrum of her heart sounded like a distant bell through the hollow, slow and fading. She wanted to close her eyes, to sink into the embrace of the ground, but a stir ran beneath her fur—a spark of something older, something she could not deny.

Her paws moved almost on their own, tracing patterns across the moss-streaked earth, symbols that belonged to the deep memory of the Hollowkin. An old wind shifted through the roots, carrying a song older than memory itself, and the air hummed with a pulse that seemed folded into the stones and soil.

Gnash crouched tense, ears pivoting at every small sound. Smig's nose twitched, claws scratching lightly against stone, fur standing on end in sharp anticipation. Both kept their attention on Wisp, knowing the next moments might decide all.

Bracken stepped softly through the shadows, pausing when he reached Fang, who crouched like a coiled spring. "Fang," he said, voice low but steady. "What have you done?"

Fang's eyes glimmered in the moonlight. "It's ended," he said, jaw tight. "Surrender or she will face her end."

Bracken edged closer, but Ashfur blocked him. "Wisp, can you hear me?" he asked gently.

Wisp's lips parted in a thin, tired smile. "Yes," she muttered. Her paws trembled, tracing another faint pattern across the ground. "The Hollow calls. I cannot stay down."

Bracken nodded. "Then we move together. You will lean on us, and we will not let the night claim you."

Fang raised his head slightly. "Surrender or I'll make sure she stays down . . . forever."

Wisp drew a slow breath and let it out, and somewhere in the darkness beyond the hollow roots, the air seemed to bend toward them, as if the old songs themselves were urging them onward.

Then, across the clearing, the bone-dry silence fractured.

Bracken's form began to tremble, muscles tight beneath fur as if some hidden current pulsed wild within his veins. His breath hitched, shallow and sharp, and his muzzle quivered. The trembling grew violent, his limbs twisting in convulsions that made the leaf-strewn earth echo with quiet thuds. A gasp—a shudder—a fierce cry tore from somewhere deep and wild.

The Bone Warren rabbits scattered at the sight—a trembling beast beyond their fear, pulsing with an ancient and terrible power. Some faltered, eyes wide and hearts slamming against ribs, senses scrambling to grasp the impossible. A few stumbled backward, no longer certain how to face this rising storm.

Gnash hissed low, muscles coiling, while Smig's sharp claws scraped the ground in nervous rhythm. Yet Wisp, weak and pale, lifted her gaze to meet Bracken's distant stare. In that moment, she knew what was awakening: the White Buck—the ancient guardian long whispered of in the Hollowkin's fading breaths, the creature of Bracken's dreams, bound to earth and legend and the tide of things yet to come.

Bracken's body stretched and changed beneath the moon's steady gaze. His fur brightened, shimmering first like lawless snow half-melted with shadows, then pure as the frost-coated grass under winter's hand. His eyes gleamed—cool and hypnotic—the dark obsidian of old nights and new dawns. Where once there was a rabbit shaped by ordinary bounds, now stood the White Buck, tall and lithe, regal and terrible in the silver light.

Fang's throat rumbled with disbelief mingled with grudging awe. "So, the legends walk again?" His voice, cracked and ancient, carried across the clearing, steady even as the ruffians wavered. "You wear the Hollow's mantle now, Bracken . . . but the Hollow demands payment in blood."

From deep within the Bone Warren's ranks, the Ashfurs began to retreat, breath caught and legs trembling, backs bending away from the might stirring in their midst. Fear, raw and keen as spilled starlight, rippled through the scattered shapes like a hunting wind.

But the White Buck did not pause; not for a moment did he falter beneath the pale sweep of moonlight. With a lithe and sure bound, he sprang forward—an unyielding storm of shining fur, silent and swift as the cold wind running through autumn leaves. Beneath the whispering boughs, he became a white tempest, a flash of frost charging through shadow, relentless as the coming dawn.

One by one, the fleeing rabbits' hurried steps were brought to sudden, shuddering ends beneath the long, sure bounds of the White Buck. His powerful limbs struck like a gathering storm, swift and unyielding, as he seized each desperate shape and hurled them against the cruel embrace of jagged cliffs. Those rocks clawed upward like ancient teeth—sharp, cold, and implacable—ready to swallow all who dared to defy the hollow's will. Some let out trembling whimpers, voices fragile as autumn leaves caught in the dying wind, while others fought with ragged snarls, their wild eyes blazing defiantly into the darkness. Many others fell silent at last, lying still beneath the heavy shroud of night, their stories fading away like the final sigh of a forgotten dream.

Yet at the ragged edge of this final, shattered field stood one alone—Fang. Like a weathered monolith of old bone and tangled bramble, he remained firm, rooted deep in the soil's stubborn heart. His eyes burned steady with the chilly fire of ancient defiance, unbowed by time, scarred but unbroken—a sentinel who dared the tempest to come.

"So you hunt me, too," Fang snarled, stepping forward, shoulders squared. "You think the white legend can drown the years under snow? You think I will bow to a ghost?"

The White Buck's voice was a clear bell, echoing in the still air, calm and certain. "Memory is the land. The blood, the breath, the bone. We are nothing without it."

Their eyes locked—silver against night-shadow, old hunger against bright, fierce spirit.

The battle began without a sound, a quiet dance beneath the pale glow of moonlight, where each strike was carefully measured, and every breath seemed held as if the world itself waited. Fang moved with the slow certainty brought by many hard seasons, his limbs striking sharp and sure—claws raking low, teeth snapping at the air, body coiled with the desperate strength of years worn deep into sinew and bone. Each motion carried the echo of countless struggles past, a weary force pressed hard against time.

The White Buck met each assault with a flowing grace that spoke of wind-worn meadows and nights thick with rustling leaves. He twisted and bounded, parrying with the light precision of a breeze teasing the grass, every movement swift and sure as the shadows themselves. Beneath their locked combat, the earth trembled soft and low, roots shifting quietly in the soil as if whispering ancient songs—songs of struggle and kinship, of battles waged long ago beneath starlit skies.

Fang hissed, voice low and ragged, "You carry stolen power. The Hollow will remember me, as I remember it. We all pay our dues."

The White Buck responded, tone steady and even, "Then I will settle the debt . . . for us all . . . for eternity."

With a final, shattering bound, the White Buck closed in, claws flashing like winter lightning. Fang met him, the collision ringing sharp and raw through the clearing. The fight spiraled swift and relentless, each turn and parry the echo of countless passages—of lives lost and loved, of stories spun beneath the watchful moons.

But the White Buck's strength waned beneath the steady onslaught, his breath growing ragged, his eyes clouding with the dusk of ages. Fang lunged again, teeth bared and claws raking at the air, and for a moment it seemed the larger buck might falter. Yet the White Buck moved with a sudden, terrible precision, sidestepping and striking with the surety of one who has fought a hundred battles. He seized Fang at the neck with his teeth, holding firm as the world seemed to narrow to the thud of pounding hearts and the rustle of disturbed leaves. Fang twisted and thrashed, but the White Buck's grip would not loosen. With a final, decisive wrench, Fang went limp, his body folding to the moss and soil beneath, life extinguished as quickly and utterly as a flame snuffed in a gust of wind.

The fur of the White Buck shone pure against the dark soil as he stood tall—a sentinel of the Hollow once more.

Behind the fallen, the few remaining Ashfur fled as whispers, hunted by shadows darker than night itself. But no sooner had they broken than Ginger—the cunning fox of whispered tales—stepped from the thicket like fire given shape. Her eyes gleamed fierce and bright, her teeth bared in wild grin of hunter and protector. None who fled escaped her keen stealth. One by one, their flight was ended, bodies taken back to the safety of her den—her cubs' promised feast.

Ginger turned then, her fiery gaze softening as she met the eyes of the White Buck and Wisp. The blaze in her eyes gentled, and for a heartbeat there was a stillness between them—a wordless knowing that ran deeper than warning or thanks.

Then, as the wind shifted, the air took on a strange chill. From the space between shadow and light, the pale shape of Dregg came forward—no tread upon the earth, no breath stirring the grass. His eyes were grave yet kind.

"You have done as was needed," he said, his voice carrying the weight of some far-off hill. "The trial is past, and you have not faltered."

Before either could speak, he was gone, as though the wind itself had carried him away. The grass bent where he had stood, and the silence after was deep enough to hear the blood moving in their ears.

"The Hollow's debt is paid tonight," Ginger said quietly, voice laced with the calm pride of one who guards the fragile turning of worlds. She ran off, her final words carrying through the night. "Rest easy, friends. Your walls hold strong, and your future burns bright."

Suddenly, beneath the burnished glow of the waning moon, the great gleaming form of the White Buck began to slow, muscles unwinding their tautness like the soft loosening of twilight's grip. The fierce radiance in his eyes softened, dimming gently to the familiar pools of Bracken's own calm gaze. Fur that had shone bright as fresh-fallen snow slowly settled into the earthier tone of a rabbit shaped by countless seasons. Inch by deliberate inch, the luminous spirit folded back into the quiet strength of the creature he had been—no longer a legend in thrall to wild power, but a steadfast guardian bound to the land, breath and heart steady as the hollow earth beneath his paws.

Bracken lowered his head, the moonlight brushing silver across his transformed fur. Wisp, still pale but strengthened by her part in the magic, lifted her chin. Together, they stood—the last breath of Ash Hollow's old magic alive in the hush of the night.

The stars above whispered their tired songs, and the Hollow, for all its scars and shadows, breathed softly again.

# Chapter 12
## Sorrel

The first light of morning crept thin and hesitant, seeming to hold back from what had passed in Ash Hollow. Mist lay heavy in the grass, clinging in slow wreaths that curled and drifted between the brambles. Somewhere, far beyond the Hollow's rim, a skylark began its song—not bright and trilling as in high summer, but a slow, questioning note, like a creature peering out from shelter after a long storm.

The Ashfurs were gone. Not merely scattered but gone in the way driftwood is swept from a beach by a receding tide. The bodies of the fallen lay where they had dropped—among the stones, in the pits, in the snares and traps, curled in the hollows of roots—but there were fewer than one might expect after such a night. The rest had fled before dawn, taking their wounds with them, back into whatever waste or dark burrow had spawned them. The Hollow did not grieve their passing.

Yet, something had changed.

The grass along the edges lay still now, no breath of wind to stir it. A narrow track that yesterday had led out into heather and gorse now ended in a tangle of hazel shoots and young bramble where no such growth had been. The dip in the land that opened to the eastern downs was choked with thorn and nettle, green shoots glistening with dew though they had not been there at dusk. It seemed the Hollow had drawn back upon itself, sealing each gap and seam, curling in tight against the chill.

Gnash stood in the stillness, the fur along his spine rising. "It's shut itself," he said. "The place has . . . locked."

Smig lifted his nose and drew in the damp air. "There's a strange scent. Like rain long past, left to lie."

Wisp had moved a few paces ahead. She stood among the wet grass, head turned toward the heart of the Hollow. "It's not only the land," she said softly. "It's him."

All of them looked toward Bracken.

He had been silent since the first trace of dawn, his eyes lowered, his body still in the cool air. There was no sign now of the figure they had followed through the worst of the battle—the towering white form, eyes lit from within, moving with the calm certainty of something not wholly bound to flesh. That presence had gone, leaving only Bracken: mottled gray-brown, narrow-shouldered, dusted with dew.

Gnash regarded him as one might study a mark cut into stone. "It was you," he said, low but certain. "We all saw it. The White Buck."

Bracken blinked, the name stirring something buried deep inside. "I . . . I don't know what came over me," he said. "I only knew what to do . . . where my paws should fall, how my teeth should strike. It felt like recalling a trail I'd run long ago, though I never had."

"You were different," Wisp said, her voice quick and light with wonder. "Your eyes . . . they were lit like the Hollowkin's. And the way the Ashfurs ran from you . . ." She trailed off, shaking her head. "They didn't just fear you. They knew you."

Smig's whiskers twitched. "There's knowing, and there's fearing. I reckon they felt both." He gave a short, sharp laugh without mirth. "Whatever it was, I wouldn't want to face it."

Bracken glanced toward the cliffs, then to the tall grasses, his brow furrowing. "Sorrel."

The others fixed on him at once, ears tilting forward, tails tucked closer, as a faint shiver ran through the group. Sorrel's name on Bracken's tongue brought a hush over them. Their eyes quickly shifted from Bracken to one another, unease prickling in the cool air. It felt as though the world had held its breath around them. No one spoke, waiting for his next word, their paws tense on the turf and their hearts quick with worry.

"I put her in a burrow," he said, the words coming fast. "She was hurt. . . badly, deep along the flank. I left her there while the fight still raged. How could I have forgotten her?" His voice tightened. "I am so foolish."

Without warning, he bounded toward the inner slopes of the Hollow, his paws thudding on the damp earth. The others went after him, slipping through the bramble runs and around the roots of an old hawthorn where dew fell in cold drops from the branches above.

The Hollow seemed stranger now, as though it watched them pass. The air was close and heavy, and every sound—the snap of a twig under Gnash's paw, the brush of Wisp's fur against the hazel shoots—seemed to linger a moment too long. The ground sloped down toward a jut of cliffstone, its face streaked with moss the color of old copper. There, at the base, lay the entrance to the burrow: a place of white stones, ivy-fringed hole almost hidden among the dead leaves and briar.

Bracken went down on his belly, pushing through the veil of ivy. "Sorrel?" His voice echoed once in the earth, then fell flat. He waited. No sound came back.

"Is she . . . ?" Wisp began, but Gnash flicked an ear at her for silence.

Bracken crept inside.

The air was warm, still carrying the faint scent of Sorrel's fur, but it was laced with something else now—the dry, metallic tang of blood, and beneath it, a smell he could not name but which made his chest tighten. He moved forward in the gloom, the packed earth brushing against his whiskers.

The hollow lay empty.

For a moment, he simply stood, his mind refusing to fit the fact into shape. She had been here. He remembered the way her breath had rattled, the twitch of her ears when he had told her to stay quiet. He had pressed his shoulder to hers, felt the hot throb of the wound. He had left her in this place.

Now, only the faint marks in the earth—the scuffed scrape of hind paws, a shallow hollow where she had lain—remained.

Bracken backed out into the morning light, his fur ruffled, eyes searching the others. "She's gone."

Wisp's ears flattened. "Gone? Gone where?"

"She was hurt," Bracken said, his nose twitching as he sniffed the air, scanning for any trace. "She couldn't have gone far."

Gnash stood with his head turned toward the slope, eyes half-closed as though listening. "Maybe she didn't go," he said. "Maybe something came for her."

No one spoke. The mist had thickened once more, threading along the ground in pale, curling tendrils. Somewhere overhead, a raven let out a single, hoarse croak before falling silent, its wings cutting through the damp air with a faint rustle.

Bracken's eyes roamed the tangled edges of the Hollow, where brambles twisted into knotted shapes and shadows pooled beneath fallen trunks. The notion that something had slipped through the gloom unseen tightened his chest and made his ears twitch. Even the wind seemed subdued, slipping softly among the roots and stones, carrying with it the faint scent of damp earth and old fur.

"We'll find her," he said, his voice calm yet firm, low enough that the sound did not stir the Hollow too much. "Wherever she is."

And without another word, he turned toward the shadowed heart of Ash Hollow.

Bracken led the way, his head low, ears shifting to catch every stir of the grass, his pale eyes fixed on the faintest marks that showed through the damp earth like scratches drawn by a trembling paw. They told the tale well enough: Sorrel had dragged herself from the burrow, each print uneven, her body sinking heavier into the soil with every faltering step. The trail bent away from the slopes and carried them into a run of wild grass, where tall seed-heads swayed above their ears, whispering against one another in the faint stir of the breeze.

The other followed, moving slowly through the Hollow, every step held by the heavy quiet that follows a vanished scent. The mist clung low, brushing their bellies, and the grass was wet enough to soak the fur of their paws. Now and then, a droplet would fall from an unseen leaf with a small, quick sound that seemed far too loud. The Hollow was neither hostile nor welcoming—it merely watched them, its breath slow and hidden.

"She was moving toward the glade," Wisp murmured.

"But why?" Gnash asked, though there was no sharpness in his tone.

The trail grew weaker among the grass, the damp smell of blood coming and going in the drifting air. A blackbird clattered from a nearby thorn-bush and arrowed low across their path, its alarm-call breaking the hush before fading away. Bracken slowed, and the others drew up behind him.

She was there.

Sorrel lay on her side beneath a shelter of a hawthorn, the branches above her hung with the shriveled remains of last year's haws. Around her stood a thick growth of tall grass, whispering faintly in the breeze. Her coat still showed its russet glow, though darkened here and there by the stain of dried blood. One foreleg stretched forward, as though she had thought to rise again, but the stillness of her body spoke more plainly than words. Her eyes were half-closed, the lashes beaded with tiny drops of dew. She had come of her own choosing—there was no sign of struggle, no scent that told of any hunter.

For a long time, no one moved.

Bracken stepped forward, the damp earth cold beneath his paws. He could feel the old instincts at work in his body—to touch her, to nudge, to stir her—but some deeper knowledge held him still. He lowered his head until his nose touched the fur of her shoulder. There was no scent of life there. Only the cool, clean smell of water, grass, and the faint tang of the wound.

"She went alone," he said softly, his throat rough with grief. "Wanted one last touch of the grass, green and sweet on her tongue."

"She would have chosen no other way," Wisp answered, her voice carrying sorrow like a song that has lost its ending. Her eyes shone, and a tear ran down her cheek.

Smig shifted uneasily on his small paws, staring at the ground. "She was strong," he muttered. "Strong as any I've known. But the end finds every one of us. Even the strong." His voice broke, and he turned his head away.

Wisp lowered herself beside Sorrel's still form. She brushed her nose tenderly to the doe's ear, as though leaning close with some secret comfort, then sat back, tears dripping from her whiskers. "She never turned from danger," she said. "Not once. Even when any other rabbit would have flinched."

Bracken closed his eyes hard, and tears forced their way out, slipping down the curve of his cheeks like rain running over stone. Memory rose in pieces sharp enough to cut: Sorrel's clipped tone urging them down among the briars; the heavy thrum of her paws striking the earth when she ran; the steady look she had given him in the hour before dawn, when all had seemed lost. He thought of how she had stood beside him with no hint of doubt when the Bone Warren closed upon them. Sorrel had been more than the Hollow itself could carry—yet now the Hollow carried her, and the grief of it broke through him, streaming down in hot tears that dampened the soil where he crouched.

He straightened and stepped away. His chest felt heavy, though no sound escaped him.

"She's part of the Hollow now," he said.

They stood a moment longer, the four of them, with the mist shifting slowly about their legs. A hush lay upon the hawthorn glade, so complete that even the blackbird had fallen silent. Somewhere deep below, Bracken fancied he could hear the slow breathing of the Hollowkin, the old dreamers who watched without eyes.

Wisp lifted her head. "Will she . . . see them . . . the old ones?"

Bracken looked at her. "If she does, she will know them as friends," he said, "and they will embrace her as their own."

Gnash turned, ears twitching toward the dark mouths of the bramble tunnels. His eyes shone with sorrow, and when he spoke, his voice shook with it. "Come now. I've no wish to linger here longer than need drives us. Let her keep her silence. Let her have her peace."

They left without looking back—for to look back was to call something to follow—and padded into the green-shadowed ways. Behind them, Sorrel lay where she had chosen, the hawthorn boughs and the tall grass stirring faintly as the morning light grew stronger. A single haw, loosened by the movement, dropped to the ground beside her and lay there in the wet grass, bright as a drop of blood.

The mist thinned as they left the hawthorn glade, opening onto a long, dark sweep of grass running down toward the Hollow's heart. The air carried a strange fullness, as though the Hollow listened in its own way. Bracken kept to silence, his shoulders sore from more than the fight just passed. Sorrel's absence tugged at him with every step—the place at his side that should have held his friend felt hollow and raw. He thought of Sorrel's quick talk, her sharp ears always turning first to danger, and the memory struck like a thorn under the skin. There would be no Sorrel to share the morning light again, no quick bark of laughter when the fear passed. Bracken's paws moved over the damp grass, but his heart lagged behind, heavy with loss that words could not shape.

Wisp came up beside him, her paws light on the wet ground. She glanced at him once, then fixed her gaze ahead. "Without Sorrel," she said, without hesitation, "you'll have to lead us back to Glenmere."

Bracken stopped. The thought seemed to hang in the air between them. "Glenmere . . ."

She nodded. "The others are still there. We can bring them here . . . to Ash Hollow. The land is rich here . . . plenty of tall grasses for cover and good feeding, and the earth is soft and deep for burrows. No hard roots to tear the paws, no sour ground to starve on. It's the sort of place a rabbit can live and not spend every day fearing for his life."

Bracken's eyes dropped to the ground. "Safe," he echoed, but the word felt heavy. "Wisp . . . you don't understand. I'm tired. The fight, the Hollow . . . even before that, the journey here . . . it's in my bones. The way back will be long. Dangerous."

"You think I don't know that?" Her voice had the edge of someone who had already made up her mind. "But if we don't go, they'll never come. Glenmere is all they've ever known. They won't believe they have another home unless we go to them and tell them. You saw what the Hollow did . . . what you did. You are the one they will follow."

Bracken shook his head, a low sigh escaping him. "I don't even know if I can make it. The way is worse now. Winter's claws are soon to still the ground. And . . ." He trailed off. There was something unspoken in his tone, a doubt deeper than weariness.

From behind, Gnash padded closer, his dark coat rippling in the first streaks of sunlight. "You're afraid of more than the road," the cat said quietly.

Bracken gave him a sharp look, but Gnash only blinked.

Wisp turned her eyes back to Bracken. "You led us through the Crooked Wood, through the Bone Warren," she said. "You stood against the wicked ones when no one else could. You became the White Buck."

Bracken's ears dipped flat against his skull, and he looked at the ground where a beetle crawled between the roots. "That wasn't me," he said, voice catching like dry grass in the wind. "Not truly.

I cannot even tell you what it was. One heartbeat, I was myself, and then . . . something old was moving through me. Older than the hills, older than any warren. It spoke with my tongue and used my paws. And now it's gone, leaving nothing I can grasp."

"Gone?" Wisp's tone softened, but there was a spark in it too. "Maybe not. Things like that do not fade so easy. Maybe it left a mark, even if you cannot feel it. Maybe it planted something in you . . . a path, or a memory, waiting for its hour. I have heard stories: the White Buck doesn't speak without reason. You dreamed true, Bracken. I can tell."

Just then, the sun broke over the cliffs, spilling gold over the Hollow. The light caught in the frost still clinging to the taller grasses, and for a moment, the land seemed to glimmer with a cold, slow heartbeat.

And high upon the cliff's rim, stark against the sky, stood the White Buck—motionless, watching, a figure drawn sharp in fire and frost.

He stood taller than Bracken remembered, greater even than in the half-light of his dreams—his coat not simply white but shining, as though the first light of morning had settled into his fur. His eyes shone with a pale fire. When he spoke, his voice carried through the Hollow like wind over many warrens, rising from the stones beneath their paws and from the sky above them at the same time.

"Behold, the rabbits of Glenmere."

All turned.

At the gates of Ash Hollow—where the old bramble-choked tunnel rose from the earth like the roots of a fallen tree—they saw them.

First was Bramblehide, her right ear notched and her coat faded to thistle-gray. Her movements were stiff, but her eyes shone with the sharpness of one who had seen danger many times before and learned to stand against it.

Beside her stood Briarback, strong-shouldered. His coat was still the deep brown of youth, but his sides were drawn in and his steps careful, as though the journey had cost him more than he could spare.

And then, from behind, came Thatch and Reed—unmistakable, the pair still moving in step with one another as they had since kithood. They nosed through the crowd, ears pricked and alert, scanning the Hollow with a mixture of caution and awe.

More followed—half-familiar faces from Glenmere: old does who had once nursed in the low sunlit runs, bucks Bracken had seen patrolling the hedge-lines, a handful of yearlings whose eyes darted to every shadow. Their fur bore the dust and scent of long travel.

Bracken's heart gave a jolt. "They came . . . "

Bramblehide stepped forward, her breath steady but her sides working. "We followed, Bracken. Not right away . . . a few days after you left. We might have stayed, but . . ." She hesitated, her ears flattening. "The Twolegs came. They broke the earth of Glenmere. Dug down through the heart of the warren. We could hear it caving in. Those who stayed . . . I don't know if they are alive."

A low murmur passed through the Glenmere rabbits behind her.

Thatch added, "Glenmere was lost. Reed and I . . . we remembered the way you'd gone. It wasn't easy. We nearly turned back twice."

Reed gave a small nod. "But we didn't."

Bracken glanced at Wisp. She said nothing, but her eyes told him all he needed to know—You have to lead.

Then out from the undergrowth came Gnash, moving in that unhurried, sure-footed way of his. He settled himself upon the short grass, tail folded neatly across his forepaws, and regarded the gathering with the calm detachment of one who had watched many such meetings before and knew he would watch many more.

The Glenmere rabbits froze every limb strung tight, their noses twitching at the sharp tang that drifted on the still air.

"Cat," Bramblehide said, ears flattened, the word thick with fear.

Bracken turned back to the Glenmere rabbits. "He is a friend," he said. The words came easier than he'd expected. "You are safe here. This place . . . Ash Hollow . . . will protect you. But it's not like Glenmere. It won't open for everyone, and it won't stay open forever. You've come at the right time."

Bramblehide studied him for a long moment. "You sound different, Bracken."

"I am," he said simply.

Thatch's ears flicked forward, and he lifted his head. "But there is something else that is different. Where is Sorrel? She should be here."

Reed stepped closer, his nose trembling. "Yes . . . where is she?"

Bracken felt the earth tug at his heart. He looked toward Wisp, and for a moment neither spoke. Then Wisp drew a long breath and said, "She is gone. She fell in battle, and not against fox or cat, but in fighting her own kind. It was here, for this ground. She would not yield."

Bracken added, his voice low and heavy, "It was Ashfurs that we faced. Sorrel stood with us, and she would not turn. She gave everything she had . . . her claws, her strength, her very spirit . . . to win this place for us. And though the fight was cruel, she did not fall until the Hollow itself had chosen."

The Glenmere rabbits lowered their heads, ears drooping in sorrow. Their silence was a still pool, broken only by the rustle of grass.

Bramblehide spoke at last. "Sorrel was strong," she said, "stronger than many of us knew. She carried her trials like a doe twice her age. There was thorn in her will, and fire in her blood. I knew since her first days. Even then, she had the mark of one who would not be turned aside. We will remember her. Ash Hollow itself will remember her."

Wisp lifted her head, eyes shining. "When she ran," she said softly, "her paws always struck the ground ahead of mine, as though some path was opening for the rest of us. She never looked back, not once. Sorrel knew the way, even when none of us could see it."

A soft wind moved the grass then, and though no rabbit spoke, each of them felt that Sorrel's name had been laid down among them, not to be lost.

Bracken shifted, his heart tight, and a great question leapt onto his tongue. "But what of your travels?" he asked, ears lifting high. "The Crooked Wood, the angry river, and the warrens twisted under the Bone Hill, the Dark Ones, the Ashfurs with their cries for blood and chase . . . how did you pass through all that?"

Thatch tilted his head, whiskers quivering, as though weighing Bracken's worry in the balance. "My friend, the land lay strangely hushed. We met with small hindrances only . . . no more than a quick stoat darting and gone, or a fox's spoor grown stale in the dew. Rabbits were scarce, far scarcer than I once remember. The fields stood empty, save for wind over grass and the quiet shapes of rooks."

Bracken lowered his ears. "I cannot make sense of it. The ground beyond Glenmere was never so still."

"It was not chance," Wisp said, speaking steady, her eyes catching the dim light. "Step by step, we cleared the path. The hollow logs, the nettle beds, the banks where enemies might wait . . . we left none unturned. The ground was made clear, so the way would stand open when they came to follow. If they walk smooth now, it is because our paws cut away the snares before them."

From the cliff above, the White Buck kept his watch. Sunlight poured about him so that his shape and the day's brightness seemed to mingle. Bracken felt the pull of those eyes, not harsh with authority, but older—like the steady turning of the seasons over earth and root.

The White Buck's voice rose once more, gentler now, yet it reached every ear in the hollow: "The Hollow remembers."

And then, the brightness of the morning seemed to swell until he vanished, leaving only the rustle of leaves and the scent of earth behind.

For a heartbeat, all was still, as though the Hollow itself were listening. Then its breath came again—the soft slide of wind combing the grass, the shy rustle of bramble-leaves as they shifted against one another.

Wisp broke the silence. "Well," she said, her voice not without a note of wonder, "it seems the journey's been made for us."

Bracken looked once more at the Glenmere rabbits—tired, worn, but alive. In their eyes, he saw what he had felt himself the first time he had stepped into the Hollow: the faint, flickering hope that they might still belong somewhere.

By midday, a great stillness, heavy and portentous, had fallen upon the Hollow. The light was a pallid gleam washed thin by a low-lying haze that clung to the high cliffs in a woolly veil and pooled in the sheltered glades. It was not the stillness of fear, nor the brief, empty pauses that punctuate the life of a wild rabbit; rather, it was a silence so profound and deliberate that it seemed the very Down itself had slowed its breathing to a near stop, waiting.

In that quiet, the rabbits of Glenmere, their numbers fewer than in the sunnier seasons, were assembled. They were gathered in the lower meadow, a place where the rich grass, now bowed and sere, swept in gentle swells toward the great, tangled bastion of the bramble-gate. The air, cold and damp, bore the keen, earthy scent of frost-dampened mosses and the sharp, resinous perfume of hawthorn, a perfume that hinted at seasons long past. Among them were the four who had come from afar: Bracken, with his twitching nose and watchful eyes; the small, nervous Wisp; the dour and scarred feline Gnash; and the tiny mouse Smig.

Bracken stood apart at first, a solitary figure whose keen eyes, sharp and watchful, moved with a steady gravity across the settling warren entrance. He saw the yearlings, a restless knot of them huddled together, their nervous energy barely contained as they awaited the final light. Further on, the elder does rested on their haunches with a profound and quiet ease, the composure of those who have seen many seasons pass, their very stillness a testament to the old ways. And beside them, Wisp, small and bright-eyed as a newly turned leaf, was speaking in hushed, quick tones to Briarback, a buck of serious mind.

On the slope above, where the light faded first from the sky, Gnash lay sprawled, his great body a dark shape stitched to the deepening earth, his tail curling and uncurling with a slow, deliberate rhythm, a patience born not of rest, but of a quiet, predatory confidence. And in the formidable warmth of Gnash's fur, Smig lay nestled, the small rise and fall of his breath lost against the great cat's side.

They had chosen Bracken to lead the new warren, for they knew he had carried himself with the steadiness of an old oak, one who weathered storm and frost alike. They saw how his ears caught every sound in the burrows, how his nose read the air before danger showed itself, and they knew he would teach the younger rabbits to watch where their paws led. In days of hardship, he would not falter, and if food was scarce, it would be he who would uncover the hidden roots beneath the frost. The others looked to him without thinking, and so it was no surprise when the choice came upon them. And Bracken, with the same calm that marked his ways, chose Wisp as his second, saying only, "She is the seed . . . . the future."

There had been no stamping, no thump of hind legs against the turf, nor any cry to make it plain. Such is not the way of rabbits, who distrust loudness and open show. Rather, it came upon them in a quiet, certain settling, like dew gathering by night until every blade is heavy with it. All rabbits know—deep in their bone and blood—when the time has come for one to step forward from the circle, and in that hour no word is truly needed.

Bramblehide dipped his head, fur along his shoulders bristling with the small shiver of agreement. Briarback moved up close, loosing a short grunt and what might have been the flicker of a smile before his teeth snapped down on a stalk of dry grass. Wisp came beside Bracken then, and though she said nothing, the meeting of her eyes with his carried both trust and the long memory of loss. One after another, Thatch and Reed touched their noses to his flank, a rabbit's way of saying more than restless words could carry.

Around them, others fell silent until the air seemed changed. Even the trembling of grass in the breeze felt altered, as though the field itself were listening. Such a hush is known to rabbits—the kind that comes before storm or fox, when all stand waiting for a sign. Yet now it held a different meaning: not the threat of death, but the arrival of a choice.

Bracken let the air fold over his ears. His heart clenched, not with fear but with the sober thrum of duty. The ground ran on before him in shadow, obscure and dark. Yet he knew the path lay beneath his paws already, carved by all who had fallen and all who still remained. The first task rested before him, plain and hard and shining, clear as starlight over the field.

"We will go to her now," he said, his voice low yet carrying, like water flowing over stone. "It is time."

No one asked whom he meant. Every rabbit there knew.

Sorrel.

Her absence clung among them like the gap in an old story, felt in every pause: a note missing from the tune of the warren. From the moment Bracken had borne her fallen body from the fight, her nearness—and then her stillness—had been as real as the frost that rimed the grass and the smell of thawed soil rising among the roots. No one had stood beside her at the end, but they all carried the sense of it. She was gone, and yet still among them, like a name softly spoken even when no mouth formed it.

They moved together now, a slow procession, rabbits to the last keeping their line. Their paws muffled in the damp ground; their ears folded low to hold off the bite of the cold. No one broke the silence. Only the dry hiss of grass-stalks sliding against fur, the dull thump of hind-feet along the hollows, and, now and again, the sigh of air threading through the thorn-heavy brambles gave sound to their passing. It was as though the Hollow itself drew breath on its own great rhythm, taking note of what went forward beneath its boughs.

In the gathering, a doe moved through the morning mist, her paws sinking slightly into the softened earth. Two kits followed close, ears flicking at every sound.

"Mother," the smaller one asked, pausing to nudge her side with a tiny paw, "where are we going?"

She looked down at them, the pale light glinting on her fur. "We are going to honor a hero of our new home," she said. "She kept us safe when the shadows came, who gave all so that others might live."

The kits tilted their heads, ears brushing against her flanks. "A hero?" the elder one asked, eyes wide. "Did we know her?"

"Yes," she replied, her tone steady, though her heart stirred at the memory. "Her courage shaped the paths we walk now. Today we remember her, and every rabbit who follows will carry her deeds forward."

They moved together, a small line of soft bodies through the dew-slick grass. The air smelled of damp roots and frost melting into the soil, and each step was careful, thoughtful. No words came, only the sound of paws pressing through the undergrowth and the sigh of wind threading among the thorned bushes.

The doe paused at a rise, her head lifting to the pale sky. She glanced back at the kits, who watched her with quiet wonder. "This is the way," she said. "Every path we take honors those who showed us how to tread."

The kits followed once more, tails trailing along her flanks, hearts full with the gravity of the journey, carrying the story she had shared within them. The morning stretched wide and chill, the air carrying the quiet of the warren's past with each careful step.

At last, they came upon Sorrel. She lay on her side beneath the shelter of a hawthorn's low, thorny branches, the grasses about her smoothed by wind and rain. Her rust-red fur had dulled beneath the frost, yet there remained something of her in the angle of her limbs—that lean, ready strength that had never wholly left her, even in repose.

The rabbits formed a circle around her, each taking a place in the ring without needing to be told. This was the way of such things—the circle as old as their kind, the shape of watchfulness and belonging.

Bracken stepped forward first, as was his right and his burden. He lowered his head, touching his nose gently to Sorrel's shoulder. "She was the one who saw when I could not," he said. "When I doubted, she was certain. When I would have turned aside, she would not let me. Sorrel . . . there is no Ash Hollow without you."

He stepped back, and Bramblehide came forward, her gait slow but steady. She rested her nose against Sorrel's flank, her eyes narrowing slightly as if looking back through seasons. "When she was scarcely more than a doe, she saved two of my kits from the ditch beyond Glenmere, when the water ran high. She never told the tale herself. That was Sorrel . . . the deed done, the telling left to others."

Others came in turn, speaking in the low, deliberate way of rabbits who understand that some tales must be handled gently, as if they were fragile leaves in the wind. When it was Briarback's turn, he shifted his paws and cleared his throat, ears half-laid in thought.

"It was near the hedge-line," he began, his voice still thin from his long journey. "I'd been fool enough to wander there alone, looking for marjoram shoots. Didn't smell him till he was nearly on me . . . stoat, quick as a striking hawk. I'd no time for the run. He'd have had me, sure as winter frost."

Briarback paused, his eyes narrowing with the memory. "Then Sorrel comes . . . all thump and teeth, straight at him like she meant to tear the day itself apart. Stoat turned tail, went slipping back into the ditch. I reckon it wasn't her speed that chased him off, nor her size . . . it was that look she gave him. Made him think he'd bitten off more than he cared to chew."

He gave a short, almost embarrassed laugh, looking toward the others. "Truth is, I'm here because of her. That's the plain of it. Without Sorrel, you'd be telling some other story now, one without me in it."

Wisp was the last to step forward. She hesitated, her white-patched fur catching the dim light. "She . . . she was the first to believe in me," she said. "When I was small, smaller than I am now, the others said I was too easily frightened. Sorrel told me that fear wasn't weakness, only a way of knowing the world. She said I'd grow into it, and I think . . . I think she believed that before I did."

Silence fell. It was not the silence of emptiness, but the deep, steady quiet of earth and stone, the full, resonant stillness that comes when all that needs to be said has been spoken, and the land itself pauses to listen. Even the thin winter breeze seemed to ease away, as though unwilling to intrude.

Custom was older than any of them could name. The dead were not carried away, nor hidden. That was not their way. Sorrel's body would remain where she had fallen. The grass would cover her, the thorns guard her, and shrew, beetle, and the small feeders of the undergrowth—would take her back into the slow-turning cycle of the earth. That was the way, the oldest truth the rabbits knew: that a rabbit's strength returns to the earth in death, just as it draws from it in life, and the soil holds no shame in its taking.

Bracken looked around the circle, at the faces turned toward him—some bowed, some fixed steadily upon him, all waiting.

"This place is called Ash Hollow," he said. "Yet a warren must bear its own name, one that binds those who live within it. We have come from Glenmere, from the road, from the dark places between. We have lost, and we have found. But from this day, we will live here . . . together. And this place . . . our new home, will be called Sorrel Warren."

A ripple passed through the circle—not a sound exactly, but a loosening, as though the naming had taken something weightless and set it down among them, solid and certain. Wisp's eyes shone with the bright wetness of pride. Bramblehide's head dipped in solemn assent. Even Gnash, watching from the slope, gave a long, slow blink, the nearest thing he would give to reverence.

The wind stirred again, just enough to rattle the hawthorn's dry leaves, scattering a few over Sorrel's still form. They came to rest upon her like a final gift, a blanket from the Hollow itself.

Bracken stepped back into the circle. Around them, the high cliffs caught the weak sun, holding its warmth a little longer than it might have lasted elsewhere. And from somewhere deep in the rocks, a voice—or perhaps only the turning of the wind— seemed to murmur, carrying her name away into the stones.

The day's glow was sinking fast, drawing long shadows across the slope above the Hollow. The sky over the western ridge burned in streaks of orange and copper, fading into the slow bruising of night. Bracken sat among the hawthorn, his paws tucked close against the cooling earth. Beside him lay Sorrel.

The air carried the faint scent of crushed grass and the sharper tang of blood, already fading. A soft wind stirred through her rust-colored fur, lifting it in small ripples before letting it fall back still again.

Wisp was with him, quiet as the dusk. She'd been silent for a long time, staring at Sorrel as though half-expecting the doe to stir and look back at them. At last, she spoke.

"She would have wanted us to keep moving," Wisp said, her voice low. "She never liked stopping, not even in the middle of the day."

Bracken's ears twitched. "She'd have told us we were wasting time," he agreed. "But she'd have made sure we stopped anyway . . . to help those who had a thorn in their paws."

That drew the faintest smile from Wisp, though it faded almost at once. "I don't think I've ever known anyone who could be so . . . hard and soft at the same time."

Bracken nodded. The truth of it sat between them, quiet as the settling dark. Sorrel had been the one to carry them forward when all else seemed hopeless, the one who had believed in nothing but what she could see with her own eyes—yet had carried them all the same.

"She kept us alive," Bracken said. "More than once. Without her, we'd never have reached the place."

"And without you," Wisp said softly, "we wouldn't have kept it."

Bracken's pale eyes shifted toward her. "That wasn't me. Not really."

"It was." She turned toward him now, her white-patched face catching the last edge of sunlight. "Maybe the White Buck is something ancient, something . . . bigger than us. But it was you who carried him. You who stood when the rest of us would have run."

Bracken looked away, his gaze resting on Sorrel's still form. "It didn't feel like me," he murmured. "It felt like . . . I'd stepped into a place I didn't belong. Like standing in another rabbit's skin. And when it was over, I wasn't sure if I'd brought him, or if he'd just . . . used me until he was done."

"Does it matter?" Wisp asked.

Bracken thought for a long while. "It matters if he's gone," he said at last. "If this place called him once, maybe it can again. But what if it can't? What if next time, it's just me?"

Wisp's ears lowered slightly. "Then it will be just you. And that will be enough."

For a time, they stood still, letting the wind speak in the dry grass. Far below, in the snug, hidden runs of their new warren, the rabbits were bedding down. Now and then came the faint thud of paws on firm-packed soil, a homely sound, warm with the sense of life going on.

But comfort could not keep fear away.

"Do you think the Twolegs will come here?" Wisp asked suddenly.

Bracken's body stiffened. "I don't know. But their hunger is endless. Nothing is truly safe. Yet this place . . . it is unlike others . . . different. It does not welcome everyone. You've seen it yourself. The brambles shut tight if you do not know the path. And there are corners within it that even I cannot comprehend."

Wisp drew her paws closer to her chest. "Different doesn't mean untouchable. I keep thinking . . . what if they start to break the ground here like they did there? What if when the warren closes, some of us are outside?"

Bracken's breath came slow and deep. "If that happens . . . we'll find another way. We always have."

The last light was gone now, leaving only the indigo sweep of night and the first shy stars. Sorrel's body was a darker shape against the grass, and already the night air was heavy with the scents of soil and stone.

Wisp leaned closer to Bracken, her voice dropping to a whisper. "I miss her."

"So do I," he said. His voice was rough, but steady. "I think I'll miss her most when things are quiet. When there's no one telling me, I'm about to make a stupid choice."

That drew a faint laugh from Wisp, though her eyes shone. "She'd tell you that right now."

Bracken let out a long breath, watching the stars grow brighter. "Then maybe she's not gone after all."

And they sat there until the moon lifted above the cliffs, the wind moving through the warren like a low, endless sigh. Then, from far off beyond the ridges, there came a sound—low, steady, and unnatural. Bracken's ears pricked, and Wisp's nose lifted from her paws. It was only a murmur against the night, but both knew it well: the slow, hungry crawl of machines, those of the Twolegs, somewhere out there in the dark. Neither spoke. The warren seemed to hold its breath, and the sound faded, or else slipped deeper into the land, leaving them to wonder whether it had ever been there at all.

# ABOUT THE AUTHOR

**P**hilip Mazza is a novelist with a boundless imagination, captivating readers with the epic fantasy series *The Harrow Saga* and the sci-fi thriller *The Neon Hive*. Born in New York in 1959, he earned a degree in Business from LeMoyne College and an MBA, later holding leadership roles in human resources and operations. Now a professor at the Madden School of Business and Economics, Philip dedicates his time to his students and writing. *The White Buck* is his sixteenth literary work. He and his wife enjoy travel and continue to live in upstate New York.

www.ingramcontent.com/pod-product-compliance
Lightning Source LLC
Chambersburg PA
CBHW020843020726
47497CB00005B/1231